THE FIRE YET BURNS . . .

Outside, Sara knelt on the driveway, holding something down with one hand. It thrashed and fought, and she started to curse. *Where did my little girl learn all those words?* Elliot didn't wonder for long, because then he heard a blood-curdling meow.

"Oh, God," he groaned, glued to the spot. His mind leapt back in time to the day Shelley had torched the family pet, Fluffy, a kitten barely three months old. "Jesus, not again—not Sara."

Sara struck a match against the concrete drive. She put it against the cat's tail, and it went up like a roman candle.

Released by the sudden flash of light, Elliot headed for the screen door. *"Sara!"*

He ran down the porch steps and stopped in confusion. Images and time merged, superimposed over each other. *Sara, Shelley, or both? . . .*

"DARK LULLABY has an original and enthralling plot, a blending of pathos and horror; an appealing heroine and a hair-raising climax. Jessica Palmer is a new author with a glorious future."

—R. Chetwynd-Hayes,
Bram Stoker Award–winning author of
The Monster Club, The Grange, and *The Other Side*

"An unsettling book filled with power and terror."

—Charles Grant,
author of *The Pet*

DARK LULLABY

JESSICA PALMER

POCKET BOOKS
New York London Toronto Sydney Tokyo Singapore

This book is a work of fiction. Names, characters, places and incidents are either the product of the author's imagination or are used fictitiously. Any resemblance to actual events or locales or persons, living or dead, is entirely coincidental.

An *Original* Publication of POCKET BOOKS

POCKET BOOKS, a division of Simon & Schuster
1230 Avenue of the Americas, New York, NY 10020

ISBN: 0-671-70309-9

First Pocket Books printing May 1991

10 9 8 7 6 5 4 3 2 1

Printed in the U.S.A.

For the children of violence and abuse

---

the survivors
and
especially those who did not . . .

Sorrow's song for you.

ACKNOWLEDGMENTS

With special thanks to:

Thomas Lee Beatty and his mother, Marge, for their continued belief in me; Charlie Grant and his wife, Kathy Ptacek, for their encouragement and support during the long arduous journey from the completion to publication; the late Ray Peuchner, who provided the original inspiration when he said: "why don't you write a story about a child? . . ."; John Bradshaw, who inadvertently provided the story line; Lori Perkins, a minor miracle worker; and Sally Peters.

*"Every child has the right to protection and . . .
to a life free from violence, exploitation, and abuse."*

*—1989 The United Nations Convention
on the Rights of Children*

DARK LULLABY

CHAPTER 1

Sara sat in the darkness surrounded by boxes, her fortress against the world. The unpacked cartons contained all that could be called hers in her almost nine years of life. With her thumb tucked sloppily into her mouth, she pulled herself into a fetal position. She hid. Sara hid from the sights and the sounds. She hid from the house and from a reality that seemed too bleak to bear.

The only illumination came from a street lamp, splashing across the floor as an oblong box dissected neatly in quarters. The light danced eerily, interrupted by the snakelike shadow of the gnarled branch as it brushed against the pane, whipped into an occasional fury by the wild December wind. Sara paid no attention to the erratic staccato. Instead her ears were trained on the voices coming from downstairs. Her parents were fighting—again.

". . . so what do you expect? It was your bright idea to move a little more than a week before Christmas. What sort of Christmas can we have? I can't even find the damn coffeepot much less the Christmas decorations, and you want to put up the tree. Well, screw you, buddy." Her mother's voice dropped to an unintelligible murmur.

"You know why we had to get out of that house as well as I do." Her father's shout carried easily. "We couldn't spend Christmas there. What sort of Christmas would that have been? If you had taken better care of your children, we wouldn't have had to move."

"Why you bas—" The word was cut off, and Sara heard the sound of a hand cracking against flesh.

Sara burrowed deeper into the corner, trying to compact herself into the smallest possible bundle. So she hid, hoping fervently that the fight would end, but she knew it wouldn't until one of her parents succumbed to a drunken slumber. She hoped also that their attention would not bring them to her room where she would be pulled into a tug-of-war of intoxicated recriminations.

But more than anything else, Sara wanted her sister. She pulled her thumb out of her mouth and whispered her name. "Shelley?" Only the empty room answered back.

If Shelley were here, then things would be okay. Sara would still be in her own home, and in their shared room. They could huddle together under the covers and tell each other stories to drive out the sound of the battle below. Shelley had been the adventuresome one, the leader. She had been strong.

She had been smart. After all she was almost eleven years old.

Sara looked ruefully at her wet thumb—only then aware that she had been sucking it—and started to cry. She'd be in for it if her parents found her here sucking her thumb, a habit they thought long since past.

Sara put her hand in her mouth and bit hard. The shock of pain stopped her tears. She had to be quiet or she would bring them in on her, and with them, their wrath.

Her mother's voice came in fits and starts as she gulped for air between words and sniffles. "How dare you say that? There was nothing I could have done." The last part of the sentence disintegrated into great heaving sobs.

"You should have checked them, but no, you were too drunk that night to take care of your children."

"Drunk." Her mother's normally husky voice had risen to a shriek, powered by anguish and rage. "How about you, Mr. Sobriety? You were drunk then, too. You're drunk tonight."

"Tonight, hell. We're talking about then and you were snockered. They had to carry you out of the house. You were out cold. You're their mother, fer chrissakes."

The tempest outside drowned out the voices for the time being. A good storm was brewing. The stars were cold little pinpoints of light in a brittle sky except where the clouds had begun to roll in. The branch tapped plaintively at the window, like someone or something wanting to be let in from the cold.

Sara sat up, hopeful. "Shell?"

Rat-ta-tat, tat. Then silence. Sara settled back to wait.

"You know we had to move," her father snarled.

Sara heard her mother's shocked, muffled cry, followed by a simpering whine. Witness to their many battles, Sara could easily imagine the actions which accompanied the sounds as her father savagely wrenched her mother's arm, twisting it—his face flushed with fury, his teeth clenched. Pressing the heels of her hands against her eyes, Sara attempted to blot out the images, just as she willed the voices to silence.

"We—we—we could have stayed with your mother," her mother stuttered, "at least until after Christmas."

"Sure."

Sara's thumb had found her mouth again. The tapping against the window had reached a frantic crescendo. Something stirred inside the box closest to her, and Sara bolted for the door.

Gertrude Goering lay half on and half off the crumpled sheets. White tufts of hair stood out at odd angles from the shiny scalp. The small blood vessels undulated across her skull. Her eyes darted around the room looking for something. A small night-light glowed in the corner near the bedside table.

She raised her head weakly and peered toward the ceiling now obscured by the darkness. The lamp cast ghostly shadows which stood over her like soldiers over a captive. She didn't like this room. Maybe she should since, with its Victorian style, it brought with it memories of her youth; but she did not. Something about it wasn't quite right. Its corners appeared to be joined at irregular angles. The overall image was asymmetrical—the distortion disconcerting.

Age had dimmed her sight, but she sensed something skewed about the room. It brought to mind a picture Sara had brought to show her of a girl and a rabbit. In one shot, the girl looked huge; in the next, the rabbit dwarfed the little blond Alice. The caption said it was done with trick photography. Well, this room was like that. *Trick photography.* Somehow it didn't fit; the perspective was wrong.

Tired of trying to pierce the gloom, the old woman turned to the light. From a box of Pampers, an unblinking baby stared blissfully back at her. Its contentment belied the battle that raged below.

She listened intently. Again she cursed her body that left her shackled to this bed, lying in her own filth. She wanted to get up and shout at them. They hurled insults and barbs about a daughter who had been destroyed by their continuing warfare. But Sara remained. Didn't they know what this must be doing to her? If Nana—as her grandchildren called her—could understand every word, then the child could also. Only the howling of the wind gave an occasional reprieve from the sounds of the fierce struggle downstairs.

If only this body would permit, she would get up and give them a piece of her mind; but she could not. What the initial stroke had not accomplished, the second stroke did, and it had done its work well, leaving her mind intact and lucid, but crippling her body. Even if they had come to her room, she couldn't have told them her thoughts. The power of speech was denied her. Her thoughts roamed and paced without an outlet like a caged animal longing to be free.

Time had finished the job. Contractures from the long confinement to bed had twisted her body and contorted her limbs until she resembled something more insectile than human. She lay tangled in her sheets like a fly caught in a web. Great weeping bedsores sprouted on her hips and elbows which her daughter treated twice daily with creams and salves.

She couldn't fault her daughter for her care. Jane had been taking care of Nana for five years with as much tenderness as a young mother of two could spare on a wasted heap of human flesh. Jane would normally come in each hour or so to change her, to powder her, and to talk—bitter bile from a bitter woman. Nana was safe, for Jane didn't expect her to comprehend.

Sara avoided Nana now—Sara who had once climbed into her bed as much to give comfort as to receive it when the periodic episodes of violence exploded around them. Sara—who alone seemed to know that behind the useless body the mind remained—would join her despite the urine-soaked sheets. A tear squeezed out from the corner of Nana's eye.

Stop it! Stop it! she screamed within her mind. It was drink that had done it; alcohol had turned this home into a combat zone. Nana thrashed around in the bed and loosened the dressing haphazardly placed on her left hip by a daughter who was too drunk to care whether or not it remained in position. Nana's frantic, futile action brought the unprotected sore into contact with the saturated sheets.

Stinging tears flowed freely. The tears were not a response to the physiological pain, but rather to Nana's helpless frustration. What did it matter who was to blame? Shelley was gone, dead, having died in a self-made funeral pyre, and while they pointed fingers at each other, Sara was slipping away. Couldn't they see that?

Elliot Graves opened his eyes to the sound of fire engines, flashing red lights, and the suffocating smell of smoke. Flames danced on the second floor in Bacchanalian ecstasy. *Fire!* He felt a familiar sense of dizzying, spinning disorientation. He lifted himself from the bed and headed for the stairs. *The children.* He had to get the children. He was only vaguely aware of the banging on the front door as an ax shattered the cheap wood.

He bounded for the upstairs bedrooms, but a blackened, grimy hand grasped his shoulder. He turned to find an apparition clad in a yellow slicker and huge boots. Its wheezing breath came through the hollow tubes of a mask. The soot-shrouded specter pushed him toward the door.

"But my kids!" Elliot protested.

Flames roared and crackled over their heads. "We'll get them and bring them to you. We are trained for it. You'd just get hurt. Now, get outside; you'll only be in the way." The fireman shoved Elliot roughly toward the splintered door.

Normally Elliot would have taken a swing at any man who dared push him around like that, but in the confusion of the crisis, he allowed himself to be propelled out to the front lawn. Someone, a neighbor perhaps, guided him to a fire truck. He spun around to watch in despair as what remained of his hopes and dreams were consumed by flames. A face appeared at the window. Blistered hands beat against the bubbling glass.

"Shelley!" His voice was drowned out by the conflagration and the hiss of water as it hit the flames. He headed for the door, but unknown hands held him fast. Then Elliot realized with a start that this wasn't his former home, but his new one where he and his family were going to make a fresh start. He choked back a sob. "No, not again," he groaned, "it's not fair."

His stomach began to churn and roil. He keeled over from the pain. Firemen ran back and forth in agonizing slow motion around him. Absorbed with the human fascination for disaster, no one noticed as Elliot collapsed, clutching his abdomen. "God, my stomach!"

An ulcer! he thought wildly. Elliot knew about ulcers. They had killed his father. As a teen, he had watched as the pain tore his father apart, sapping his strength and vitality. He watched as they took out his father's stomach piece by piece in surgery that was meant to cure but never did, leaving his abdomen a crosshatch of scar tissue. Elliot watched as his father dwindled and died. The "fine, upstanding citizen and Rotary member" was repaid for his strict adherence to the work ethic with torment and death.

The straight nine-to-five job was not for Elliot. He was a musician and a damn good one. He would not give up his dreams. He had compromised more than he had planned to support his family. Instead of playing with the greats, he drummed music appreciation into the heads of indifferent and semiliterate students. Instead of a band, he stood in front of a choir filled with tone-deaf nuns at the local parochial school.

Helluva lot of good his ideals were now as he lay on the ground, gripping his tortured belly while his house went up like an inferno. It felt as though something were eating him alive, from the inside out. He writhed in visceral misery. "Please, God, let it stop," Elliot whispered, forgetting his professed agnosticism in the agony of the moment.

Just then a small figure completely engulfed in flames threw itself shrieking from the second-story window as a fireman burst out the front door carrying the smoldering, blanket-wrapped body of his . . . his mother-in-law. *His mother-in-law, for Godsakes.* What the hell were they doing with her, her body spent and her life essentially ended years ago? What about his children? He didn't notice as someone led a bewildered Sara over to him. His attention was fixed on the fiery form before him that twitched with spasmodic movement. It flopped around in the mud which extinguished the flames but not the pain. A continuous wail came from the molten orifice that once had been a mouth.

A fireman emerged from the house with the comatose body of his wife slung limply over his shoulder. All of Elliot's anger centered on her as he struggled to his feet, pulling himself up from the water-soaked ground. Something gnawed his innards, and his intestines boiled in response. Elliot looked down at his belly just in time to see the snakes exploding from his navel. That was when he started to scream.

Elliot awoke bathed in sweat. His neck ached from its crooked position where it rested on the arm of the couch, and his stomach protested that night's canned chili dinner, mixed with too many Scotches. He laughed weakly. *Only gas—no ulcer, no snakes. No fire.* Yet the dream's images lingered—seared indelibly into his psyche.

"Oh, Shelley." He buried his face in a pillow and let the tears flow. As he thought of his eldest born, Elliot felt a familiar stirring in his groin.

A few moments later he sat up and sniffed tentatively for the all-too-familiar smell of smoke. *Nothing.* Elliot got up from the couch to check the house before he headed upstairs to bed. Behind him, hidden by the curtain, a small, blond form thrashed in the shadowy recesses—unheard and unseen.

Jane Graves woke up to a rhythmic throbbing in her right shoulder. She sat up, holding her arm gingerly against her chest. A bracelet of bruises ringed her wrist where he had grabbed it. The upper arm was swollen. With gentle fingers, she kneaded the flesh, wincing when she reached a particularly delicate spot.

Thank God, no broken bones. Jane could still remember the doctor pulling off a wide band of adhesive tape after Elliot had broken her ribs. She couldn't decide which had been worse, the original break or the tape. Gritting her teeth, she lifted her arm up and out to test its range. She was able to stretch it over her head. "Goody," she muttered under her breath. "It's going to be fun unpacking."

She went to check Sara. The bed was empty and neatly made, looking as though it hadn't been slept in. Jane shrugged. *Must be downstairs, playing.* She cocked her head, listening for the sound of the television. Silence. Maybe she was outside. Jane, already poised in front of another door, took one longing look at the stairs and sighed. She had to take care of Mother first.

Her mother was tangled in the sheets. Her feet caught in the bars of the hospital bed that Elliot bought when it became clear that she was going to become completely bedridden.

"Well, he did it to me again, Mama," Jane said. Her mother looked at her and blinked. Jane started, surprised. Sometimes she would swear that her mother understood what she was saying and that frightened her. To be aware and alert while trapped inside that body would be sheer torture.

With brusque, jerking movements, she rolled her mother over to one side and started to sponge her off. "Yes, he did it again. What am I supposed to do? I don't care what they say in these women's magazines; I can't leave him, not with you and Sara to support. I keep asking myself what am I supposed to do."

One side bathed, Jane peered into her mother's face. She stared blankly at the opposite wall. Jane reached for the salve and the gauze bandages. She must have been mistaken. Her mother didn't understand a word she was saying. Perhaps, that was for the best. Yet it was good to have someone with whom she could talk. Jane could still remember her mother as a healthy young woman, and secretly Jane hoped that beneath Nana's desiccated exterior some limited comprehension remained, at least of Jane's unexpressed love.

"He blames me, you know. He blames me for what happened. How can he blame me? It wasn't my cigarettes or matches. I don't even smoke. I'm not the one who has a cigarette perpetually hanging out of my mouth or burning in the ashtray. I don't keep matches or a lighter which the children can steal and play with. I may have my bad habits, but smoking isn't one of them."

She placed the bandages on Nana's hip and then rolled her mother over to her other side to repeat the process. Her movements revealed her anger, quick and sharp. Her tongue felt furry and her head throbbed in unison with her arm—adding insult to injury. *Boy, a Bloody Mary would taste good right now.* Jane turned her mother over to her back, pulling the clean sheet under Nana as she did so. She stooped and tucked in the corners.

Her voice took on a querulous quality. "He blames you, too, you know, but how could the fireman have known? And I wasn't awake to tell him that my babies were in the back bedroom. If you had been in the back bedroom instead of the front bedroom . . ." Her voice drifted off. "I'm sorry, Mama. What am I saying?" She choked back a sob and sat in the chair next to the bed. "Oh, God."

She patted her mother's hand reassuringly, but it wasn't Nana who needed reassurance. Jane marveled again at the pale luminescence of her mother's skin.

Blue veins and arteries traced a mosaic under her paper-thin flesh. She looked at the white wisps of hair that floated like a halo around her mother's head.

"I'll brush your hair later, Mama. Right now I need to go find Sara." Jane leaned over and kissed the dry, flaky cheek—and shuddered.

Gertrude followed her daughter's progress to the door. A single tear slid slowly down her face, following the path of a wrinkle until it reached her parched lips.

Jane left the door cracked open, and her footsteps receded down the hall. Nana lay quietly imprisoned by her thoughts. The what if's—what if she had been in the back bedroom instead of the front?—what if the fireman hadn't found her first?—what if Shelley hadn't been playing with matches? What if? The questions always led in smaller concentric circles back to an unanswerable and unforgiving reality.

A creaking noise attracted her attention. Her eyes searched the room, trying to locate its source. The closet door swung on its hinges, groaning slightly. It seemed to laugh at her personal grief. First one inch, then two, four, six inches. Gertrude's eyes widened in terror, for she saw two glowing embers in its pitch-black interior staring back at her.

Jane walked gingerly down the stairs, cradling her arm against her chest. The action of changing the sheets had brought back the pulsating pain, and anger replaced sorrow. *How dare he?* Jane thought in self-righteous indignation. The living room was dark. The curtains drawn. It helped hide the mess. Boxes were stacked everywhere, along the wall, on chairs and tabletops; only the couch was free of them. Some were open, spilling their contents across the floor. She wondered idly what Elliot had been looking for this morning and if he had found it. There would be hell to pay if he had not.

Fear nagged at her, threatening to overwhelm her. She had better have the house cleaned by the time he got home. *All this to be unpacked before Christmas.* Jane sighed. If she had thought it would do any good, she would have sat down and had a good cry. Instead she walked through the kitchen and out the back door.

"Sara. *Sara!*" she called into the lowering gloom. A fierce wind whipped at the hem of her frayed robe. It seemed to swallow the sound of her voice. *"Sara!"* The clouds were a leaden gray. It was going to snow. They were going to have a white Christmas after all.

Thoughts of the song and the old Bing Crosby movie with its homespun, wholesome theme brought tears to her eyes. "Merry fucking Christmas," she chuckled mirthlessly and turned to go inside. She hoped Sara was all right and that she had known to bundle up against the cold. She shouldn't be out on a day like this, but it wouldn't do to have her underfoot while Jane was trying to get things settled. *Sara is a bright girl,* she thought. *She can take care of herself.*

Once inside, Jane headed for the liquor cabinet. A Bloody Mary would get rid of the fuzzy feeling inside her head.

CHAPTER 2

Drink in hand, Jane sat on the couch. She shuddered as she took the first sip of her Bloody Mary. The living room itself was gloomy, the gloom unrelieved by the mahagony-stained woodwork and the somber green walls. The woodwork, however, was beautiful and it had been a major "sales" point.

Still Jane preferred her little tract home with its big picture window. Even with its stark white walls, it seemed cheerier than this. *Kelly green. Who in his right mind would paint this room, any room, such a color?* Maybe she would paint the place, if they stayed long enough. *Hah! That's a laugh.* And she fervently hoped they wouldn't.

The place was cold, clammy. A draft seemed to run through the house, but that was to be expected in an older house. "I bet the heating bill is outrageous,"

Jane said to no one in particular. She shivered and drew her robe more tightly around her. It had a bone-chilling quality. She wondered how much of the frigid air current the drapes kept out and wondered too which she would prefer—the dark or the cold.

Setting the completed drink down, she opted for light and a sweater. She started to get up and then stopped. The house seemed to press down on her despite the high ceilings. This place was oppressive. Or was it how she had come to be here that oppressed her? How had she let herself be talked into this? The swirling umbra closed in around her, and the cartons took on a life of their own.

Jane jumped at the low moan that came from the veiled recesses of the drapes behind her. She could barely make out her daughter's prone form clad in her pink flannel pajamas. She was curled in a tight knot, her face covered by tangled blond hair.

Sara clawed her way to the surface of a dream in which a charred and burnt sister stood grinning at her, a lit match extended out over her parents' bed. *"No, Shelleeeey! Don't!"* Sara shrieked as she sat bolt upright.

Her mother stood above her, eyes wide and frightened, her face a pale smudge against the shadows. Jane knelt and grasped the wet hand. Sara was sucking her thumb again. Her father had better not find out.

"Sara, honey, it's all right. Come on, baby doll." Jane picked up the small form, grimacing as her arm cried in protest and pulled the child into her lap. "It's all right, baby. It was just a bad dream. It's all right. Momma will keep all those ghosts away. Trust Mama, baby."

Sara sank into her mother's comforting arms and stuck her thumb in her mouth. Jane pulled it firmly away. "You mustn't do that. Daddy will spank you if he finds out." She looked down at her child's tear-stained cheeks and felt like an ogre. She considered questioning Sara about her dream and decided against it. Whatever it was, it would keep.

"Why don't you go get dressed and I'll get your Cheerios out for breakfast?"

"Okay."

"And stop in and say good morning to Nana. Brush her hair for me like a good little girl and give her something to drink. I'm afraid I forgot."

Sara turned sullenly away. It was an odious chore. She didn't like Nana anymore. She knew that she should—after all Nana was her grandmother and you were supposed to like grandmothers—but she always felt cheated because she didn't have one of those grandmothers like they have on TV. Those grandmothers were fat and jolly, always bustling about in the kitchen, making good things to eat and kissing hurts to make them better.

Sara hadn't always felt this way. Back when Nana still could get up and around in a wheelchair, she had told Sara stories and played in Sara's games. Sara was her little princess, and Nana, the child's protector. It had been such a long time ago, before her sister had gone through the transition to semi-adulthood and was too big to play with her younger sibling.

Then Nana got sick again. Sara went in to greet her one morning and she was gone. "A stroke," they said. In her five-year-old mind, Sara had wondered who had hit her. She envisioned the hand of God smiting the aged woman. What had Nana done that God should punish her, spank her like her father did Sara? Sara was bereft, unable to understand. She only knew that Nana was gone. When she returned, she was alive—barely—and held captive inside a dead body. At first Sara would go visit her grandmother, but she would just lie there.

Sara knew that somewhere Nana registered her presence. However, Sara found no comfort in the knowledge. Her grandmother couldn't play with her; she couldn't even speak. Only Sara knew Nana was alert. She had watched her grandmother respond with subtle movements of her eyes. One blink for yes, two for no. It was their own little code, a secret. At night when her parents fought, Sara—the quiet child, the empathetic child—would go into Nana's room to hide.

Eventually, Nana was transformed into something arachnid which Sara found disgusting. Lately though, Nana had grown even more repugnant and now she looked like a great daddy longlegs sitting in its web waiting for an unsuspecting fly. One day Nana would surprise them all by moving sprightly and devouring Sara whole. Yes, Nana knew what was going on. Sara could see it in her eyes that were both hurt and hurtful.

Teary-eyed, Jane watched her daughter saunter slowly to the stairs. How long would they be haunted by these dreams? She had them, and she knew that Elliot had them too. Always the same: Jane would watch as her daughter dropped—like an overcooked marshmallow from a stick—flaming to the ground. Her stomach lurched, and she blocked the image from her mind.

After that she needed a little something to steady her nerves. She opened the drapes and let in th sickly, gray light. The sky was menacing, threateni The first great snowflakes, driven by the wind, s along a diagonal path to the ground. It was going to be one helluva storm.

Washed and dressed, Sara entered her grandmother's room and said, "Good morning, Nana." Repressing her revulsion, she gave her grandmother the obligatory kiss on the cheek. Nana didn't seem to notice. Instead she stared in fixed, horrified fascination at the open closet. Sara turned to look.

"Do you want that closed, Nana?" Gratitude reflected in her grandmother's eyes. Sara closed the door.

"Do you want something to drink?" Nana responded with a single blink. Sara grabbed the glass off the bedside table and guided the straw into her grandmother's mouth and watched her gulp at the water greedily. "Mother wants me to brush your hair. Do you want me to brush your hair?"

Nana blinked once.

"Okay." Sara took the soft bristle brush and tried to get the few strands of hair to lie flat against Nana's head. What little she had left was as soft as down. Sara looked at Nana's pink scalp. The blood vessels pulsed along the surface. *Such a delicate skull,* she thought, *so fragile.*

* * *

Nana stared at Sara and saw her expression turn d and cold. The little girl gave Nana an evil grin. g her lips next to her grandmother's ear in a ratorial pose, she whispered, "Why don't you d woman? Don't you know that you are already ' Sinister, throaty laughter—emanating from closet—echoed about the dimly lit room, and Nana shook.

Sara straightened, turned her grandmother over onto her side so that she faced the closet and went to open the curtains. "Is there anything else you want, Grandmother?" she asked innocently. Nana blinked once, then twice. She trembled underneath the thin blankets. Sara left, shutting the bedroom door behind her.

Nana found herself looking at the bedside table and the diaper box with the terminally smiling baby. It seemed to mock her. She heard the clicking of tumblers and a slight creak as the closet door opened slowly. One inch, two, four, six. It stopped. Nana closed her eyes so she wouldn't have to see the burning eyes.

Jane finished her drink as she mused about where to look for the Christmas decorations. Grudgingly she had to admit Elliot was right. Despite the obstacles, it would be best if they could make this as normal a Christmas as possible. She snorted at the idea. Nothing was normal now, and she wondered—not for the first time—whether things would ever be normal again.

Sara walked up. "Mama?"

"Don't bother me now, honey. I'm trying to remember where I put the Christmas ornaments." She gave Sara a sick smile. "After I finish unpacking, would you like to help me decorate the tree? We can surprise Daddy."

Sara looked down at her feet. "Sure."

Jane got up and started toward the kitchen. "It's snowing. It looks like we're going to have a white Christmas after all. Isn't that great?" Her mother rambled mindlessly.

Sara followed on her mother's heels. She wasn't fooled. She recognized alcohol's false cheer. The exuberance would soon be replaced with barely repressed hostility and anger of which Sara had to be wary.

"Here's your Cheerios. Eat them up and then help Mommy by unpacking some of the boxes in your room like a big girl. Put your toys away, anywhere you want to keep them. Okay?"

Sara stared sulkily into her cereal bowl. "Do I hafta?"

Jane pulled up short. It wasn't often that her daughter questioned her. "Why not? Don't you know where you want to keep them? Put them in the closet, if you can't decide."

"No, it's just that last night I heard something in the boxes. There was something moving around in there. I don't want to unpack those boxes. What if it's still in there?"

"Now what could possibly be in there? I tell you what, I'll go up with you after you're finished with your cereal, and we'll both take a look. Then we'll see what mean old monster is lurking in those boxes. I betcha Batman wouldn't let any ol' monster harm you." She reached for the vodka bottle. Her daughter eyed it suspiciously. Guiltily but not without a surge of resentment, Jane put it down. Sara was right, too much to do to overindulge today, no matter how badly she thought she needed it.

Jane herded her daughter through the living room, up the stairs, and into the front bedroom. They had learned the lesson well—no back room for their daughter this time. "Now which box did you hear the sound in?"

Sara walked across the room to last night's hiding place. She sunk to the floor and looked at the boxes around her. "That one." She pointed.

Jane picked up the box and dumped its contents onto the bed. Toys fell out in a jumble. A battery-operated radio flared to life, blaring out the strains of "Jingle Bell Rock."

"See, nothing's there." She snapped off the radio. "Now, you go ahead and unpack. This place will start to feel like home once you have your toys put away."

Sara fingered the hot pink transistor radio. "Sure," she said without enthusiasm.

As she turned to go, Jane wondered whether or not she had lied, for she doubted that this place would ever seem like home to either of them.

"Oh, Mom," Sara called after her mother. "The Christmas ornaments are in the hall closet."

Jane looked back at her curiously. "How do you know that?"

Sara shrugged. "Dunno. Maybe I saw you put them in there."

Jane went to the hall closet. There it was, the box with its faded blue stocking which never seemed to stay in place. Each year, the stocking hung defiantly out of the confines of the carton and greeted her as though it eagerly awaited the season—like its former owner. She pushed back the tears. It was Shelley's stocking. The more docile Sara had a pink one. Next to the box of decorations was another, plainly marked "ornaments."

Jane glanced over her shoulder at her daughter who busily inspected the radio as if she were looking at some particularly nasty insect. Lugging the package with her, Jane descended the stairs and peered out the etched-glass panel in the front door. The snow blew in big billowing clouds which moved parallel to the ground, so thick that it obscured the house across the street. Jane flipped on the radio and got to work.

Sara examined first the radio and then the other toys. She held them away from her, grasping each between her index finger and her thumb. Once it had passed inspection, she drop-kicked it into the closet. If her mother found her doing this, she would be angry; but Sara didn't care. This whole thing wasn't her idea, anyway. She wanted her old house and her old room. She wanted her sister. It wasn't fair of them to hide Shelley just because they had been naughty.

Sara's mind followed the convoluted path which had led them to this spooky house.

Her short life had always been pockmarked by violence, but the violence increased until it erupted with volcanic force. Her sister mirrored this change and became more distant and remote. Shelley outgrew dolls and playing house, and her toys became dangerous. Sara tried to interest Shelley in the old games, but without success. Instead, Shelley preened in front of her mirror. She never tired of telling Sara that Daddy liked his eldest daughter best because she was so grown-up. Shelley had been no fun then, always sighing over her picture of Michael Jackson.

He's a wimp, anyway.

No, Sara didn't like it at all, this creepy old house and a sister who stayed out of sight. She wondered if she could change it, make it better; but it was too late. They were being punished.

Thwock! She punted Raggedy Andy into the closet.

Sara had been so relieved when her sister deigned to let her into her little sorority that she promised not to tell her parents no matter what Shelley did. She had even pretended to like Michael Jackson. *Puke!* She made a gagging noise.

Thwock! Raggedy Ann followed her abused brother into the gaping maw of the closet.

After all, it had been Shelley's idea just like all those other times, like the time with the cat. Only this time, something had gone terribly wrong. The next thing Sara remembered was those men in yellow raincoats, with faces straight out of a science-fiction movie, who had carried her out of their bedroom while her sister screamed unceasingly in the background.

Boy, they had gotten in trouble, hadn't they? And Dad sure was mad. Sara rubbed her rump in remembered pain. But then Dad was always angry about something. Well, she had been spanked and so, she assumed, had her sister. So what was the big deal, anyway? What was all this garbage about not letting her come home? Sara knew Shelley wasn't in the hospital because they no longer went there to visit her. So where was Shelley now?

Thwock! Sara's stuffed panda fell to the floor with a thud. "Damn them, anyway," she said out loud and immediately clapped her hand over her mouth. That was one of those words that mothers and fathers could say, but little girls couldn't—one that would get her mouth washed out with soap.

Thwock! The panda flew into the closet. Peeking over her shoulder, Sara said a bit louder, "Damn!"

Three hours later, Jane paused to admire her handiwork. She almost smiled. It was starting to look like a home after all. Except for the books, everything in the living room was unpacked and put away. Those boxes were artfully concealed behind the couch and the recliner. The last two were pushed against the wall near the door. The books she would get to after she had unpacked the boxes in the kitchen and the master bedroom.

Sara's clothes were unpacked last night, and if she had put up her toys, her room would be done too. Jane moved into the kitchen, noticing that most of her muscular stiffness and soreness was gone. She tested her injured shoulder, rotating her arm in its socket. Only a slight twinge remained. Humming, Jane started to empty the dishes from the first box.

A subtle change in light brought her from her fevered activity. She looked outside. Everything was coated in white. Nearly a foot of snow had fallen already. She checked the clock. *Two.* She had better get lunch and see to Nana. Empty boxes littered the kitchen floor, and she realized that she had only one box left to unpack—the miscellaneous box.

She chortled. *Miscellaneous is right.* She hated that box. Always the last one packed, it contained whatever had been left over in their last sweep through the house. Who knows what one would find there? A dirty sock stuck to Critter's saliva-slicked chew bone—and she added calling the kennel to the ever-growing mental list—a coffee cup with the dregs of the coffee they swilled down the day of the move, and any toys that the kids left out.

She paused. *Kids?* The smile faded, along with the pride in her work. Well, she'd just finish this last box and then she'd make a sandwich for Sara. But first, a pick-me-up.

She heard something stirring behind her. Nervously she looked over her shoulder. *Nothing, just the house settling. All old homes creak and groan,* she thought, *especially in a wind like this.*

Sara sat in the window seat in her grandmother's room. "Do you want me to sing you a lullaby, Nana?" Nana blinked once. Sara started to sing in a hypnotic monotone:

The old gray mare,
She ain't what she used to be,
Ain't what she used to be.

Thwock! She had retrieved Raggedy Andy from the closet and to punctuate the refrain, she slammed him into the wall. "Ain't what she used to be." *Thwock!* "Ain't what she used to be."

Her mother's voice drifted up from downstairs. "Is that you, dear? Check Nana and see that she's dry. Oh, yes, and it's time for her blue pill. Will you give it to her for me?"

"Yes, Mama."

"Then come on down. I'll fix you a peanut butter and jelly sandwich. Critter will be home from the kennel soon. Won't he be glad to see us?"

Sara wrinkled her nose at her mother's saccharine tone. She was drinking again. She took out a pill and placed it on Nana's tongue. Her eyes narrowed.

"What would you do if I made you take all of them?"

Nana swallowed hard with an audible gulp. She trembled slightly as she looked anxiously at the jar on the bedside table, and Sara smiled. Her mother called to her, interrupting her thoughts.

"Sara, come down and eat now."

Sara bounced out of the room, dragging Raggedy Andy behind her. *Thump, thump, thump, thump*—his head hit each step as she ran down the stairs.

The overjoyed Critter got underfoot as Jane put together the Christmas tree. She ignored the blue stocking and put up Sara's. Jane had had time to "relax" and was feeling quite jovial—a feeling she knew wouldn't last. She put a record on the cheap, plastic stereo that she and Elliot swore they were going to replace one day just as soon as they had the money. Soon the soothing refrain of Bing Crosby's "White Christmas" drifted throughout the room. She started putting ornaments on the newly assembled tree.

When she was finished, Jane flopped down on the

couch. *Enough is enough.* She was through for the day. Even Elliot should be pleased with her progress. Critter curled against her feet, keeping them toasty warm. She nursed her drink—Scotch now that it was close to five.

Everything was getting hazy, with that nice rosy glow she got from a couple drinks. Sara played quietly upstairs. She had been a little angel today, and Jane decided to pick up a special present for her when she went shopping tomorrow.

A car pulled into the driveway. The crunch of snow and rattle of chains heralded her husband's arrival. Elliot stormed into the house, sputtering and fuming.

"Christ, what weather!" he raged. "I had to put the chains on just to drive home. Damn near froze to death."

Jane shrank against the couch, and the dog shrank against her legs. He glared at his wife.

"You're lucky you don't have to work. All you've got to do all day is sit on your duff and watch soaps." Without so much as a second look, Elliot went up the stairs two at a time.

Jane's mouth dropped open. *He didn't even notice. Sit on my duff indeed!* She got up to fix herself another drink.

Elliot dumped his coat on the bed and walked over to Sara's room to give her a hello hug. He opened the door and peered into inky blackness. He switched on the light to reveal her crouched in the corner, thumb stuck in her mouth, staring into space. He grabbed her hand and wrenched her thumb out of her mouth, dragging her to her feet. He followed her gaze and saw the pile of toys on the closet floor.

"Jane. What the hell is this?"

Jane grimaced. *What now?* Keeping her voice even, she answered him as she started up the stairs. "What's what?"

"This mess in Sara's closet. Can't you unpack any better than that?"

"She did it herself, Elliot. Wasn't that big of her?" Jane moved quietly into Sara's room, eyes searching frantically for the source of her husband's anger. "She unpacked all her toys—she's becoming quite a little adult."

He pointed at the closet. "If you call that unpacked, you're a bigger slob than I thought."

Sara cowered behind him. He turned on her. "What's the matter with you? You scared of the closet? Well, I'll show you." Elliot pushed her through the closet door, slamming it shut and locking it behind him. He pocketed the skeleton key. "I'll let you out when you've cleaned up your mess."

Jane rushed toward her husband, clutching frantically at his arm. Sara banged against the door, pleading and crying. "Daddy, let me out. Please, let me out. I'll be a good girl, I promise."

Elliot stopped his wife with a look. He turned back to the door. "You clean up that mess and I'll let you out. Not a moment sooner." He walked out the door, saying over his shoulder to his distraught wife, "Is dinner ready yet?"

Jane shook her head no. He caught the gesture and yelled at her. "What the hell did you do with yourself all day? Can't you even have dinner ready on time?" He threw up his hands in disgust. "What I have to put up with. The least you can do is fix me a drink. I'm bushed."

Jane waited until Elliot disappeared into the master bedroom and then scurried to the closet. She leaned against the door. "Sara, Sara? Hang on, baby doll, I'll let you out as soon as I can."

Sara leaned against the door. She felt hatred and anger—muted by guilt—at her father. She searched the floor for Raggedy Andy and froze. Two pinpoints of green light winked in the background. She pressed her body against the wall. They moved closer. "Scat!" she shouted. They paused for a brief moment and began to inch cautiously forward. Sara swung, and her hand touched something warm and furry. It leapt. Sharp claws scratched at her legs. A scaly tail slithered along bare skin. Something crept over her thigh, and Sara started to scream.

CHAPTER 3

Jane peered owlishly at her husband. He sat slumped next to a plate of cooling Hamburger Helper. Lost in a semistupor, he snored over the coagulated greasy remains. Sara's cries had stopped hours ago after Elliot went bellowing up to her room to beat on the closet door. All that could be heard was an occasional sick whimper which floated dolefully down the stairs to the dining room.

Earlier, Jane had tried pleading with him. "Let her out, Elliot. She'll miss her supper."

He only glared at her, and she was silenced, thinking that he must have gone out for drinks after work. Otherwise he wouldn't be so mean this early. He went on to prove her theory by getting quietly sloshed and passing out even before they had finished their meal.

She toasted his limp form. "And Merry Christmas to you, too, my dear. May you rot in hell."

If possible, the snow was falling harder. The wind blew it in tinkling patters against the pane of frosted glass. Great gusts tore at the shutters. The Christmas lights on the house across the street were only murky little patches of bleached color floating eerily in the whiteness.

Jane rose unsteadily to her feet. Using the table as a prop and a guide, she walked carefully to his side of the table. Swaying gently over him, Jane waited to make sure he was asleep. In confirmation, he let out one loud snort and set his head down on the tabletop.

She groped in his pockets while he took a few drunken swipes at her. "Sh-toppit, I'm not in the mood."

No key. She staggered up the stairs. She found it where he had left it on his dresser. With the feigned stealth of the totally drunk, she tiptoed sloppily to her daughter's room. She hit the switch, releasing a flood of light.

Jane aimed at the keyhole and missed. Biting her tongue and closing one eye, she tried it again and hit. She threw the door open ready to be received by Sara's eager embrace. She did not expect what she saw.

Surrounded by her toys, Sara squatted on the floor, thumb firmly planted in her mouth. She sat motionless, catatonic, as though entranced. Glassy-eyed, her pupils didn't even appear to register the change in illumination—neither did she notice her mother's presence.

Her look of horror was daunting. Jane took a step backward and almost fell. What manner of ghosts and goblins had visited her in the closet? What manner of beast had haunted her waking nightmare during her confinement?

For the second time that day, Jane picked up the little girl in her arms, crooning softly, "It's all right, baby. It's all right, baby. Mommy's here now." *Liar,* her mind shrieked at her, *nothing's all right. How can you tell your own child such lies?*

As she struggled to stand, carrying Sara's dead weight, Jane felt the hair on the back of her neck rise. It felt . . . it felt as though someone were standing directly behind her. The unseen presence emanated a malign hatred. With a surge of adrenaline, Jane whirled around. If it was her husband, she was ready to fight.

Nothing.

Sara moaned. Legs shaking with fright, Jane carried her daughter over to the bed and lowered her gently onto the spread. She stretched out beside Sara, whose breath come in short, ragged little gasps. *Damn, that was spooky.*

Her rational mind wanted to deny her gibbering panic, but the feeling was too real to be dismissed. Jane searched the room for some plausible explanation. It eluded her. She told herself it was only an overactive imagination brought on by exhaustion, and put her head upon the pillow next to Sara's to descend into an unquiet slumber.

Nana squirmed on the bed and waited. Afternoon deepened into twilight, and evening into night. She needed to be cleaned, to be repositioned, to be fed. Nana thought with some indignation that she hadn't eaten at all that day. Her arms and legs were cramped. She shifted restlessly, but it provided no relief. The sores burned where bandages had become saturated with her own wastes.

As she watched the day's progression, Nana had time to ponder the move and time to regret its result. For her, it meant living in this fusty old house with its dank closets and its musty smell. It meant hunger. It meant thirst. It meant being forgotten and left to rot. Nana cocked her head and listened to the ominous silence following Sara's deliverance.

Surely someone will come soon. She lifted her head on a weak and wobbly neck. Agitated, she would have liked to rattle the bars of her urine-soaked cage, but couldn't. If she hadn't been a Christian, she would have cursed. Her family, it seemed, was too busy to worry about her.

Tired, Nana leaned back against the pillow. At least, the eyes were gone. No burning coals glowed to disturb her thoughts and her intermittent naps. It must have been her imagination. That's all. Nana tried to move and only succeeded in tangling herself further in the sheets. She moaned, followed by a sharp intake of breath. *The eyes, oh no, the eyes. They're back again!*

Jane awoke to a rhythmic, resounding clanging. In her semiconscious state, it registered as the clatter of chains, a ghostly manifestation which brought her from her sleep like a bolt. The strange banging surrounded her, coming from no direction and all directions at the same time. What was it? She felt disoriented until she heard the muffled rumble of Elliot's curses during a lull.

She looked at Sara's soft wheat-colored hair. Her thumb was firmly planted in her mouth. Jane gently extracted the thumb. Remembering last night, she felt ironically relieved that the closet had been a mess. It had funneled his anger into a less physically harmful, if not less humane, punishment.

She would have to clean Sara's closet today before he got home. She smiled at the sleeping figure and felt an overwhelming love accompanied by an equally overwhelming sense of shame. Jane felt the fierce protectiveness of a lioness with her cub, followed by a certain helplessness. Were they not both prisoners of the same hell? She bent over and kissed her daughter's cool forehead.

"You deserve better than this," she whispered.

Sara moaned.

Jane kissed her cheek, leaving her daughter to sleep. Moving quickly, she tracked the eerie noise to its source in the basement, only to be confronted by the ludicrous sight of her husband in boxer shorts and a pair of moon boots, hammering on the pipes.

"The goddamn pipes froze." He took another swing at the pipe with a wrench.

She suppressed a laugh. "I don't think that's going to help, do you?"

"Probably not." The words came out as short, frosty puffs.

"Why don't you go upstairs and get dressed? If it's this bad, school is probably closed."

"No, they would have called."

"Perhaps they did," she said. She vaguely remembered the telephone ringing but it seemed filtered through the haze of a dream. "I'll put on coffee and turn on the radio. If there are any closings, it'll be announced."

He turned and trudged up the rickety stairs to the kitchen, and so life went on as if yesterday had never happened. In the morning, they became two civilized people, an ordinary couple, carrying out the trivialities and banalities of daily existence—except for the rage which lurked just below the surface.

Jane started the mechanics of morning preparations, only to stop dead. *Damn! Frozen pipes. No water. No coffee.* The calm of early morning changed to anger. She switched on the radio with a swift twist as Elliot walked into the room, dressed in jeans and a sweatshirt.

"Well, you can forget about coffee." She fiddled with the knobs at the kitchen sink. The faucet replied with a belch and then mute silence. "No water."

"How about a glass of milk, then? My stomach's churning this morning."

She stared down at him without sympathy.

Elliot watched her stiff-backed anger with growing resentment. It was going to start now, the rebukes and the recriminations, the I-told-you-so's. She said nothing, yet her rigid posture spoke louder than words.

"Why don't you say it?"

"Say what?" Jane spoke, her voice controlled, her jaw taut. The radio announcer's voice droned in the background.

"That this is all my fault. That we could be safely

tucked away at my mother's house if we hadn't moved."

She scowled at him. "Well, it's true, isn't it? I know we're getting this house out of charity. What a deal. One of your teaching pals offers you this rental at a cut rate, and we're stuck in a place without water. Water! We can't cook; we can't wash; we can't even have a glass of water if we want one. What am I supposed to do about Mother?"

His shoulders sagged in defeat, and for a second Jane could recall how she once felt for him—before the marriage had soured and the love turned to hate—but she caught herself.

"Claremont High . . ." They both turned to face the radio. "And that completes the list of school closings for the day. Basically, if you're home, you might as well pour yourself a cup of coffee and curl up with your favorite radio station, W—"

She clicked off the radio. *Grand, no water and a husband underfoot all day.*

"I wonder why they didn't call," he mused. As though in answer to his query, the telephone rang. Jane's heart started to pound. What if they had called last night and she hadn't answered? She pushed the thought away. In a throwback to childhood, she crossed her fingers against bad luck. Elliot's voice drifted into the room. He returned.

"That was Dardenelli. They didn't call last night 'cuz they didn't know they were going to close." He folded his arms across his chest, adding acidly, "Their pipes froze."

Jane stood up a little straighter and met his gaze

steadily while she uncrossed her fingers which she had hidden behind her back.

Continuing the previous conversation, he said, "Anyway, you know we couldn't live with my mother forever. She drives you nuts. This was the best deal in this town. Sam could get a lot more for this house than he's getting from us, and that's all I'm going to say on the subject. I've got pipes to unfreeze."

Bundled like an Eskimo against the cold, he went to the garage and managed to resurrect a blow torch and a hammer from the wreckage which would probably remain unpacked until spring's first thaw. Jane fixed a small plate of food and went to check on her mother. She realized sheepishly that she hadn't fed Nana at all yesterday. She must be starved.

Jane felt a dark sense of foreboding as she approached the door. *Who closed it?* Inside, it was freezing and her mother lay on top of the covers—staring in stark terror at . . . what? Jane followed Nana's gaze to the closet. The door was ajar.

She hurried over to the bed. "Oh my God, Nana, I'm sorry." The reek was horrible. A bowl of stagnant soapy water stood next to the bed. Jane cleaned Nana as best she could and then covered the spindly woman with a blanket. She bent down with the glass, but Nana did not move, only stared at the closet. Her breath was thready and bubbling. *Pneumonia.* Jane groaned as she recognized the telltale symptom. Well, at least Medicare covered that.

"Come on, Nana, you must eat. You must drink." Nana continued to stare at the door. What strange fluke yesterday had made her think that her mother understood? She shook her head. "Does that bother you, Nana?" She turned from her mother to the closet. Her question was answered by a sharp intake of rasping breath. "It does, doesn't it? I'll close it."

"Funny, you know," she said as she returned to feed her mother. "I could have sworn that I shut the closet door yesterday, at least once. I guess the house has settled and the door no longer hangs right. Old houses will do that, you know. Nothing to frighten you, though, Nana. It just happens."

Her mother greedily gummed the peanut butter and jelly sandwich Jane had brought her for breakfast. "No oatmeal today, Mama." She switched to the more familiar term as yesterday's guilt receded and her confidence returned. "No water. No bath, I'm afraid, either. Pipes froze. Elliot's in the basement fixing it. School's closed for the day."

Sandwich finished, Jane put the last of the water to her mother's lips which she gulped down eagerly. "I hope he gets the water running soon. I'll bathe you as soon as I can."

Sorting through the clothes in the bedroom, Jane's repressed fury returned. *No water. That's just great.* She threw his shirts on the bed. She tossed his socks and underwear next to the shirts.

She didn't like this place. She didn't care that it had been a good deal. Jane didn't particularly like being the recipient of Sam Halloway's condescending charity. She had argued against the move. In the long run, though, Elliot had won. He usually did—if not by veto and violence, then by attrition. So there was nothing for Jane to do except unpack—and wait. For what, she wondered. She shook her head and crammed his shirts and socks into a drawer.

Sara came out of her bedroom a short time later. Rubbing sleep from her eyes, she bounced down the stairs ready for breakfast. She met her father as he emerged from the basement. He ignored her and turned on the tap. It choked and sputtered, and finally spat out rust-colored fluid.

He called up the stairs. "It's thawed, Jane. You can wash now."

Elliot turned to Sara. "How are you today, sleepy-head?" He bent down for a good-morning kiss and Sara had to resist the impulse to back away. Elliot hugged her and pondered her frigid response.

"You okay, honey?"

"Sure. I'm hungry."

"One bowl of Cheerios coming up," he said with faked good humor.

Sara watched as her father made a ceremony of her breakfast. With exaggerated motions and an elaborate bow, he attempted to make her laugh as he presented the cold cereal to her.

Her look was incredulous. He honestly didn't remember, she could tell. He didn't remember what had happened last night or why she was mad. How could he forget?

"You okay?"

"Yeah." Elliot smiled a small, sad smile, and Sara could read it in his eyes. He didn't know. He knew he had to be forgiven, but he didn't know for what. She wanted to cry.

"Okay, pumpkin, I'm going to go help your mama unpack."

She was left alone in the cold, silent room.

The day's progress was marked by an ever-increasing mound of empty boxes and a faint change in hue of the steel gray sky. Her mother unpacked clothes and filled closets while her father unpacked books. Sara stayed in her room where she occasionally meted out more abuse to Raggedy Andy, dribbling him around the floor in a bizarre parody of soccer.

She helped her mother bathe, feed, and change Nana. Jane strapped the newly powdered, dressed, and pressed woman into the chair and wheeled her over to the window while she changed sheets.

"See, Nana, we're going to have a white Christmas. I'll leave you here where you can look out the window."

Sara peered over Nana's shoulder at the street below. The holidays would soon be upon them, but to Sara it didn't feel like Christmas despite the tree in the living room. Its lights lied as they flashed seasonal cheer. The stockings hung limp and empty. She glanced at her mother, wondering if there would be any gifts this year.

With the books unpacked, Elliot wandered aimlessly around the study berating a fate that left him home and the papers he needed to grade at the school. He would have to work during Christmas break.

"Damn!" he muttered. With the day's chores completed, he had started on his second Scotch and prowled.

Jane listened to his restless footsteps. She patted Sara's head. "You go downstairs and see if you can't get your father interested in watching TV. See if you can keep him out of trouble." She straightened, a frown on her face. "Go on, honey; I've still got a few things to do up here." Sara watched as her mother moved down the hall to her room. With a sigh, Sara headed for the stairs.

Jane opened Sara's closet and felt the same rush of icy fear she had before. She shivered. Well, this was the last of it. All she could do before Christmas. After Sara was tucked in bed for the night, she had presents to wrap, and tomorrow, more presents to buy. She had picked up a few gifts in the hurried days before the move, but it was going to be a Spartan Christmas. She wasn't sure even now if there would be enough time.

It wouldn't take long to fix this up, just put the toys up on the shelf. Jane wondered why her usually fastidious child had just dumped her toys on the floor. It wasn't like her, probably some belated juvenile rebellion against the move. After all, wasn't Jane herself going through a rebellion of her own against the cruel and unrelenting wheel of fortune which held them both?

The motions of straightening and unpacking were mechanical now. Jane grabbed first one toy and then another and placed them neatly on the shelves. She wanted no more scenes like the one yesterday. Something moved behind her. She stood up. Silence.

"Sara? Is that you?" Sara was not around. Jane shrugged. *It's the house settling, that's all.* She returned to her work, picking up toys two at a time. Jane felt, as she had last night, someone watching, staring at her with barely repressed hatred. She glanced nervously over her shoulder. *Nothing there.*

The last few toys she simply threw onto the shelf, stepping out of the closet and shutting the door. She leaned against its cool wooden surface with a sigh of relief.

From the hall, Jane heard a slight creaking sound. She tilted her head. Her heart fluttered in her chest. The slow creak continued. Again she sighed. It was nothing, just the closet door in Nana's room opening. If Elliot was getting bored, maybe he'd take the time to fix the door.

That evening while her mother wrapped packages, Sara twisted under the sheets in a slow, sinuous, serpentine movement. She was bathed in an uneven sheen of sweat which slicked her forehead and soaked her hair. Shelley stood before her, a grisly apparition.

The left half of Shelley's head was stripped of hair. Her scalp was covered with oozing blisters and was interrupted occasionally with pieces of angry, reddened skin. Flames had eaten through the flesh at the jawline, revealing pink gums and grinning teeth, and the eye on that same side drooped like a molten Halloween candle. It was sealed shut. The one open eye wept copious tears in eternal mourning.

"Shelley?"

The specter smiled. "You miss me?"

Sara cried, "You know I do. When ya gonna come home?"

"I can come play with you sometimes, but I can't stay. Mom and Dad wouldn't like it. They don't want me anymore; I'm too ugly." The charred head bent near. Sara could smell the strong odor of burnt meat, like a steak left on the grill too long. "It's Christmastime, and Santa Claus is coming to town. Want to see Santa, Sara? He's coming for you."

Shelley came closer, opening her one good eye, and incredibly, Sara could see into it. A figure in a black cloak straddled a huge black steed. He reined his beast, and it bolted forward. The cloak billowed back to reveal a skeleton. The great destrier reared, and the skull snapped back, dropping to the black-clad shoulder and rolling down a bony arm. It landed in the wraith's hand. The phantasmal Saint Nick raised his outstretched arm, holding the decapitated skull like a lantern before him.

Sara turned her head and squeezed her eyes shut. "No. Santa Claus is fat and jolly. He dresses in red, has a white beard, and rides in a sleigh. Don't you remember, Shelley?"

Shelley uttered a short bray of laughter and paused thoughtfully—what was left of her brow furrowed. She stared down at Sara. "You don't mind the way I look, do you, Sara?" Sara nodded uncertainly.

"Look at me!" Shelley roared. Sara looked. In the retina of her weeping eye, Sara saw the ghost of the black rider.

Shelley smiled. "Okay, kid. I'll be back for you."

Elliot teetered over his daughter's sleeping form. "Shelley, oh my little Shelley." He stumbled over to the bed. He bent down, his hand caressing her shoulder.

Sara opened her eyes and sat up with a small cry. His sour breath washed over her and she felt a surge of nausea. "Daddy?"

He jerked upright, nearly losing his footing. His eyes cleared, and he let out a strangulated sob. "Sara, is that you?"

"Yes, Daddy." He pivoted and fled from the room.

Sara watched the empty doorway for a while and

then settled back to wait for sleep which seemed farther away than ever.

Outside the wind howled and wailed. A small figure dressed in blue dungarees flitted through the trees that bordered the property. Wisps of blond hair formed a pale nimbus around a misshappen head. The child's form moved in erratic fits and starts across the unfriendly landscape as the storm raged around it.

A rabbit froze in the field beyond. *Something approached.* Still as a statue, it waited for the danger to pass. Its nose twitched as it scented the frigid air, noting only the crisp, clean aroma of freshly fallen snow. The rabbit relaxed its stance and started to hop toward its burrow. An inhuman shriek reverberated off the trees and the ground. Ever alert in a hostile world, it streaked across the rough, broken soil.

A clawlike hand grasped it by the neck, and the animal screamed. Probing figures pulled at the animal's windpipe, ripping the delicate throat. Blood pulsed and flowed in projectile spurts. The hands tore it, pulling convulsing limbs from the blood-soaked torso.

CHAPTER 4

Sara awoke with an unearthly, pain-wracked death cry echoing in her mind. Visions of a skeletal Santa Claus on a black horse bearing charred Christmas gifts remained from last night's dream. She rubbed her eyes. The soft, muffled silence that accompanies a heavy snow hung suspended about her; no agonized wail disturbed the apparent calm outside. She lay quietly in the darkness listening to the wheezing groans of the aging house and waited—waited for Shelley to elbow her in the ribs so they could go off on some new adventure, but Shelley never came.

With a sigh, Sara slipped out of bed, putting on her bunny slippers in a single fluid motion. She padded over to the window. The small brick house across the circle was dark, its Christmas lights having been turned off sometime during the night. From this vantage point she could see no other houses. Through the little crystals of ice that had formed on the pane, she could just barely make out the naked trees and stubble-filled field behind the house. It was a lonely, dreary view.

As she peered at the frozen landscape, she detected a flicker of movement. Sara strained to see. Something tugged at the edge of her consciousness. She felt suddenly frightened and alone. As though in response to her isolation, a small square of light popped on in the house across the way, a beacon in the darkness. The branch so like knobby arthritic fingers tapped languidly against the frosted glass, quiescent in the calm following the storm. Sara tapped back. "No, I won't let you in," she muttered under her breath.

She reached for Raggedy Andy who looked a little battered after yesterday's abuse. Sara held the doll close to her breast, rocking back and forth as she hummed the melody to "Brahms' Lullaby." Raggedy Andy stared back at her, his painted eyes relentless and unyielding.

"It's all right, baby." She mimicked her mother's husky croon. "It was just a bad dream. It's okay. Mama will keep all those ghosts away." Raggedy Andy persisted, his eyes filled with silent reproach and accusation because the dreams hadn't gone away. They were worse than ever. Sara threw the doll down in disgust. "You've got to understand. Now, you be good. If you're bad, you get punished. I'll . . . I'll lock you in the closet with your sister."

Raggedy Andy continued to stare, reticent, judgment withheld for the moment. Tired of playing mother to the mute and unforgiving doll, she turned again to the window. Sara pressed her nose against the glass. Two widening, curved columns of condensation appeared under each nostril. After a second breath, the vapor obscured the sleeping world beyond. Sara pulled away and blew against the frosted pane, writing her sister's name in the mist.

Outside a battered station wagon crept into the cul-de-sac. The car's window rolled down and a disembodied arm appeared, heaving the morning paper onto the white lawn. The paper bounced and then slid to the porch stairs, marring their flawless, chaste surface. As the tired old wagon accelerated, it backfired, leaving a dark cloud in its wake and a ring of black soot on the street. Sara watched as it turned in the circle to make its slow progress up Elm Street. *A new day had begun.* The streetlights winked off as the first rays of the sun gleamed over the horizon.

Sara sighed again. Soon her parents would be up. She liked this part of the day before the world—and her parents—would awaken and destroy the tenuous peace. She liked being alone when she could think her own thoughts undisturbed. Sara could pretend that she lived in another place, another town, with another family like Beaver Cleaver's. Her pretend father would listen patiently to her tales, and better yet, he would understand. He would nod appreciatively and give her sage advice. This ideal daddy smoked a pipe and didn't drink. Instead, he read the paper, while her pretend mother cooked a roast in a spotless kitchen. She wore a dress with a full skirt and pearls, and was the head of the PTA.

Sara punched Raggedy Andy. "You bad boy. Quit looking at me like that or it's the closet for you." He fell noiselessly onto the floor. "Well, that's that." She seized the doll roughly and strode over to the closet and threw him onto a back shelf. Her eyes lighted on her overnight case. With a joyful cry, she extracted it, dragging it over to her bed. She admired the shiny red vinyl. It was just like Barbie's. She opened it to check the contents—a pair of pajamas, a shirt, jeans, sneakers, and a clean pair of undies—just like Mommy told her: *Always put on clean undies; you never know when an accident might happen.*

Not that she understood the association. Sara had often wondered if clean underwear was some sort of talisman against disaster—like a rabbit's foot—until Shelley told her it was so Mommy wouldn't be embarrassed if she got hit by a car and had to go to the hospital. That made her wonder even more. If she got run over by a car, wouldn't her underwear get dirty, anyway? Sara giggled. It made about as much sense as all the starving children in India.

As Sara looked at them now, she wondered, too, if Shelley had been wearing clean undies when . . . when . . . Her mind went blank. *When what?* Sara shrugged, unable to follow the thought through to its conclusion. Maybe Shelley hadn't worn clean underwear and that was why her parents were so mad at her that they wouldn't let her come home.

Sara dug to the bottom of the case until she revealed a package of crushed Twinkies. *Good, they're still there.* She would have to replace them, but it made no sense to let these go to waste. She opened the package and scraped the gooey mixture from the cellophane, shoving crumbs and all into her mouth, looking surreptitiously over her shoulder at the door to the hall. It wouldn't do to get caught eating Twinkies before breakfast.

Neither did she want her mother to discover the neatly packed case. How could Sara explain it? The case had been neatly packed for years, long before . . . *before what?* Sara shook her head. It had been her safety valve, her lifeline to sanity in a world of disruption and violence. Her eyes became unfocused as the memories came back, unwelcome and unbidden.

Sara and Shelley sat at the kitchen table while her parents fought. Both played nervously with the food that had grown cold. Their appetites decreased as the volume of their parents' voices increased. Sara didn't know what they fought about today. The scenes were so frequent, Sara no longer listened to words. It didn't matter since a topic that was okay yesterday easily became dangerous today.

Shelley rolled her eyes toward the ceiling and slipped quietly away. Sara, through some perverse sense of loyalty, stayed. She hoped somehow that her presence would avert the violence. She stayed to protect her mother, trying to become invisible while she pushed her mashed potatoes around her plate. Her father became more agitated, and her mother more belligerent. She sculpted a small castle with the sodden white lump. Her father noticed the forbidden activity. His heavy hand fell on her fragile arm and pulled. "Quit playing with your food!"

Sara stifled a cry of pain and slipped unobtrusively under the table.

"Leave the child alone. She ate most of her dinner."

"Well, if you knew how to cook better, she'd eat all of it. Instead you serve us this slop." He picked up a spoonful of potatoes and threw it on the table.

Sara clung to her mother's feet. The battle raged on overhead. Occasionally, she tapped on her mother's knees hoping to divert her attention.

"Don't fight," she whispered plaintively. "I'll eat my potatoes." Jane brusquely brushed her away. The cuts and parries flew between them. Her father got up to pace feverishly back and forth.

Her mother's voice rose, and she flung Sara's glass of milk in her father's face. "I've had enough of this. I don't have to take this shit from you."

Elliot flushed, his face turning purple in fury. His hand grasped the handle of the serving fork and swung. Sara watched, eyes round with terror as the prongs sank deeply into her mother's arm. Sara saw the blood well to the surface, dribbling down her mother's forearm, and splash onto her upturned face. Her mother screamed. Sara fled.

She found herself running down the street into an unfeeling night. Stars blinked placidly. She reached the corner and stopped. It had been her milk, her milk, that her mother had thrown into her father's face. She felt responsible—maybe if she had finished the milk, it wouldn't have happened. Yes, it must have been her fault.

She stood panting and weeping in the circle of illumination given off by the streetlight. She felt naked and exposed. She turned to her left and to her right, confused. Where could she go? Sara bawled great hiccuping sobs as she realized there was no place else to run or hide since she wasn't allowed to cross the street.

Her mother, arm wrapped in a dishtowel, found her sometime later sitting on the curb under the streetlight. She spanked Sara and brought her home. Her mother's eyes were filled with dour, disapproving reproof. Sara packed her things that night.

At first, Sara had tried stuffing her things into a hankie and tying that onto a stick, just like Huck Finn, but she couldn't fit all the clothes she thought she'd need—not much else, in fact, besides clean undies. So she discarded the stick in favor of her overnight case. If it was good enough for Barbie, it was good enough for Sara Graves. She packed everything she thought she might need, including the hankie.

Sara licked the cellophane. A ring of white filling and crumbs surrounded her mouth, reaching from her nose to her chin. She grabbed the hankie, closed the suitcase, and shoved it under the bed—just in case. She had wiped off the last incriminating evidence as the door to her parents' room whispered open and then closed. She listened to the footsteps which stopped outside her door.

A soft tap was followed by her mother's gentle voice. "Sara, are you awake?"

Her heart beating wildly in her chest, Sara stuffed the sticky handkerchief and wrapper into her slipper.

It scratched against the bottom of her foot. "Yes, Mama."

Jane opened the door and smiled down at her daughter. "Why don't you come down to the kitchen? I'll make pancakes for breakfast. You'd like that, wouldn't you?" Sara nodded. "Come on down, then. Bring your toys. I don't want you playing up here. Your father's still asleep. You might wake him. I'm going to go check on Nana, and I'll be right down."

Sara waited for her mother to shut the door and pulled the soiled handkerchief and crumpled wrapper from her slipper. She wrinkled her nose. "Yuck." She listened as her mother began a quiet conversation with Nana. Sara slipped into the hall. In the bathroom, she dropped the handkerchief into the hamper, the cellophane into the wastepaper basket, washed her face and hands, and after a few seconds' thought, her foot. She met her mother in the hall.

"Did you wash your hands?"

"Uh-huh."

Jane bent down and kissed Sara's cheek. "You're such a good girl. Go get your toys now and come to the kitchen."

Sara watched her mother begin her creaking descent and then returned to her room. Once again in her own bedroom, she surveyed its almost sterile cleanliness. All her toys were put away. She pulled a coloring book and crayons from the bedside table and headed for the stairs.

Critter greeted her in the kitchen, all wiggles and good spirits. The large brown mutt jumped up on Sara's chest, kissing her enthusiastically, tasting what remained of this morning's Twinkie. Sara sniggered and hugged him.

"Make him get down, Sara. You know he's not supposed to jump up like that."

"Aw, he's just happy to see me."

"I suppose so. Maybe tonight we can let him into the rest of the house. I didn't find any puddles in the kitchen this morning."

Sara plopped down on the floor where Critter did a quick little jig, butting her shoulder with his head and licking her fingers. "You kept him locked up last night?"

"I didn't want to, but your father thought it would be for the best. He was afraid Critter would have an accident. You know with all this excitement he might . . . well, forget."

Sara patted Critter's shaggy head, scratching behind a black-tipped ear. He gave her the doggy equivalent of a smile, tongue lolling. "Good old boy. You wouldn't forget now, would you?" Critter wagged his tail. "You can sleep with me tonight."

Her mother frowned. "Not in bed he can't. At least, don't let your father catch you." Jane dug out the frying pan and stood next to the sink scratching her head. She looked down at Sara and laughed. "I found the frying pan all right, but I can't seem to remember where I put the spatula. I'll be so glad once we're settled in here. It'll be weeks before I can find anything."

Sara pointed at a drawer. "Did you look there?"

Jane looked quizzically at her daughter and opened the indicated drawer, removing the spatula. "Aren't you amazing? You seem to know more about where I put things and what's going on in this house than I do."

Sara rolled on the floor with Critter. "Honey, don't do that. You'll get dirty. Why don't you go plug in the Christmas tree? It makes the house look so cheery." Sara looked doubtful. Jane noticed the expression and immediately understood. "I know, honey, it all seems strange right now, but you'll get used to it. I promise."

Sara stood up and went into the living room. Critter trailed closely on her heels. She plugged in the tree. The little Italian lights sprung to life, holding steady for a minute and then started to blink on and off. She stroked Critter's soft fur and said, "I'll never get used to it. Never!"

Her mother, having located everything else she needed, was whipping the pancake batter into a froth when Sara returned to the kitchen. Jane hummed gaily along with the little transistor radio which echoed the tinny refrains of "O Little Town of Bethlehem."

"Your dad and I are going shopping today. Anything you need?"

"Nope."

"You won't mind staying here with Nana, will you? We've got some Christmas shopping to do."

Sara perked up. "Oh, yeah?" She looked at her mother out of the corner of her eye and asked nonchalantly, "Whatcha gonna get me?"

Her mother glanced over her shoulder. "You're a sly one, aren't you? You know I can't tell you that. Anyway, you won't mind staying here, will you? Even though it's Christmas break, your father will have a lot of papers to grade after losing a day from work, and he'll probably want to pick them up today."

Sara stifled a groan at the mention of Christmas vacation. Her dad would be home for almost two weeks. It seemed like forever. Her mother voiced Sara's unspoken thoughts. "He'll probably be a real bear until he's got his papers done, but we can leave him alone and go shopping ourselves. After all, we have to pick up a surprise for him too. How about tomorrow or the next day? You can go see Santa."

"I suppose." Sara shook her head without enthusiasm and dumped her crayons onto the kitchen table. The next week and a half stretched before her like an empty wasteland.

"We won't be gone too long, just a couple of hours. But you're a big girl now, you'll be okay by yourself." Sara proceeded to color Fred Flintstone's face blue while her mother poured the batter into the frying pan. Jane Graves sang "O Tannenbaum" happily as the hot oil sizzled and hissed.

Sara eyed her mother curiously. It was odd for her to be so cheerful. She glared at the liquor cabinet as if by looking hard enough, she could see through the wood to the bottles within and discover if something was missing. Critter lay at her feet. When Sara shifted in the chair, his tail thumped against the floor.

"You feeling good today?" Sara said.

Jane stopped, spatula poised over the pan. "I guess I am. It's so bright and sunny." She peered out the kitchen window. "Look at how the snow sparkles and shines. I love it right after a snow, before it gets all dirty and gray."

Sara thought obliquely of the ring of soot from the backfiring car and remained silent. Two hands covered her eyes, and she jumped.

"Guess who?"

"Daddy."

"How'd you guess?" He lifted Sara out of the chair and threw her toward the ceiling. "How's Daddy's little girl today?"

"Don't be too rough with her, Elliot," Jane chided. Her father put Sara down on the floor and scowled at his wife.

"Okay," he replied sullenly, then turned and winked at Sara. "Paper here yet?"

Sara climbed back onto her chair. "Yup."

Elliot headed for the front door while Sara started to color Barney Rubble purple. The front door opened. Cold air filtered into the kitchen. The door slammed shut and her father sprinted into the kitchen.

"Jeez, it's cold out there."

Jane turned around as she slid a pancake onto a plate, passing it to Sara. "Elliot, you didn't go out there barefoot." He looked abashedly down at his toes. Snow turned to water and pooled around his feet. "Honestly, you're as bad as the kids."

Her voice faded off as she caught her error. She threw Elliot an apologetic look, and he returned it with a wistful smile. "You ready for coffee yet?" she asked with forced cheer.

"Sure," Elliot said as she plugged in the coffee maker. He poked her ribs. "You mean you haven't made it yet? I thought your heart wouldn't start without your morning coffee."

She poured another round cake into the sizzling oil. The coffee maker began to sputter in the background, and the DJ announced another sale where he promised you could find *that perfect Christmas gift.*

"Ever notice how everything turns into a perfect gift at this time of year?" Elliot rolled his eyes. "I mean everything, even toilet paper." He switched off the radio.

"Daddy!" Sara protested. "I was listening to that!"

"Well, excuuuuse me." He turned it on again. The coffeepot started to shake on the countertop. It gurgled, churned, and spat. Water seeped from its plastic seams, dripping onto the hotplate, which hissed its indignation. Sparks flew from the back of the gyrating device. "Holy . . ."

Elliot wrenched the plug from the wall. It gurgled and coughed a few more times, then fell silent. "Crap."

"How about instant?" Jane pulled a pan from the cupboard, and Elliot bent to examine the smoking pot. She joined him as he studied the burnt wires.

"What do you think happened?"

"A short, I guess. Instant will have to do." He straightened. "We can buy a new one this afternoon." Critter perked up, listening intently. He started to growl.

Jane turned to the dog. "What is it, Critter?"

"Shhh, listen." Elliot held up a warning hand. Sara looked up from Barney Rubble. They heard a soft pattering noise like fingers drumming gently against a tabletop.

"What is it?"

Click, click, click, click.

Elliot shook his head. "I don't know."

Jane returned to the sink. The pan fell, clattering from her hand. She pressed her fingers against her lips and gasped.

"What is it?"

Jane grimaced and pointed at the sink.

Elliot strode over to her side, only to step sharply backward. "Christ."

"What! What is it?" Sara scrambled down from her perch and peered into the sink. "Oh, gross!" She backed away.

Hundreds of cockroaches emerged from the drain. They formed a roiling, squirming mass that covered the bottom of the sink. Elliot opened the cabinet under the sink and pulled out the insecticide. He covered his mouth with his hands and started to spray while Sara and Jane moved aside. A small cloud formed around him. He gagged at the fumes, but continued to spray until the writhing insects grew still.

Jane and Elliot exchanged troubled looks. Jane picked up what was left of breakfast and dumped it in the garbage.

CHAPTER 5

Nana thrashed convulsively on her bed. Her hands and feet twitched spasmodically. She let out a short, shrill cry.

Critter raised his head from his paws, tilted it, and listened. A muted groan drifted down to the landing where he lay. He got up, padded softly up the stairs and into her room. He sniffed at her hand and smelled only urine. Her gnarled, semiclenched fingers jerked into a fist and then opened slightly. He watched the rapid furtive movements of her hands and feet. The *Lump* dreamed, and Critter wondered what animal chased the old woman in her sleep.

The dark! God, it was dark! *And the blackness held terrors within its confines. Nana scrambled on hands and knees toward the thin sliver of light that emanated from under the door. She was in the closet. Her fingers felt stiff and raw from digging at the hard, brittle wood.*

A husky, but unrecognized, female voice whispered outside the door. "Be quiet, honey. You'll only make it worse."

Nana uttered a strong, high shriek.

"Quiet, William, Father will hear."

Nana didn't even notice the strange appellation as she clawed at the oak door. Her fingers felt tacky. She put them in her mouth and tasted salt. Blood. Her fingers hurt, but her stomach hurt worse. It gnawed at her, begging to be filled. Nana sucked her fingers, knowing the fluid itself provided some nourishment. Her stomach rolled. She bit her hands.

How long had she been here? Days. It must have been days, but it was hard to tell except by the light which filtered under the door. It became weaker, and the woman's voice silent. Thus, she knew night had fallen.

Nana placed her mouth to the keyhole and begged, speaking words which had been spoken a long time ago. "Let me out. Please, let me out. Pleee—" The word was choked in a fit of coughing. Her throat was so dry, and she was sooo thirsty. Her stomach rumbled again, and she wept. What had she done wrong? Did it matter? She got up on her knees to beat against the door until her strength gave out. Nana collapsed in an untidy heap, her nose pressed against the crack illuminated by the small sliver of light.

Fresh air. The closet reeked of feces and urine.

She felt a surge of shame that she was reduced to this. Childlike anger flowed over her and she slapped at the wall. "Noooo!" *she wailed into the unrelenting artificial night.*

"Hush now, or your father will get angry."

Angry? Let him get angry. He was angry, anyway. Again, Nana tried to remember the sin for which she was imprisoned, but could not. She didn't understand. What crime could possibly deserve this punishment? this hunger? this thirst? Nana got up on all fours. Her head swam with the movement; her parched throat rasped, and her stomach lurched.

Outside she heard a man's resonant voice. "Can't you keep that son of yours quiet?"

"Son?" Nana recoiled and spun, eyes trying to pierce the umbra behind her. She was not alone! Nothing moved, and she relaxed slightly. It must be some kind of mistake.

"Let him out. He'll starve."

"Let him out? I'll be damned if I let him out. I'll beat him within an inch of his life. You spoil him. Listen to him whimper."

Nana held her breath. Maybe if she was good . . .

"Dear . . ." The sound died, followed quickly by a heavy thump against the door.

"How dare you? That's right, lay there! Cower on the floor. You and your son are just alike."

Nana listened to the woman cry. Nana felt consumed by an empty, hollow feeling which she no longer recognized as hunger. She crept away from the door. Her hand hit something soft. She grabbed it and crammed it into her mouth, only to spit out human excrement.

She would have prayed to God like Mama had taught her, but she couldn't remember the words. She collapsed. Her hand strayed to the disgusting mess, but she restrained herself. Still, she knew it was there, and maybe if she got any hungrier . . . She never completed the thought, for two rabid red eyes winked in the darkness.

Rats! *One hand groped for a slipper, a toy, something to throw at the glowing apparition. It found nothing besides the stinking pile. She sat up and flung it at the eyes. They just blinked and seemed to grin at her. She swooned.*

Pain! *Searing pain brought her around. She stared down at the place where she knew her legs to be, even if she couldn't see them. The fiery eyes gazed at her. "Ahhh!" They closed and she felt the pain again. The rat was eating her alive.*

Nana awoke mouthing a silent scream. She lay bathed in sweat. She had wet herself again. Critter gazed implacably at her. Nana tried to raise herself from her bed, but couldn't. She coughed. *William?* she thought, *who is William?*

Critter nosed her hand. Nana made a weak swat at him. He turned to leave the room. The Lump was awake again, and feisty. Nana turned to face the closet door as Jane walked into the room with a cup of hot cocoa.

Sara stood in Nana's room and watched from the window as her parents drove off in the Nova. Behind her, Nana's breath came in harsh gasps. Sara turned, cocked her head, and looked from Nana to the closet. She moved across the floor. Picking up the blankets, she checked one last time to make sure Nana was dry. She gently lifted Nana's head and changed the disposable diaper they put there. It was stained with the hot chocolate her grandmother had just finished.

"You okay?" Nana blinked twice and looked at the closet door. Sara pondered it. "Won't stay closed, will it?" Nana blinked twice. Sara pulled the rocker from the corner of the room and wedged its back under the knob. "Better?" Nana blinked one time. "I'm going to go out and play, okay?" Her grandmother blinked again.

Sara went into the hall and closed the door, thought better of it, and left it open. She got her yellow insulated jacket, red mittens with matching scarf, and her boots from the hall closet. Critter capered around the hall. "You want to go outside, Critter?" He barked. She looked over her shoulder into her grandmother's room. Nana lay quietly on the bed, eyes closed.

The knob on the closet door started to rattle. Nana's eyes popped open, and she made a small gurgling noise in her throat. Horrified, she watched as the doorknob twisted and turned, but the door remained closed, held in place by the rocker.

In the foyer, Sara sat on the stairs lacing up her boots. She heard a soft thud coming from upstairs.

"Nana? Are you all right?" She listened. She looked at Critter. He panted at her. She put on the other boot, wondering whether she should go back up. Sara waited. Silence. *It's nothing, probably came from outside. Nana is too old and crippled to climb over the bed rails, anyway.* Sara chuckled, donning her coat. "I'll be back in a little while," she called up the stairs and went out the front door.

She stood on the porch, blinking in the bright sunlight. Her father had shoveled a sickly looking path to the driveway and to the mailbox. A sorry sight, the battered and rusty box was stuck on a post which leaned precariously into the street. When he finished this chore, he had announced that he would shovel the drive tomorrow, but Sara wondered. He had a habit of leaving work undone and promises unfulfilled. He forgot, Mama said. Sara thought that he forgot lots.

Critter bounded down to the yard. Up the street, children shouted and squealed. Someone had tied a toboggan to a bike which some big kid pedaled through the snow, pulling the toboggan behind. Sara kicked ferociously at the snow piled near the door. Critter ran barking out of the cul-de-sac toward the group.

"Critter, no! You bad dog." Critter froze in his tracks. He turned from the children to Sara and back to the children again, giving his head one forlorn shake. "You get back here." Dejectedly, he trotted back to the bottom of the stairs, tail tucked between his legs. She sniffed as she joined him in the front yard. She took a swing at him which he quickly dodged.

"Stupid mutt." She pursed her lips. "Come on. Those kids don't want to play with us, and I certainly don't wanna play with them.

"Let's go exploring." He started to jump around frantically. "Race ya!" She took off at top speed toward the corner of the house. He streaked along behind and soon sped past her. She slowed once she was out of sight of the other children. She paused and stuffed her mittened hands in her pockets. Her breath came out in billowing puffs. Critter, realizing that he had lost his companion, stopped and waited expectantly.

She looked around her. The large oak—at least that's what Mr. Holloway said it was—reached for the sky. All its branches, except the one that reached her window, were broken. Mr. Holloway said it was going to be cut down come summer. Bird tracks surrounded the tree. Her gaze followed the spoor. Critter walked over to her side.

"Let's pretend we're Lewis and Clark lost in the wild, and we're looking for food." She pointed to the faint trail. Critter promptly looked at her finger. Sara rolled her eyes and let out an exaggerated sigh. "Dumb dog," she murmured under her breath. He tilted his head to one side, waiting patiently for her to continue, unperturbed by the criticism.

Sara stomped twice and followed the spindly, indistinct path into a shallow stand of trees. Something fluttered in the distance. The other children's voices became distant echoes. Through the bare branches, she could see the empty field which stretched across the horizon. Despite the heavy snow, clods of black dirt were still visible in the plowed tract. Broken stalks pushed through the snow's irregular and blemished surface. The field looked barren and forlorn.

A bunch of crows pecked at the earth. Sara burst from the small grove and ran toward them waving her arms and shouting. They rose in a single dark cloud. She stopped. They settled. Again she raced at them. "Hey!" Her voice was swallowed up in the vastness of the field, caught and scattered by the wind. The birds screeched a cacophony of complaint, but this time didn't move. Critter, discovering her game, bounced toward the flock of birds. They ascended with a raucous protest only to light farther away. Critter followed them.

"Critter, come on. We don't wanna eat crow. Let's go see if we can hunt up a turkey for Christmas dinner." Critter was only too happy to oblige as she raced along the tree line. Sara stumbled over the torn earth while he ran in circles around her. Watchfully, the crows meandered back to their feast. Sara wove in and out of the stand of trees. Finally, however, her curiosity got the best of her. She paused, her chest heaving up and down while she caught her breath. She turned toward the milling crows. Something on the ground held and maintained their interest.

An unknown, unnamed fear pulled at her and drew her unwillingly toward the flock. She felt more than saw an ethereal, amorphous image floating along behind her. In a lightning flash, sinewy hands grasped her throat. Overwhelming pain flooded through her, and she fell to the ground, twitching in terror. Her heart thundered in her chest and sent blood roaring to her brain. Vertigo enveloped her. Critter trotted over to her prostrate form and whimpered. He prodded her with his nose. She wheezed, and then just as quickly as it had come, the impression was gone.

Befuddled and befogged, she was only dimly aware of Critter's nose pressed against her cheek. She sat up on the hard frozen earth, her eyes scanning the gray landscape. *Something about the birds,* she thought. Sara stood up and brushed the snow from her jeans. She headed for the center of the field. The birds paused over their delicate repast.

With an indignant caw, most of them took to wing, hovering protectively overhead. One stayed behind, eyeing Sara balefully. It stooped over and plucked something from the gray-and-red blotch before it. Sara choked and coughed. Dangling from its mouth was a dripping, oozing eye. It flew to join its fellows. Then the two largest crows separated from the rest and soared over the Graveses' house, one carrying its gruesome burden. They circled several times above the peaked and gabled roof. Their voices rose in harsh, lonely cries before they flew away.

Sara shivered in the snow, staring at the ground, suddenly aware of the cold. A mass of matted gray fur lay at her feet. Empty sockets stared blankly at her. The area around what once had been a rabbit was stained crimson. Its torso covered with blood. The limbs, flecked with dried blood, were torn from the body and scattered among the frozen stalks. She glanced apprehensively over her shoulder. Her gaze returned to her gory discovery.

It was transformed. From the blood-soaked snow, Sara saw two eyes—one permanently sealed, the other eternally open. The drooping face leered at her, its scarlet surface bubbled and blistered. Shredded gray fur turned to charred flesh. Tufts of frozen straw became wisps of blond hair. Sara rubbed her eyes with the heel of her hands, whispering, "Shelley? Are you here?"

Critter sniffed at it and the distorted image grew hazy. It swam and became just another dead bunny. He tried to pick it up. Sara cuffed him on the nose. "Gross. You don't want that. It's . . ."—she searched for the right word—"dirty. Let's go back to the house."

Reproved, Critter just stood there. "Come on, Critter." With one last longing look at what he thought would make a great snack, he obeyed. Discouraged now with her explorations, Sara pushed her way through the trees and broke into a run after she reached the yard. She careened around the tree. Critter loped along beside her. Breathless, she slowed to a walk. She bent over, picking up a handful of snow. Sara patted it, trying to make a snowball, but the snow wouldn't pack. It fell in little powdery clots to her feet.

The big kid riding the bike skidded to a stop in front of the Graveses' house, the toboggan and its protesting occupant banging into the rear tire. Sara and the two boys simply stared at each other as though sizing up an adversary. Critter, however, felt no reservations and ran happily toward the other children. He wanted to make friends. He wanted to play.

"It's too dry to make snowballs," the larger boy said disdainfully.

Her heart beat wildly in her chest. She walked to the curb and casually scratched Critter behind the ear. His presence provided some small comfort. Sara peered at the boy on the bike, looking down her nose at him with as much bluff and bluster as she could manage. His cheeks and the tips of his ears were bright red. A colorful cap covered his head from which a few strands of dark brown hair escaped.

"I know that," Sara said.

"Well, then wha'cha doin' it for?"

She shrugged. "Dunno, 'cause I wanted to."

"This your dog?"

"Yup."

"What kind?"

"My dad says he's Heinz 57."

The older boy laughed. "That's just a mutt."

"Well, maybe, but he's a good mutt."

"You live here." He pointed at the house.

Sara stood a little bit straighter. "Sure. What's it to you?" The big kid toed the pile of snow the sled had made in its wake and said nothing. She changed the subject. "How can you ride that thing in the snow?"

"It ain't too bad once you get the hang of it."

The smaller boy, silent until now, climbed off the toboggan, extending a gloved hand. He was blond and plump. He exuded a ruddy-cheeked glow. "You gotta watch him, though. He's dangerous. I'm Tommy; he's my big brother, David."

Sara gave the larger boy a cool, appraising look and took Tommy's hand. "I'm Sara."

"You just move in?"

"Yeah."

David nodded toward the house. "Ain't you afraid of living there?"

Sara turned and looked at the cracked peeling paint and the distorted gingerbread eaves of her new home. It stood over them, dark and foreboding, a stark shadow against the bleached white sky and snow-covered earth. "Nah, why should I be?"

"It's haunted," David said, and Tommy hissed at the older boy.

Sara spread her feet wider apart and placed her hands on her hips. "No, it's not. Says who?"

"Says everybody."

"Well, it's not. If it were, wouldn't I have seen a ghost—or something—by now?"

"Well, have ya?"

"Have I what? Seen a ghost?" She waved his question away. "That's silly."

"Is not! That's what everybody says; it's haunted." He prodded Tommy with his foot. "You coming?"

Tommy climbed back on the toboggan and turned to look at Sara, his expression serious. "Well, some pretty bad stuff's happened here."

"Like what?"

Tommy shrugged.

"Don't even talk to her. Little Miss High-N-Mighty won't believe you." The older boy stuck his tongue out at her. "The ghost's gonna getcha, I bet, I bet."

"That's silly."

"Ha!" David got on his bicycle and pushed away from the curb. Sara watched. As they left, Tommy pointed at David, then at his own head and made a slow circling motion with his finger. Sara smiled.

"Come on, Critter, let's go inside."

Sara sat in the rocker in Nana's room, watching her sleep. Saliva dripped from her grandmother's open mouth. Sara pulled herself into a ball and stuck her thumb in her mouth. David's voice rang in her ears, "haunted," while dead red-and-gray bunnies danced in her mind's eye and raucous crows screamed derision over torn corpses. Beaks with oozing eyeballs flashed at her, and pieces of bugs became her crisped sister.

She pulled a broken locket out of her pocket, fingering the chain. A whole Shelley smiled up at her. The other half once had held Sara's picture, but it was gone; Sara had broken it and given the other half to Shelley as she lay in the hissing oxygen tent at the hospital. Sara wondered if Shelley still had her half. She would have to ask. Sara's hand closed tightly around the small heart. She felt protected with the photo in her grasp. Almost as though her sister were here with her, ready to chase the evil spirits away.

Sara didn't move when her mother's voice floated up the hall. "Sara, we're home. You stay up there until your father and I bring the packages in."

Sara said nothing, extracting her thumb from her mouth and wiping it on her blue jeans. She listened as the front door banged open and shut several times.

"It's okay now. You can come down." She moved listlessly to the head of the stairs.

Her father struggled in the front door with a large package. Jane Graves held the door open, shaking her head. "I don't know why you picked such a big one."

"You know we've wanted one for years," he said as he put his burden down. "Why not get the best?"

"But that little component system would have been just fine. For that one"—she pointed—"you're going to have to put the rack together and everything."

He snarled, grabbing her chin and turning her to face him. His voice was threatening, oily and deceptively smooth. "What's the matter? Don't you think I can do it?"

Jane kept her thoughts to herself, but she knew with Elliot's mechanical ability it might be days before the stereo was assembled. He released her and slid the box toward the living room. "Look, like I said, why get second best. With the insurance money we can afford it."

She winced. She would rather not think of the source of the funds. Shelley's life insurance policy had been small, just enough to cover the . . . her mind refused to form the word. The few hundred dollars that were left, Jane felt could be better spent elsewhere. She dropped the subject. To argue further would only invite his fury.

Then Jane noticed her daughter standing at the top of the stairs. "What's up with you, kiddo? Nana okay?" Sara nodded. "We got a fancy new stereo, isn't that something?" Again Sara nodded. Jane turned back to her husband. "Do you think you'll be able to put it together before you have to leave for your gig tonight?"

"Christ, I almost forgot about playing at the Christmas shindig for the Elks. At least the lodge is here in town and not in the city. I don't know why you want to live in the suburbs, all 'for the sake of the children.'" His voice changed in tenor to a high-pitched imitation of Jane's, descending when he continued. "We wouldn't even be in this house if you hadn't insisted we stay in the same goddamn town. It would be so much better for me in Chicago. What with Shelley gone . . ."

Jane backed out of his way. It was an overworked

topic and a major source of contention. Not about to be cowed, she countered, "It's not the middle of nowhere."

"What do you mean? There's a goddamn plowed field right behind the house. It's about as far out as you can get and still be in the suburbs."

"It's better for Sara here." At the sound of her name, Sara started down the stairs. Her father glared at her mother, who didn't notice. Instead, she continued to defend her position. "The schools are better and besides it's closer to your work. Which would you rather have, a long drive to the city whenever you have a gig or a long drive to school every morning?"

With lightning speed, he stepped away from the living room door. His arm snaked out and he grabbed her by the throat, shoving her against the wall. He held her, his fingers locked around her neck. Every muscle quivered with repressed tension. He wagged a warning finger at her menacingly while Sara started to whine. Critter beat a hasty retreat. "Look. I don't have the time to argue with you. I got a stereo to manufacture before I work tonight."

Jane nodded mutely. Elliot relaxed his grip. He returned to the box, which he "walked" the rest of the way into the living room. Sara scampered to her mother and hugged her waist. Elliot ignored them, intent on getting the stereo into the proper, most advantageous position. Jane put her arms protectively around Sara, who examined the box dubiously. Sara silently agreed with her mother. She didn't think he could put it together, but she held her peace.

Jane bent over and whispered into Sara's ear, "Why

don't we go bake some cookies and leave your father to his own devices?"

"Sure."

Jane propelled her daughter toward the kitchen, giving Elliot a wide berth. "How about gingerbread men?" Jane asked as she pulled Sara into the kitchen behind her. In the living room, Elliot began to swear.

CHAPTER 6

Christmas morning dawned cold and clear. Water basin in hand Jane paused in front of Nana's door, savoring the silence. Yet something about it was unnatural. She pulled the peach chenille robe more tightly around herself, trying to put her finger on what seemed out of place. Other Christmases usually began with Shelley and Sara climbing into bed with Elliot and herself, but not this year—no Shelley. The stronger, older sister had been the ringleader for whatever misadventure the two thought up. Jane felt the pressure build behind her eyes and the tightening in her throat that signaled the onset of tears.

She squelched it. She had to get Nana up, dressed, and ready. It was one of the few days during the year that she came down to join the family. Jane wished they could have set up a bedroom on the first floor.

She was sure Nana would have enjoyed being part of the daily bustle and activity, but Elliot had insisted on his combined music room and study away from the bedrooms.

Steeling herself, Jane tapped lightly on the door and entered. She moved around the rocker which remained where Sara had wedged it under the doorknob. For some unknown reason, Nana seemed to prefer it that way. Jane walked over to the bedside table, carrying the cooling basin of water. Nana peered up at her.

"Did you sleep well?"

Nana blinked.

"Nana, it's Christmas. Time to get you ready so you can come downstairs to watch Sara open her presents. I'm going to wash your hair and get you all prettied up. It looks like it's going to be a beautiful Christmas, an extra special day, and we're going to have turkey with all the trimmings."

Jane patted the few sparse tufts of hair. "Would you like to have a drink of water before I start washing you?"

The watery blue eyes blinked again.

Jane picked up the water glass, guiding the straw to Nana's mouth. It was a disconcerting habit of Nana's to blink in response to questions, almost as though . . . Jane brushed the thought aside with an unconscious gesture. She placed a capsule on Nana's tongue. "Time to take your antibiotic. The doctor says you should get through this cold quickly since we caught it in time. Says if we could get you up more often that you wouldn't be as prone to colds." She gave her mother another sip of water. "I'm going to try, Mama, really try to get you up every day once things settle down again."

She bent over the prostrate form, thinking as she did how quiet things had been. With Elliot playing at Christmas parties nearly every night, it had been almost peaceful. She wondered how long it could last. She sprinkled the lukewarm water on Nana's thinning hair. Deft fingers gently massaged the baby shampoo into her mother's scalp. As she went through the motions, she chattered away.

"Things have been better for Elliot and me since we finished the move. He's been working most nights, playing at different gigs. Oh, he still comes home drunk sometimes, but he leaves us alone. Usually, Sara's in bed, and I know when to stay out of his way."

Jane dismissed the scene with the stereo with a wave of a soapy hand, but it reminded her of the purchase, and she rattled on. "We bought a nice stereo. We've wanted one for years, and now when he's home, all he does is listen to music. He's happy with it. He put it together all by himself, can you believe it? Even wired the old speakers into his study." Her voice revealed her amazement at this prodigious feat. "A lot of times he just falls asleep in the study. Sometimes I think maybe everything's going to be okay, but I worry when he doesn't come to bed at night. You know how it used to be when Shelley was . . ."

Jane stopped. Frowning, she looked out the window at the brightening day. She lifted Nana's head, placed a towel underneath it, and started to rinse her hair with the water she brought over in cupped hands. She looked down again at her mother. "Why, Mama, what's wrong? You're crying."

Jane stroked Nana's cheek. "I wish I knew what you were thinking."

When her mother's hair was rinsed, Jane grabbed another towel and wrapped it around Nana's head, feeling her own tears welling to the surface. "It's going to be all right, I'm sure. I'm probably worried about nothing. Like I said, he's left Sara alone. I check on him at night, and there he is in the study, snoring away." She patted the towel-wrapped head. "Let's see . . . a quick sponge bath and we should be all set."

Jane switched to automatic, lost in thought as she bathed Nana, applied the salve to her sores, and changed the sheets. "Well, Mom, what do you want to wear today? How about that lovely pink robe, the warm flannel one?" Jane quickly dusted her mother with talcum powder and wrapped her up in the robe. She then brought the chair next to the bed, placed some disposable diapers across the seat and liberally sprinkled them with talc.

She lifted the light form to the chair. "You know, Mom, you're a real featherweight. I wonder how much you weigh now. Maybe I'll have the doctor weigh you the next time we take you in." Getting her mother seated on the chair was more of a challenge. She arranged the distorted limbs in some semblance of a sitting position, propping her up on pillows. Finally, Jane tied her mother into the chair.

"There. We're all set." Jane picked up the dirty linens and took them into the bathroom to soak. When she returned, Nana had somehow managed to twist herself around so that she faced the closed closet door. "Sometimes I think you are more spry than you let on. Don't worry about the closet. I'd get Elliot to fix the door, but I'm afraid he'd botch the job." She bent over Nana's wheelchair to open the door.

"Oh, he would, would he? Who are you to talk?"

Jane jumped. Elliot stood right outside Nana's door in his worn red-and-blue-checked robe and slippers, his arms folded across his chest. He smiled ominously.

She put her hand to her chest, willing her heart to slow down to a trot. Elliot didn't like to be reminded of this lack of aptitude. "You startled me."

"I bet I did. I figured you'd need some help getting Nana down the stairs." He turned to Nana. "Hello, how are you today?" Nana's eyes followed him as he walked past them into the bedroom to examine the door. "I did okay on the stereo; I can probably fix the door."

"I didn't mean anything by that. It's just that it needs to be rehung, and that's difficult, isn't it?" Jane wheeled Nana into the hall.

His voice drifted out to them. "No, I think it should be okay if I just replace the latch."

Jane stood next to the heating vent and shivered. *Damn, it's cold here.*

Elliot walked back out of the bedroom and bent over Nana. "Do you want me to fix the door for you?" Nana blinked and smiled. "I thought you would."

Jane frowned. "It's almost like she understands, isn't it?"

Elliot looked down at his mother-in-law with her contorted body and warped limbs. "I think she understands more than you give her credit for." He looked back up at his wife. "You're shivering."

"Yes, haven't you noticed how cold it is here? It seems to be colder here than any other place in the house. It's strange, too"—she nodded at the heat register—"in the closets you expect it, no vents, but not here so close to where the heat comes up from downstairs."

He surveyed the hall. Pieces of the faded medallion rose wallpaper had started to peel away from the wall. "Probably a draft coming down from the attic." He pointed at the trapdoor in the ceiling a few feet away.

Jane's gaze followed his hand. "That's stretching it a bit, don't you think? I mean I'm standing next to the main vent, and the attic door is almost six feet away." She wondered if she should mention the noises she had heard in the attic and decided against it.

Elliot shrugged. "The old gravity furnace isn't the most efficient means of heating a house."

"You're right there. Do you think we could persuade Sam to put in a new heater before next winter?"

Elliot rolled his eyes toward the ceiling. "Jeez, let's not start making demands already, shall we? We've only been here a week." He gestured toward Nana. "Let's take her downstairs."

Jane rolled the chair to the head of the stairs. Elliot grabbed the base of the chair and lifted while she held the handles. She contemplated the spot on the top of his head where his hair was starting to thin. With a barely audible snicker, Jane remembered the once-curly, untamable brown mop which used to fall to his shoulders. It had been such a long time ago; fashion's dictates and their lifestyle had changed considerably.

Then she had believed they would be happy, that they would make a life together—her musician husband and her. She would stand by his side while he bowed to an adoring audience. He drank a little too much, but he had seemed so fun-loving, robust, and decisive in comparison to her father, whom she remembered rarely, and then only as a blur. Her images of her paternal parent consisted mainly of his sleeping off a drunk—on the kitchen table, sprawled on the floor, or wrapped around the toilet—while his wife and children slaved to keep the farm going.

"You know this is nice of you," Jane said. Elliot looked up, surprised. "Not many husbands would be so tolerant of their wives' invalid mother."

"What do you mean?"

"I don't know, just that a lot of them would rather have her in a nursing home."

"I like your mother. She's a tough old bird. She deserves better than that. Life really hasn't dealt her a fair hand."

Jane almost dropped the chair as she watched Nana feebly lift a stiff and shaky hand from where it was propped on a pillow and pat the air in front of her ineffectually.

Elliot saw it, too, and smiled. "You see? I told you she understood more than you gave her credit for. Isn't that right, Mother?"

The hand waved weakly a couple more times and then dropped back to the arm of the wheelchair. Elliot bent to put the chair down at the foot of the stairs and Jane brushed a couple of tears away. *What is wrong with me today?* she thought.

Elliot looked around the foyer. "Quiet, isn't it? Where's Sara?"

"Still sleeping, I guess," she said over her shoulder as she steered Nana toward the living room. Elliot trailed along behind and sighed. Jane didn't have to guess what he was thinking—how different it seemed from other Christmases?

"Why don't you put on a pot of coffee?" Elliot suggested. "And I'll go get the sleepyhead."

Jane watched as he ran up the stairs, and she wondered why things couldn't be like this all the time. She dismissed the thought with a shake of her head. *They just couldn't be and weren't; no point worrying about it.* She positioned Nana next to the tree and went to brew the coffee.

"Hey, slug-a-bed. You going to sleep Christmas away?" Sara stretched and yawned. He lifted her out of bed, glanced over his shoulder, and then tossed her into the air. She squealed. He threw her up again and caught her on the descent.

"Again, Daddy, again."

He grinned at her. "Okay, one more time, but don't tell your mom, promise?"

She looked solemn and made an X over her heart with her finger. "I won't. I promise." Up she went, and then he set her gently on the floor. Little flannel-clad arms reached up to him.

"Once more, pleeease."

"No, your father's getting too old for that sort of thing." He stooped over and did a quivering imitation of an old man walking with a cane. He wagged his finger at her, pulling his lips over his teeth. "Besides, little lady, you're getting much too big." He broke into a witch's cackle.

"Aw, Dad, you're not *that old.*"

"Not yet, dear, but soon." Sara looked disgusted. Elliot grabbed the tiny hand. His eyes became glazed and he squatted next to Sara. She took a quick step backward, but he held her fast. "What's the matter?" He patted her cheek with a sweat-soaked palm. His hand dropped to her shoulder and followed the contour of her body until it rested on her hip.

"What's wrong? Don't you love your daddy anymore, Shelley?" His hand slipped between her legs. "Give your daddy a great big kiss."

"Daddy? Daddy, I'm Sara."

His eyes cleared and he pulled sharply away. "Of course, you're Sara. Who else would you be?"

Sara shook her head as Elliot stood up. "Come on, let's see what's been left under the tree for you."

They entered the living room just as Jane finished putting on some Christmas music. Two steaming mugs sat on the coffee table. Dutifully, Sara went over and kissed Nana on a powdery cheek. Flakes of dry skin fell like snow onto her lap. "Merry Christmas, Nana."

The family stood in a frozen tableau of distress. Sara stepped away from the chair and eyed her parents. Ill at ease, she stuck her thumb in her mouth. Elliot scowled, but didn't correct her. It was Christmas, after all, and they all felt nervous. Elliot broke the silence.

"Why don't you check and see what's there?" He nodded at Sara. Formerly Shelley's job, as eldest, to pass out the presents, someone had to fill the void. Sara dove for the tree, lifting a big package.

"Ooh, is this for me?"

"That's what it says, doesn't it? But don't open it yet. Why don't you pass out the presents this year like a big girl?"

Jane excused herself and went into the kitchen to collect herself. She returned with a small plate of cookies. Elliot raised an eyebrow in mock reprimand.

Jane gave him a sheepish grin. "Aw, gee whiz, cookies for breakfast isn't going to kill us, is it? After all, it only happens once a year."

He noticed her red-rimmed eyes and walked to her side, giving her a hug. "You going to be okay?"

She extracted herself from his arms. "Sure."

Sara, meanwhile, created growing piles with their presents, placing them next to her father's recliner and her mother's favorite easy chair. She made a ceremony of it in an attempt to cover up the discomfort they felt at Shelley's absence.

"One for Daddy, one for Momma, one for Nana, and two for me." She looked up at them, seeking their approval.

Elliot nodded. "Go ahead, pumpkin."

Jane gestured toward the cups. "Coffee's getting cold."

Once all the packages were distributed, Sara settled next to Nana. "Can I open one?"

"That's what they're for."

Sara gleefully started on the largest box. Unlike her more exuberant sister who would have shredded the wrapping paper, Sara was restrained. She picked gently at the tape and stripped the package, leaving the paper intact. She grimaced at what she saw there. A Teddy Ruxpin. *Kid's stuff.*

Her mother caught her expression. "What's the matter, honey, don't you like it?"

Realizing how hurt her parents would be, she tried to smile. "It's just that I don't have any tapes to go with it."

"Open that package over there." She indicated one at the bottom of the stack. "I bet Santa wouldn't bring you Teddy without any tapes."

Sara averted her eyes, folding the paper she had just removed from the package. She didn't like Santa. For her, there was no Santa. They had lied. He wasn't a kindly fat man dressed in red, but a skeletal image riding a great horse and carrying a skull like a lantern. Shelley had shown her. *The black man.*

"You open one, Jane." Her father handed her mother a small box.

Jane took it from his hands and tore into the brightly wrapped gift. She held up a flannel nightgown. "This ought to keep me warm on these cold winter nights. Your turn, Elliot."

He opened Sara's first. "Oh goody, socks."

"Don't you like them, Daddy?"

"Like them? I love them and need them, too. Mine have holes in them."

"I know, Mommy told me."

He winked at Jane. "I bet she did. Did she tell you that I needed a new robe, too?"

Sara sniffed and stuck her nose up in the air. "I'm not gonna tell."

"Going to," Jane corrected her gently.

Meanwhile, Elliot peered at his stack of boxes. "Hmmm. Let me see. Which one looks about robe-size?"

"Daddy, that's not fair."

"It isn't, huh? Well, let's see what is in this big box here." They watched him as he started to unwrap the next package, revealing a chain saw. "Is this a hint?"

"Maybe, a little one."

"You certainly have enough for me to do—fix the door, cut down the tree. What next? Paint the place?"

Jane grimaced. To deflect his apparent irritation, she turned to Sara. "Hey, let's not stand on formality. Dig in. Sara, what else have you got there?"

Sara reached for another package. She let out shouts of delight while her parents exchanged more subdued thank-yous. Jane picked up the new food processor and showed it to her mother.

"Talk about hints."

"All's fair, eh, love?" His tone was acid.

Nana sat and watched patiently, eyes flitting first from one face to another.

"Hey, we almost forgot about Nana. Sara, put a package on your grandmother's lap," Elliot said as he paused over a small flat parcel.

Nana picked at the bow while Jane watched, amazed. Elliot glanced at her as if to say, *See, I told you so.*

Sara impatiently grabbed the package. "I'll help you." She took off the paper and opened the box, setting it back on Nana's lap.

Nana's hand fluttered over the present inside. She

grabbed a swatch of cloth and lifted it as well as she could, only to give up and look down. Jane frowned uncomfortably, then to hide her dismay she asked with feigned cheer, "What is it, Sara?"

Elliot grinned, answering before Sara had a chance to. "A robe, a nice fluffy purple one. Can't have you wearing the same old robe all the time, can we, Nana? A girl has to have a change of clothes."

Jane chuckled. She turned to Sara. "There's more. Sara, help your grandmother." Sara bent to the task of opening each package, some slippers, some talc, and one final gift that Elliot wouldn't let Sara open.

"This one's a surprise. I'll open it."

Jane watched him curiously. The box contained a tape player and several storybook tapes. "Oh, Elliot, that was a good idea."

He shrugged. "Well, it must get a little boring with nothing better to do than lay there in bed all day." He beamed, pleased with his own idea. "I'd say between the stereo, Teddy Ruxpin, and the tape player that this entire family is wired for sound now."

"Not quite," Jane said.

"Whad'ya mean?"

"Well, you still have one more package, but wait. Let me pour some more coffee before you open it." Jane returned with the refilled mugs. Elliot opened his last package.

"Oh, this is great." He stared at the batch of sheet music. "How did you know?"

Jane snorted. "You've been dropping little hints for weeks now. You're about as subtle as a bull in a china shop."

Sara stood up. "Can I put this on, Mom? Pleeease?"

She held up the package which proudly told her to *Get in Shape, Girl.*

"Sure."

Mimicking Sara's piping tone, Elliot stood up and squirmed. "Can I go get my sax, Mom? I'll use the mute. Pleeease?"

Jane laughed. "Sure, kids, have at it." As Elliot and Sara wandered off, Jane moved over next to Nana's chair. She blew on the coffee to make sure it was cool enough to drink. Jane held it up to Nana's lips, following it with a cookie. "You see, Mama. Things are going to be okay." Nana looked at her sadly and blinked—twice.

Elliot came back into the living room, sax in hand. He turned off the stereo. "How about a little Dixieland, Nana? I'm gonna rock your socks off." Nana smiled faintly. He put the sax to his lips, his eyes on the sheet music and his fingers picking out the notes, haltingly. Sara came back into the room in a leotard and tights and started dancing, waving the weights around as she moved. Jane rocked back and clapped her hands. On the second go-round, Elliot played with more confidence. He motioned with his head for Jane to come stand next to him. She did. Then he looked from her to Nana's feet. Jane looked. Her mouth dropped open. Nana's toes wiggled in time to the tune. Shocked, she ran into the kitchen, blinking the tears away. He followed.

"I'm sorry. I just thought you should see."

"Oh, Elliot. If she understands . . ." Her voice died in her throat. "How awful for her."

"Honey, we're doing the best we can. Maybe those exercises that the doctor recommended will help."

Jane wiped her eyes. "You know, this has turned out to be a pretty good Christmas. Better than I expected. If only . . ." She started to cry again.

Elliot pulled her into a gentle embrace. She stiffened at his touch. He kissed the top of her head. "I'm sorry, Jane. It'll be all right."

Jane hummed along with the music while she worked on dinner. Sara turned into quite a little dancer, doing her own interpretation of "When the Saints Go Marching In" which looked like an odd mixture of a Jane Fonda workout, the watusi, and the Bolshoi ballet. The despair Jane felt earlier had lifted, dulled by the rum-spiked eggnog she had fixed for Elliot and herself.

The kitchen windows were steamy and the mouthwatering aroma of roast turkey filled the house. She had convinced herself by now that Elliot must be wrong about Nana. To think otherwise was too painful to bear. She made periodic trips to the living room to refill her mug from the punch bowl and to join in the fun. She pointedly ignored Nana's feet, not wanting to see that she managed to keep up with the beat.

Jane set the table and put the mashed potatoes, stuffing, and vegetables in separate bowls. When the dinner was ready, she lit the candles and went to announce that dinner was served. The family assembled. Nana sat between Jane and Sara. Both fed her, one taking over while the other one ate. Dinner was jovial, but quiet—interrupted only with a periodic "please, pass the," smacking lips, and groans of delight. The candles gave the meal a rosy glow.

After eating their fill, they leaned back. Elliot let out a loud burp. Sara giggled and Jane scolded him. "Elliot! Excuse yourself."

"In the East that is considered the highest compliment one can give to the chef."

Sara belched in imitation of her father, and Jane gave her a look of mock severity. "Hmmm," she said, lifting her mug to her lips.

"Really, that was delicious, Jane."

"Yeah, that was good, Mommy."

They fell silent and contemplated the leftovers, each left to his or her own thoughts. Jane felt sated and sleepy. She wished that she didn't have to put Nana to bed, but soon she would have to take her mother upstairs and clean her up. Nana, quiet until now, uttered a short, sharp cry. Jane looked at her, bewildered. Nana stared at the candle. The candle sputtered, and the wax spewed over the lip in a wide stream, winding its way around the smooth surface.

"What's the matter, Nana?" she asked her mother. Jane followed Nana's gaze as did Sara.

A little smile played about the child's lips. The flame leapt and danced. Sara stared in fixed fascination. Unaware of what she was doing, she lifted her hand and reached for the fiery light. *So pretty.* Nana tore her eyes away from the portent of ill and looked at Sara. Their eyes met and Sara grinned a wicked little smile so reminiscent of her sister. Nana shuddered.

With a sigh, Jane stood. "You ready for bed, Mother?" The candle guttered again, the flame jumped gleefully a few more times and then extinguished.

* * *

That night Jane and Elliot made love. In the passion of the moment, she didn't notice how mechanically he ground away at her as though performing some distasteful, mandatory duty. After her cry of ecstasy, he rolled off her. As she fell into a self-satisfied sleep in his arms, his thoughts were far away on a nubile young form lost to him forever.

She snuggled against Elliot. If she could have, she would have purred like a kitten. She burrowed closer to his warm body. The wind mumbled around the walls. Perhaps another storm was brewing, but Jane didn't care. She thought she heard someone whimpering. It came from the hall. She thought about going to check Sara, but contentment held her in the soft, warm bed. A patch of moonlight fell on the door. Jane stared at it, dazed. Smoke drifted through the keyhole. She thought wildly of fire. Fear kept her immobilized. The thin tendril uncoiled and sank lazily to the ground.

She strained to watch and her nostrils flared at the stench of charred flesh. The glimmer grew until she could discern bare skin, bubbled and blistered in different places. She waited now, transfixed, a scream frozen on her lips. Crawling across the floor, she recognized the monstrous image as her daughter. Added to the burnt visage, decay had taken its toll. A delicate web of mold grew across the face; two empty sockets revealed where the eyes should be; the nose had collapsed into the skull.

It mounted the bed, and Jane scrambled back against the headboard, trying to rouse her husband, but he snored on. The scream stuck in her throat.

Held in thrall, she struggled to be free. Whispering the Lord's Prayer under her breath, she waited, reconciled. Shelley touched her legs with hands as cold as ice. Jane gasped for air. Shelley crawled onto her, over her abdomen and chest. She grinned. Two blistered, reddened hands reached for her face. Talon fingers caught at her eyes and tore at her flesh. Jane squirmed in her grip. The pain released her from the thrall and she started to shriek.

Jane sat bolt upright in bed, awakened by the horror of her dream. Her chest heaved and her hands shook. She rubbed her eyes, trying to erase the image. She glanced around the room. Her eyes rested on the keyhole where now no vaporous wisp swirled in languid undulation.

Still Jane got up to check the door. She opened it and checked the hall. *Nothing.* A curling bit of wallpaper whispered softly at the slight movement of air. Jane jumped. It seemed to be waving at her, a weeping remnant of bygone days.

Critter brushed past her to lay next to the bed. Jane backed into the room and headed for her dresser. She clawed frantically through a drawer, dumping its contents on the floor. She spied the skeleton key which she quickly inserted in the door, twisting it. Rusty tumblers groaned, rattled, and fell into place.

Leaving the key in the door, she collected the clothes from the floor and stuffed them back into the drawer. A quick turn of the knob reassured her the door was locked, and she climbed back into bed. Catching her breath, she glared angrily at Elliot's sleeping form. With the heightened senses of the recently awakened, she listened and could have sworn she heard something climbing around in the attic.

Sara awaited Shelley's nightly visitation with a mixture of dread and anticipation. She missed her sister dearly, but wished that Shelley would appear as she once had and not in the form she now possessed. In part, Sara could understand why her parents had banished her. Still she waited.

The smell of burning, as always, heralded her coming.

"Sara. Sara!"

"Shelley, is that you?"

Shelley stood before her in the moonlight. "Of course it's me, silly. Who else would it be?"

"Dunno," Sara answered, pouting.

"It's Christmas." She fixed Sara in her molten stare.

Sara turned away. "Don't show me Santa again, Shelley."

"I won't." Shelley stepped back, falling into ringing peals of laughter.

Relieved, Sara started to talk. "It was a good Christmas, Shelley, you shoulda been here. I got all sorts of presents."

Shelley scowled, nodding her agreement. "Yes, I should have been here, but I couldn't, you know. Mom and Dad wouldn't let me, and for that they must be punished."

"Punished? How?"

"Don't worry about that." She dismissed the question, abruptly changing the subject. "Daddy came to you today like he used to come to me."

"I don't understand."

"Of course you don't. You're too young."

"I am not! Tell me."

"You sure you want to know?"

Uncertainly, Sara nodded. Shelley whispered in her ear. Sara gasped.

"No!"

"He used to with me. He always liked me best." Sara felt suddenly ill. "I told you, you wouldn't understand. He does it to Mommy, too, 'cause he has to."

Sara shook her head no. Shelley lifted her hand, revealing fingers fused by flame. "It doesn't matter. You don't have to believe me. I got some presents for you, too."

Excited, Sara started to bounce around on the bed. "You do? What, what?"

"They're in the attic. Come with me."

"The attic?" Sara climbed out of bed and walked behind her sister into the hall. They both stood next to the vent. Sara shivered in the cold; Shelley seemed not to notice. She pointed at the trapdoor.

"I can't get up there," Sara whispered to her sister.

"Sure you can, dummy. I'll help you." Shelley's image started to blur until she dissolved into a wisp that drifted toward the ceiling.

Sara cocked her head. "But, Shelley, I can't do that."

"Sara, Sara." The voice came down to Sara from the attic above her head. It touched her spine with a frozen hand.

"Shelley, I'm scared," she pleaded.

The next thing Sara knew she stood beside Shelley. Bare rafters reached a point somewhere in the shadowy recesses above her head, but she ignored them. Instead her gaze fixed on Shelley's old toy box which she thought long gone. The lid opened, and a marionette floated unaided in the air. "You always liked this. You were jealous of it and wanted one just like it, didn't you?"

Sara nodded tongue-tied.

"It's yours if you'll help me."

Sara looked into her sister's blistered face with its mouth twisted into a perpetual sneer, feeling suddenly sleepy. "How?"

Shelley slipped something into Sara's hand, and she bent over to place a lipless mouth next to Sara's ear. "I'll tell you."

CHAPTER 7

Elliot stared at the gleaming sax he held in his hands. The placid Christmas was little more than a shadowy memory. He felt the dull anger rising to his throat like bitter bile. He put down the sax, stretched, and went over to the bottle he kept in his study for just such emergencies to pour himself another drink. Jane didn't know about this bottle, but he doubted she'd mind. She rarely objected to his drinking. She wouldn't dare.

Frustration throbbed behind his temples, a formless entity threatening to devour him whole. Elliot brought his fist down upon the flimsy, metal music stand with a bang. "Damn!" It crumpled under the violence of the blow and sent the music sheets scattering across the floor. He didn't notice. Instead, he placed his glass upon the shelf. Internal balance gone, he wobbled where he stood. Closing one eye, he tipped the bottle over the glass, aiming with excessive care, and missed. Scotch splashed over his books, rolled down the shelf, a little dribbling onto the term papers he came into the study to grade. He pushed the papers out of harm's way and tried again. *Success.*

Elliot teetered back over to the chair, glaring at the papers. If he read one more theme about Bach—spelled Bock—he'd puke. Come to think of it, he might puke, anyway; he felt a little woozy. He didn't want to think about the hangover he was going to have tomorrow. Elliot picked up the sax, put it to his lips, and blew a few melodious notes, only to put it down again in disgust.

What had happened to all his dreams? He was going to be famous. He was going to know Jimi Hendrix and Janis Joplin and call them by their first names. He was going to play backup for the *biggies.* But Janis and Jimi had gone and died on him, and the biggies had names that sounded strange even to him, and dressed weirder still. Elliot took another sip of his drink, musing. He was beginning to sound like his mother. *Let's face it, I'm getting old.*

He sat back in the chair, swirling the glass before him, admiring the way the light played off the amber liquid. He didn't have to think too long or too hard to remember where his dreams had gone. They had gone up in smoke. *Charcoal-broiled fantasies.* Elliot laughed without humor at this bit of alcohol-induced wit.

He remembered those wild days after college when he was a member of a rock band, playing for the same student body who once gave him a home, and then he got a little too close to one particular student body—

Jane, with her long blond hair flowing in a thick mane down her back and her even longer, lovelier legs. She had been beautiful then, whether she wore the typical student uniform of patched and faded blue jeans with a fatigue jacket, or "dressed" for an occasion in peasant blouse and skirt. Her large blue eyes could have melted butter. They had certainly melted him, and he—with all the patience he could muster—melted her reservations and scruples.

This had been his demise. Elliot could still recall the day she came to him to tell him that she was pregnant. His mind had done a quick jitterbug, jumping quickly from abortion to marriage to running and hiding at his favorite pub. Instead, he had snarled at her, "Why the hell weren't you taking the pill?" She cried and apologized; he did, too, feeling suddenly small for his rebuke in the face of dilemma.

Abortion had been unthinkable. Enough of his staunch Catholic upbringing remained that it was never a serious consideration. In the long run, he had done the right thing, the noble thing, and here he sat—dead drunk—playing with a second-rate jazz band at an occasional gig for the local Kiwanis or Rotary club.

Jane had changed little in the intervening years. She still had the same luxurious blond hair and lovely, long legs. Pregnancy had not thickened her waist, although she bore the stretch marks. Her eyes were more tired, dark circles and fine lines marred her face with the worry parenthood—and marriage—had wrought.

He wondered guiltily what her assessment of him as a husband would be. He repressed the thought, for on its heels came fleeting images of the violence that marked their marriage. Elliot chose instead to concentrate on his receding hairline. He just wasn't the man he used to be. He moaned softly. The walls seemed to pick up the sound and throw it back at him. He moaned again.

Now the reason for their marriage and the loss of his career was gone, dead—Shelley, little Shelley who had been so bright and alive despite her rebellious nature. She had had a cruel streak, true, but Elliot had turned a blind eye to most misbehavior—like the time with the cat. He called it spunk. It confirmed their bond. However, her behavior had become dangerous. *Fire! Always fire!* He shuddered.

What was it the psychologists had said? Shelley had acted out their anger, and hers. She burned with rage, and in the long run it had killed her.

Her death revealed his guilt and his failure. Daddy's little girl was gone, and he wondered again as he often did what he could have done differently. Elliot loved Sara, but Shelley always had a special place in his heart. She had been Daddy's little girl while Sara was closer to her mother; now Shelley was dead.

Thinking about her, he could still bring Shelley's image to mind with surprising clarity. It was as though she stood before him. She looked so real. He shook his head. There she stood, shimmering in the study's dim light—blond hair, big blue eyes—and he realized with a shock how much Sara resembled her elder sister. It was as though as Sara grew older she grew more like Shelley. Shelley's eyes—as he remembered them—had been a little more close set than Sara's and her features sharper, but as Sara lost the babyish look of youth, her features too became more refined.

Tears formed in his eyes as he recognized the embroidered merry-go-round horse on her once-favorite powder-blue dungarees. Elliot reached out toward the wavering apparition in a loving caress. He felt a familiar stirring of passion. "Shelley," he whispered, "come back to me." The child smiled and moved closer. She uttered a musical, yet taunting, laugh which faded. Again he reached for her; his arm passed through the phantom image and Shelley vanished. He put his face in his hands and wept.

Nana lay awake in the dark. She slept fitfully at night, which was not surprising. Most of her day was spent dozing, drifting in and out of quick little cat-naps. Night, though, was different. At night, Jane would arrange her mother in bed, arms and legs propped on pillows and then Jane also went to bed. If the position became uncomfortable, an arm cramped or a leg numbed, all Nana could do was wait until the coming dawn when Jane would arrive to release her from the agony.

The night-light glowed. Jars of salve and bottles of talc stood guard, outlined against the image of Snoopy playing the Red Baron. What had awakened her tonight? She tried to remember. Oh, yes, a crash, followed by Jane's footsteps on the stairs. Her daughter had poked her head in the door and told Nana not to worry; Elliot had knocked something over in the study.

Yes, something fell downstairs. Elliot was drunk

again. The Lord, it seemed, had seen fit to punish this family like he had punished her. Many were the hours she had spent in an earlier era wondering what she had done to be so punished. Later after her husband had drunk himself into an early grave, Gertrude Goering came to understand she married him because that was all she had ever known. Her own father had been a hard, two-fisted drinker. Unfortunately, Jane —like Gertrude before her—followed in her mother's footsteps.

The pattern wound through generations. What had been the original sin, so many generations ago, that brought this blight upon them? Did Margaret, Jane's sister, also watch her husband drink himself into a stupor each night? Was that the sadness Nana felt coming through the lines of forced enthusiasm in her letters? Jane and Elliot, however, had been doubly punished with the loss of their eldest child, Shelley. It mattered little that they had helped to precipitate the loss.

Not for the first time, Nana cursed herself, cursed the fact that she still lived while Shelley decayed in her grave. If the fireman hadn't stopped to pick up her enfeebled form, perhaps Shelley would be alive today. She had heard this discussed often enough in loud arguments when the liquor had scrambled their wits and loosened their tongues. The accusations flew. Shelley died, and Nana lived; where was the justice in that? Why hadn't they put her in a nursing home? Why keep such a burden? But surprisingly, it was Elliot, and not Jane, who wouldn't hear of it.

Nana peered around the room and her eyes settled on the door to the closet. The back of the rocker was firmly tucked under the doorknob, and blessedly it remained quiet. Meanwhile, Nana awaited the morning and the eventual change of position with avid anticipation. She dreaded each time Jane opened the closet to get a new gown.

Then she would hold her breath and watch. Would today be the day when the creature came forth, ripping and tearing her daughter limb from limb? Each day as the door closed and the rocker wedged under the knob, she breathed another sigh of relief. No, today wasn't the day when the house would wreak its revenge.

She thought of the house, not as a building, but as a living, breathing entity—a personality which was imbued with vile, malevolent life and malignant hatred. When they moved in, it felt like it had swallowed the entire family, and now it waited with sentient patience, digesting its human repast.

The house chipped away at the family's tentative hold on sanity. Bit by bit it took from them. It pried at their faltering grip on reality, waiting until the weakened, defenseless group would succumb to the madness which was all it had to offer. It watched for its moment with the forbearance and endurance of the ageless. Soon it would pounce.

Nana raged silently. She must do something—but what? This family was all she had left; she must defend them. How? She could neither speak nor move. She was helpless, powerless against this thing—her only protection, the knowledge which she could communicate to no one.

Gentle footsteps sounded outside her door—Sara. Nana had come to recognize the footfall of each family member. As she lay there, she pondered the irony. Most old folks lost their hearing, but she, who had lost everything else, still had acute—if somewhat diminished—hearing.

Nana listened for the corresponding opening and closing of the bathroom door, but it never came. Instead . . . Nana's eyes darted to the ceiling, the undeniable sound of something moving overhead and *Voices!* Although this was a nightly manifestation, Nana realized for the first time she heard not just one voice, but *two.*

Jane sat up with a start. Something had disturbed her slumber. She felt Elliot's side of the bed. It was empty and cold. "Oh, God!" She pulled on her robe. She had to check Sara's room. If he'd . . . She stepped into the hall.

Nana strained, listening. A door in the hall creaked open, and Nana exhaled the breath she didn't know she held. *The bathroom door after all.* She gasped. *No, the direction is wrong.* It was the door to the master bedroom. More footsteps and Jane's head appeared in the doorway.

"Nana, you okay?" She walked over to the bed. Out of habit Jane stuck a hand under the blankets. *Good, still dry.* She gave her mother a sip of water and spoke more to herself than to Nana. "I could have sworn I heard something."

Jane walked back out into the hall, and Nana listened as she moved down the hall to Sara's room. A slight twist of the knob released the infernal rapping of the twig against the window. Nana waited—a long pause and the door closed.

No, no, no! Nana thought. *Look again, Jane, she's not there. She . . .* Nana's eyes turned toward the ceiling.

Jane stood in the door to Sara's room and felt a rush of love as she stared at the small mound of blankets where her daughter lay. The room was bathed in moonlight, and Jane thought she saw the gleam of gold hair upon the pillow. She pulled back to close the door and then . . .

Tap, tap, tap. Jane looked around, trying to locate its source.

Tap, tap, tap. She leaned against the wall and chuckled weakly. A spindly branch knocked against the window. That was probably what she heard after all. She looked back to the bed, thought about walking over to kiss Sara, and changed her mind. *Let the child sleep. If she can sleep through that god-awful racket, then let her.*

Tap, tap, tap, the branch responded.

Uninvited, the thought arose: *Quoth the raven: "Nevermore."*

She moved back into the hallway, leaving the door cracked. *Now, that was an obscure thought, straight out of College Lit 101.* She shrugged and started for the stairs, shivering as she passed through the cold spot.

Jane descended to the first floor. She glanced into the living room. The Christmas-tree lights winked on and off. Elliot wasn't there.

She moved across the foyer to the study and slid open the doors. They shrieked in protest, resenting her invasion. She cringed. *Have to oil those.* Another thing to add to the ever-present list.

Elliot sat with his mouth half-open, snoring in the easy chair. His head bobbed up and down, nodding slowly in rhythm to the sound of his own snores. Her nostrils flared at the smell of stale Scotch. Her eyes took in the small silver flask and the puddle of Scotch on the bookshelf and desk.

Jane went to the kitchen to get the sponge. She pulled the comforter from the back of the couch as she went back through the living room to the den where she mopped up the mess on the shelf and the desk, pausing to straighten the papers on the desk. Jane turned back to Elliot and covered him with the thick blanket. *Poor man.* Sympathy welled up inside of her, and she knew some small part of her loved him still. They had been through so much together.

She noticed the music stand where it had collapsed next to the chair. The sheet music littered the floor. *So that is what he knocked over.* Jane squatted down to pick the scattered papers up and changed her mind. *It might awaken him.*

She padded softly across the room and gingerly pulled the door along its track. Jane winced as it screamed its indignation. She bit her lip and placed her ear against the hard oak surface. A loud, choking snort greeted her. *He's really sawing logs in there.* She shook her head. He would come to regret his little binge in the morning.

Jane returned the sponge to the kitchen, nearly tripping over Critter as she walked across the front room. "Well, hello there, boy. What are you doing down here? Why aren't you upstairs with Sara?" He panted and yawned.

"Come on, fella, everything's all right down here." She mounted the stairs. Critter followed, nails clicking against the hardwood floor.

She stopped at the head of the stairs. "Well, go on, Critter. Go to Sara's room." He looked at her quizzically.

Jane walked over to Sara's door, opening it wider. "Go on, boy."

He joined her and just stood there. "What's the matter, don't you want to sleep with Sara tonight?"

He looked from her to Sara's door questioningly. His tail beat out a slow, gentle rhythm against the doorjamb. "Okay, you can sleep with me tonight. I could use the company."

She turned away from the door. Footsteps echoed overhead. Critter growled. Jane stared down at him. "You hear that, too, huh?" She knelt at his side and waited. The only sound that returned to them was the frantic rapping of the branch against the window.

"Now we're both hearing things. Come on." She walked toward the master bedroom. Critter followed directly behind her until she reached the cold spot. Then he veered sharply to the left, skirting the chill next to the vent. She looked down at him, and it dawned on her that each time he went down the hall he made a turn to the left or the right, depending on the direction of the draft, so that he never walked directly through the spot. *Odd.* Jane scratched his head absentmindedly before she climbed into bed. Critter sat next to the bed, on guard.

She patted a place on the bed next to her. "Come on up, fella. You won't get caught. I'm always up before Elliot, anyway. I won't tell on you. I promise." He jumped onto the bed, circled a couple of times and lay down by her side. Again Jane heard footfalls. Critter let out another low rumbling growl. "That's right, Critter, you keep those hobgoblins away."

She settled back, draping an arm over the warm, furry body. "I do believe you make a better bed partner than my husband. At least you don't snore." Critter honored her with a wet, sloppy kiss. She wiped her face. "On second thought, maybe not." She listened as the rattling and rustling continued overhead, then slipped into a gentle slumber, whispering a quick prayer to keep the nightmares away, but the dreams of a tortuous inferno came to her, anyway.

Critter plopped his head down on the pillow with a contented sigh. The Woman's breathing became slow and even. She slept. He stayed awake and vigilant. Like it or not, this was his House. His People, his Family, needed his protection.

Eventually though, he too slept. His feet twitched as he chased imaginary burglars away from his House to the steady cheers of the Woman, the Man, and the Littlest One. A little while later, however, Critter came fully awake. Something rustled in the hall. He sniffed the air cautiously and registered surprise. It smelled like—no, it was—the Big Little One.

Critter's world revolved around his Family. His Family consisted of the Woman, the Man, the Little Ones, and the Elder—which he mainly thought of as the Lump, for she never moved. Each one of his

People had his or her own peculiar odor. The Lump reeked of urine and talc. The Woman exuded detergent and talc, and sometimes she smelled sour, like the Man. The Man always smelled sour. Had Critter had a larger concept of the world he would have recognized the stench of stale Scotch, but he didn't. He only knew that the scent varied according to the sun's position in—or its absence from—the sky. In the day, the smell was acrid, mixed with sweat. At night the smell was stronger, fresh.

The Little Ones smelled sweet; they smelled like . . . well, like Little Ones should. Yet, there was a slight variation in smell between the Big Little One and the one he thought of simply as the Littlest One. The Big Little One sometimes smelled sour like the Man, and Critter knew that the Man had been close to her the night before—close like he was sometime close to the Woman—held in a groaning union.

He smelled the Big Little One now. That was something he hadn't scented for a long time, not since the Bad Thing. After the Bad Thing, they had come here to this Bad Place. He often wondered in some vague and shadowy way where she had gone. He had missed her. He liked the Littlest One best because the Big Little One had been prone to pulling his tail or leaping on his back, grabbing his ears and shouting, "Giddyup!" This had changed, however, when the Big Little One became a Bigger Little One.

It became worse. Occasional rough playfulness turned to anger and cruelty. At one time, there had been one other in the Family—a round, fuzzy ball of fur which had been all claws and teeth until Critter had shown it who was boss. The Fuzzy Ball had been fun. It mewed and hissed. It was someone to play with, to poke with his nose or prod with his paw, while the children were away. The Fuzzy Ball liked to chase things, anything, which amused Critter to no end.

Then his friend, the Fuzzy Ball, had scratched the Big Little One and a *bad thing* happened to it—not a big Bad Thing like happened that night to the house. That had come later. No, just a little burning bright *bad thing,* and the Fuzzy Ball was fuzzy no more. The Fuzzy Ball was gone, just like the Big Little One was gone. It seemed with *bad things,* big or little, someone always disappeared. After that, Critter knew to be careful around the Big Little One and so did the rest of the family. It was as though the bigness that changed her smell had also changed her personality.

The Big Little One was here now. She had come home. Bad Things forgiven, he stood up on the bed eager. His tail thumped against the head of the bed. Maybe now that the Big Little One was back, they would leave this Bad Place and go back to what he thought of as their real Home. He sniffed the air again, sensing something else. What was it? He scented the same distinctive aroma he had the night of the Bad Thing. He snarled, got up, and jumped down to the floor. He wasn't going to let it happen again. He would bite it; he would pounce on it; he would make it go away.

Critter stopped when he heard the soft flap of slippered feet. All other thoughts chased away by the unexpected presence. *It was.* It was *the Big Little One. She was here.* Excited, he ran out to the hall to greet her, carefully avoiding the Evil Spot.

* * *

Nana stared at the door as the figure flitted past, followed by a brown blur. The brown blur she knew to be Critter, but the other? She didn't know for sure. It should have been Sara, but the . . . what? Something was somehow subtly wrong with the image. *What was it? What was wrong?* A sound from the hall broke into her reverie, and she felt a sudden mass of conflicting and confusing emotions.

It was Shelley. If nothing else, Nana recognized the blue overalls which had been her favorites. The overalls Jane and Elliot had given away to the Salvation Army, not able—in unacknowledged superstition—to bequeath them or any other of Shelley's possessions to the younger child. She closed her eyes tightly, willing the vision away, and then opened them. *It* was gone.

Nana relaxed, allowing herself to drift. A sudden pop and she was instantly alert. A yellow flame lapped at the sheets which had fallen to the floor near the foot of the bed. Nana tried to pull her feet up. She kicked. The soggy pillow slid from between her legs onto the floor. Its wet bulk suffocated the insipid flame. Smoke drifted lazily to the ceiling. Nana looked again at the hall. The space in the doorway was empty, but Shelley's specter had left disturbed memories and turmoil in its wake.

Jane tossed and turned upon the bed, in the throes of another dream. She felt the movement in the bed as Critter got down from his perch. Without waking, she reached out to stop him. Her hand found nothing, only the warm space he had left behind. She groaned. She was alone to face this *thing* that haunted her. The creature reached her eyes and tore at them. Jane sat up, sweating and panting.

Shelley, a clear-eyed Shelley unravaged by fire, stared back at her. Jane gasped. She rubbed her eyes and looked up again. Shelley was gone. Critter stood in the doorway, staring out into the hall, tail wagging in great big loops. Critter looked back over his shoulder and gave out an exuberant yelp. The noises started up in the attic and then all was silent. Jane leaned weakly against the pillows, only then noticing the faint but discernible smell of smoke.

Half-asleep, Jane stumbled from the bed, panic rising. Her skin crawled. She groped blindly for the door, throwing it open. A blast of cold air hit her and she froze, immobilized. She sniffed the air, but it was gone—whatever she smelled had dissipated like Shelley's specter.

CHAPTER 8

The late-model Volvo came to a crunching halt in front of 413 Elm Street. Sam Holloway sat quietly contemplating the Victorian home's dingy gray exterior, his skin raised in gooseflesh. The feeling was not a new one; it visited him whenever he came within a block of the place. Childhood memories, usually banished to the far recesses of his mind, included forced visits to his elderly aunt when sweets grew sour in his mouth and he clung to his mother's skirts until it was time to leave.

The two-story house dominated the subdivision which had grown up around it. It overshadowed the other homes, disdainful of its newer neighbors. Appropriately enough, Elm Street ended here in this little circle. Almost as though by common, yet unspoken, consent no houses came too close.

Sam Holloway listened to the last of the radio news

broadcast—some human-interest piece where a family too poor to afford surgery for an ailing child found a rich benefactor. He switched off the ignition. The news was rife with that sort of thing at this time of year. He'd be glad when the season was over. He was tired of Dan Rather tugging at his heartstrings while some charity or another picked his pocket.

New Year's, thank God. All the mush and the gush would be over soon. This, however, had been the last thing he had expected to do on New Year's Eve, but he could think of no polite way to turn down Elliot's invitation. His wife, though, felt no such compunction. She stayed home with the kids, saying that she couldn't find a baby-sitter. He doubted she had tried very hard. With the neighborhood tradition of sharing sitters on nights when they were at a premium, it seemed unlikely that she had tried at all. He couldn't blame her. The Graveses were nice enough people, but there was something lurking just below the surface that wasn't *quite right*—something that he couldn't put his finger on—but was there nonetheless.

Elliot was a damn fine musician, too good to be teaching music appreciation to tone-deaf and unappreciative high-school students. Like the rest of the staff, Elliot doubled up on jobs. He led choir, taught driver's ed and even one gym class. The whole concept was so ludicrous, it should have been laughable—Elliot was the first to admit that he was about as athletic as Jell-O—instead, Sam saw the waste of obvious talent as sad. He could almost excuse the younger man's drinking. He wasn't so sure about Jane, but he supposed she had her reasons, too—what with her invalid mother and all.

Because of the move, they hadn't attended this year's Christmas party. More than a few people—not just the nuns—breathed a sigh of relief at their absence. Sam couldn't count the times he, and others, had witnessed an embarrassing incident after either Jane or Elliot had a few too many. It was a standard school joke, but Sam wasn't laughing anymore. Parties with them in attendance almost always ended in a family squabble. Little witticisms cloaked in the guise of loving comments carried venomous barbs of which one spouse or the other soon tired, and so too did their captive audience.

But it was more than their drinking. It was more even than the recent death of their eldest daughter. No, it was something else. Trouble did seem to plague them, and most people felt uncomfortable in their presence. After the daughter's death, everyone had rallied around the bereaved family, but in the long run, the gap widened. Few extended invitations to them anymore. So the family became increasingly isolated, Sam was left as the only one to befriend them. He felt sorry for them, but all he could do was sit back and watch them continue their slow dissolve.

Sam let out a long, slow exhalation in the cooling car. He supposed every family had their skeletons in the closet. He winced at the thought and shook his head. *Poor family.* He had tried to help them by damn near giving them this house, but regretted the offer before the words were completely out of his mouth. Yet, Elliot jumped on it as preferable to living with his mother—he said that she and Jane were always at each other's throats—and Sam hadn't had the time to reconsider. Looking at the drab facade, he regretted it still. Sam opened the car door and heaved his bulk off the seat. Freezing in the car only postponed the inevitable.

He made his way up the path to the door. Huffing and puffing in the cold night air, his breath came out as great ovoid clouds through which he walked. The snow was no longer the clean, crisp white it had been on Christmas. Days of exposure had left it gray and dingy, like the house. Repeated thaws followed by nightly freezes produced a crust that cracked under each step. Overweight and out of shape, Sam paused to catch his breath before he rang the doorbell. Holloway had a ruddy complexion and red hair; spider veins stood out on his nose whenever he had strained himself with too much exercise. They stood out now.

While he waited, he examined the peeling paint and grotesque gingerbread trim, summoning the courage needed to step through the door. The house's whole countenance was gloomy. Between its formidable appearance and the dying oak that flanked it, the place earned its evil reputation. Out of respect or fear, the place survived intact—no windows broken by a child's stone, no graffiti graced its peeling paint.

The old homestead. As the only male heir, he had inherited this place from a matronly aunt. Her money had left him well-fixed—unlike Elliot, Sam taught because he enjoyed it—but the house was a white elephant he couldn't seem to unload. Sam had sold the place several times only to have the deal fall through due to some legal or financial fluke. He rented the place, but tenants never stayed long. They always left before the lease was up. Their excuses, underscored with sidelong glances, were more significant for what wasn't said than for what was.

Sam rocked back on his heels and pressed the doorbell. Perhaps, he hadn't been so selfless with his offer after all. Jane opened the door immediately. She looked pale and wan, more strained—if that was possible—than the last time he saw her. She smiled.

"Come on in, Sam. We've been expecting you. Where's Beth?"

"She couldn't make it, couldn't find a sitter."

"You could have brought the kids. I'm sure Sara would have loved the company."

"Are you sure she'd be ready for my lusty brood?"

"Reasonably. Let's see, it was six at last count. You don't have another one baking in the oven, do you?" She stepped back, letting him through the door.

"Heavens no, Beth and I decided that six was at least one too many—possibly two."

"Oh, well, sorry Beth couldn't make it. We should have invited you sooner. I told Elliot that. The champagne's chilling, unless a cocktail is more to your liking. Here, let me take your coat."

Muted, mournful music came from the study. "As you can hear, Elliot's practicing. Why don't you see if you can pry the sax out of his hands, and I'll get our drinks. What would you like?"

"Do you have vodka?"

She quipped as she put the coat away. "Is the pope Catholic?"

"Last time I talked to the good sisters he was."

She laughed. "You mean they deign to talk to the laity?"

"Occasionally, they rub elbows with us working

stiffs. How about a screwdriver for starters? Let's save the good stuff for the witching hour."

"Sure. Elliot," Jane called through the study doors. "Company's here." She left to make the drinks.

The doors slid open and Elliot appeared, sax in hand. "Sam, good of you to come. Where's Beth?"

"Sitter problems."

He rolled his eyes toward the ceiling. "Don't tell Jane that."

"Too late, already have."

He groaned. "There will be hell to pay after you leave. She said I should have given you more notice."

Sam made a wry face and glanced nervously at his feet. "Sorry."

He did a quick shuffling two-step, shoved his hands in his pockets, and wandered into the study. He moved idly around the room, stopping occasionally to read a book title.

"Looks like you are pretty well settled in."

"You can blame Jane for that; she approaches a move with all the complacency of a whirling dervish."

"That can be a real asset."

"Not around Christmas."

Jane glared at him as she walked into the room, drinks in hand. "I suppose you would have preferred to trip over boxes for the last two weeks."

Elliot put an arm around her shoulder. "Not complaining, dear. Just stating the facts."

"Humph." She snorted and extracted herself from his grasp, handing a drink to Sam.

Sam winced. Things weren't getting off to a great start. "Well, I think you have done wonders for the place. It's good to have someone living here. I'm always afraid that the place will stay empty long enough to become a trysting place for the local lovelorn youth."

"Not much likelihood of that now, Sam. Let's go into the living room—if you think you can tear yourself away from your music, Elliot."

Sam followed Jane out of the study while Elliot put his sax gently and lovingly in its case. "Where's Sara?"

"Upstairs playing, I suppose. She stays pretty much to herself nowadays."

"And how did your mother adapt to the move?"

Jane frowned. "Well, you know old people, they have a hard time adjusting."

Elliot walked into the living room as Sam and Jane settled on opposite ends of the couch.

"Yes, it's funny, Sam." Elliot joined the conversation. "She seems a little spooked by the place."

Sam leaned back waiting for Elliot to continue, but he didn't—only stood in front of the cold hearth.

Sara sat on the floor of her room in front of the battered Raggedy Andy doll. She had just pulled out a handful of red-yarn hair. She contemplated it a moment, lit a match, and fired one end of a single strand. It flared. The greedy flame crept along the twisted surface. Hissing molten globules of polyester fell into the wastepaper basket below. She stopped, dropping the yarn into the metal container, cocked her head to one side, and listened. Critter looked up from his place near the doorway and started to whine. Sara whispered to the empty room, "Okay, Shelley." She got up and headed for the door.

"Well, I don't suppose I can blame her for that. I confess I used to think this was a creepy old place when I came here to visit my aunt as a child." He looked around the room. "She and her husband must have had eclectic tastes and enough money to indulge them. Whoever the builder was must have had a warped sense of perspective. Those gingerbread men on the eaves always looked like they were suffering from epilepsy. Poor slob was probably scared spitless by the time he got to the decorative touches."

"Scared? Why?"

"From what I understand, two people died during its construction—scaffolding collapsed, or something like that."

"Not all that uncommon in those days. I heard somewhere that one person died for every story constructed in Chicago." Elliot counted on his fingers. "This is a two-story house—two men—that's about right. I agree with you, though, those gingerbread touches look a bit weird, out of proportion."

Jane, silent until now, chimed in. "Elliot, how about a little fire to cheer the place up a bit?" She turned to Sam. "We haven't had time before now."

Sam sat up with a start almost spilling his drink. "Didn't I remember to tell you? The fireplace is for ornamental purposes only. When my aunt had the furnace put in, the chimney was diverted to the heater."

"No, you didn't," Elliot said. "I'm glad you came here before I burned the place down."

Embarrassed, Sam cleared his throat and dabbed at the liquid which had slopped over the side of the glass with a cocktail napkin.

Elliot went to sit in the easy chair, quickly changing the subject. "I don't suppose you know somebody who could use a cord of wood. It's fresh; we just had it delivered yesterday."

"I could use it. I'll pay you for it."

"Don't bother."

"I'll borrow a neighbor's truck and come over tomorrow to pick it up."

"If you're in any condition to." He winked at Sam and laughed.

Sam chuckled too and downed what was left of his drink. "You're right."

Jane plucked the nearly empty glass from his hands. "If we are decent hosts, you won't be. Another for you, Elliot?"

"Sure. So the chimney's blocked. Too bad. Fires are so cozy on cold winter nights."

"Yes, they are. My aunt was an odd unit. I don't know why she didn't just have them put in a second chimney. She certainly could have afforded it."

"Maybe she had the same builder put in the furnace that designed the eaves."

"Who knows? Maybe she did at that." They both contemplated the fireplace. "Actually, a lot of her eccentricities were excusable. She didn't have a particularly easy life."

Jane returned and passed out the drinks. "Oh? So this place has a history. I'm not surprised." She glanced at Elliot and frowned.

"The house, I suppose, does, but this story concerns

my aunt more. It does, however, pertain to the rumors about the place."

Jane sat down and prodded. "Rumors, eh? Anything we should know about? Well, this is a good night for a story. Does yours have a lot of ghosts and goblins in it?" Sam grimaced.

"Come on, Jane." Elliot turned to Sam. "Ghosts, hah! Recently, Jane's been afraid of things that go bump in the night."

"To tell the truth, my story has its share." He rolled his glass between his hands. A deep crease formed between his brows as he watched the sparkling ice swirl in the orange fluid.

Jane curled up on the sofa. "This sounds interesting."

"Interesting, well, maybe. It's not an easy tale to tell, though. It's not something that our family is proud of, but I suppose I should tell you. You'll hear about it eventually, anyway. First, I should tell you that this place has quite a reputation. Don't be surprised if some of the neighborhood kids tell you it's haunted." Sam paused, thinking about his childhood terrors. "It certainly looks the part."

Sara sat at the foot of the stairs, listening to her parents and Mr. Holloway. She couldn't remember what had prompted her to come down, but she sat rapt as Sam began his tale. Critter sat by her side, panting loudly. Sara slapped his nose. "Hush, I can't hear."

She leaned forward, listening intently. The voices continued.

* * *

". . . Aunt Emma was my great-aunt from my mother's side of the family."

"Oh my God, Auntie Em. Is there a Toto, too?"

"Elliot, don't interrupt," she chided.

Sam took another sip of his drink and said with forced cheer, "That's right, Elliot, don't interrupt or we'll send you to bed."

Upstairs a small shadow moved as Sara pressed herself against the wall, fearing discovery.

Elliot gulped with faked servility and said, "Yes, Sam, I'll be good."

"Anyway, she was a Jorgenson—Scandinavian. She married a certain Milton Van Clausen when she was very young. The marriage was arranged by her parents—he was much older than she was—definitely no love match. Van Clausen was quite well-to-do and made his money on some pretty shady land deals."

"This is a classic!" Elliot exclaimed, and Jane put her finger to her lips.

Sam continued as though Elliot hadn't spoken. "Despite that, I'm sure Emma's parents tried to do well by her. They had eight children and were struggling to scratch out an existence on a failing farm. Van Clausen was an unknown. They probably never looked beyond the fancy carriage and rich attire, or for that matter, the thought that it meant one less mouth to feed. Who knows, maybe Van Clausen truly loved his little bride-to-be. He built this house for her, which explains the gingerbread man. The Swedes are suckers for the stuff."

"It also explains their skewed appearance," Elliot interjected. "Germans are not."

"Perhaps," Sam mused as he took another swallow of his drink and wiped his mouth with the back of his hand. "Unfortunately, the man had little else beside his money to recommend him. He had a murderous temper—was known to have had one man whipped who was late on a land payment. His first two wives had died—one in childbirth and one under rather mysterious circumstances. Emma was his third.

"He had a heavy hand. It's one of those well-known family secrets that he beat her. After the birth of their son, he got worse, and Emma was unable to prevent the violence from spilling over onto the boy. I believe in the beginning she tried to stop him, but I think later she just gave up. Maybe she was a little relieved that the violence had another outlet besides herself."

Jane squirmed uncomfortably.

"At first she stayed close to her family, visiting them once a week. She tried to help out financially, too, but they were too proud. When the beatings started, Emma went to them for help, but they wouldn't—or couldn't—help her. Later she would visit them to vent her hostilities in the only safe environment she knew, her former home. I guess the child was about four years old when her visits stopped completely. My grandmother would stop in here occasionally, and she said that Emma had changed—darting at shadows, frightened by any small sound.

"It wasn't until the child was school-age that anyone noticed he was missing. He just wasn't seen anymore. The authorities came to see why he didn't attend school. Van Clausen drove them off his property with a flurry of obscenities. No son of his was going to attend some goddamn public school with the rest of the local riffraff. His boy was in a private school out East. No one thought to question him. Van Clausen was the type you didn't question if you valued your health or your home—he held the mortgage on a great many homes in this county."

"The son wasn't in school, though, was he," Jane commented. It was more a statement than a question.

"No, he wasn't." Sam finished his drink.

Elliot tapped his empty glass. "Break time. I'll refresh our drinks. Don't scare my wife out of her wits, mind you."

Jane chuffed, turning to Sam. "How long were they married?"

"I'm not sure. They had been married a few years before the boy was born and they were together quite a few years after, too. I'd guess about ten or twelve all together."

"Poor woman."

"That's my mother's sentiment exactly."

Elliot returned. "Did I miss anything?"

"Nothing exciting, just some statistical information. I think, Jane, Milton Van Clausen died eight years after his son was born and about four years after the son died."

"Whoa," Elliot said. "You mean the son was dead?"

"Yes, dead when the truant officers came. Probably had been dead for about two years at that time."

"How did he die?" Jane asked.

"I was getting to that. When they finally got Emma to talk about it, she said he'd starved to death."

Jane rolled her eyes toward the ceiling. "Oh Christ, what a way to go, but how? I mean how could the mother let that happen?"

"I don't suppose she could do much about it. Van Clausen locked him in one of the closets, and she didn't have a key. I think it was the closet in the room that's decorated as a nursery."

"Nana's room," Jane whispered and turned to look at Elliot.

"There wasn't much left of her mind when the authorities finally found out about it. God only knows what sort of ghosts and terrors visited her. She had been living with that terrible secret for years. All she could talk about was listening to his screams and entreaties for food, for freedom, for life until at last he lost strength and became silent. You see, they didn't discover this until after Van Clausen's death, and he too died under mysterious circumstances."

Elliot toasted the air. "Aha! The plot thickens."

Jane gave her spouse a dirty look and urged Sam to continue. "How did he die?"

"He was trampled by his own horses. Emma found him in the stable. He was crushed. Only his head remained intact. I got a rather vivid description of it from my older brother." Sam leaned back and pictured the scene as it had been described—a once-large man lying in a pool of blood, torso flattened and surrounded by mangled intestines as high-spirited horses pranced around him. He smiled weakly. "It was a good way to keep me in line, I suppose, to scare the bejesus out of me like that. Not every family has its own personal boogeyman.

"They never really did find out what happened. I think along with the other discovery they didn't care. They unearthed the child's skeleton from the basement."

"All this happened here?" Jane's hand trembled as she lifted her drink to her lips.

Elliot started to hum the theme music to "The Twilight Zone."

She ignored him. "What do you think happened?"

"Me? I don't know. Some said she killed him, but that didn't seem to fit, either; she wasn't a very big woman. She certainly couldn't have overpowered him and beaten him to death. If she used some other means to kill him—poison, for example—how did she get him to the stable, and for that matter, why the stable? Why not leave him in the house? No matter, even those people who believed she might have killed him seemed to think he deserved it. He wasn't a popular man." Sam paused.

"Like I said before, it isn't very pretty. Not something our family is particularly proud of, but for the neighbors it makes for a good nighttime tale—a neighborhood haunt. This place does have a colorful history. There's not much else to tell. They buried father and son side by side. That was ironic. After she gathered some of her wits about her, Emma had the place modernized and the basement cemented. When the hired hand did that particular job, she insisted they put a wooden box about this big"—he indicated about a foot square—"in one corner near the heater. Somebody, one of the townsfolk, started the rumor that it was his skull—something to ward off ghosts."

Jane shuddered. "That's gruesome."

"Yes, it is," Sam agreed.

"There's a precedent for it," Elliot said. "It used to be a practice in medieval times to put bones—a skull was said to be particularly effective—in the cornerstone of a castle. Some of England's royalty are said to be spread all over the island as a way of protecting the country from invasion. The practice got a little watered down in later years. I believe they used dead babies."

"Oh, that's awful."

"But true," Sam added. "Even today we follow a variation on that tradition. Where do you think the idea of placing 'time capsules' in cornerstones comes from?"

"At least we're not leaving body parts. So what do you think about all this?"

"Don't know what to think. I'm not going to tear down the place to find out, that's for sure. Look at the bright side. If it is Van Clausen's skull, it'll keep evil spirits away."

"Are you sure?"

Sam didn't answer. "God, let's talk about something more cheery. How was your Christmas?"

Unwilling to let the topic go, Jane disregarded the question. "What was life like for her afterward?"

"Oh, quiet. She mainly worked in her gardens. She had quite a green thumb."

"I bet she had a lovely flower garden. Did she grow roses?"

"No, she didn't grow flowers. She grew a few vegetables and some herbs. It was one of the things, besides the death of her husband and her son, that added to her reputation as a local witch." Elliot raised a brow. Sam didn't notice and continued. "If I remember correctly, she even grew mushrooms in the basement."

A crash came from below them followed by a loud

clattering thud. The windows rattled in their sashes, and a door slammed shut. Jane shot to her feet like a bullet. Elliot put a restraining hand on her arm. "My, you're jumpy tonight. Something just fell down in the basement."

"I'd better go check."

"Don't bother. Critter just knocked something over, I'm sure."

"And he slammed a door, just for good measure, I suppose."

"That was Sara," Elliot said.

"It didn't sound like it came from upstairs."

"Calm down, Jane. It's nothing. Besides, what have we got in the basement that Critter can damage?" At the sound of his name, Critter looked around at Sara and whimpered.

Jane settled back on the couch. "I guess you're right. Sorry, Sam, what were you saying?"

"I was just telling you about Emma's garden. Not much to tell really. I think she had a few fruit trees, but those have died off. Only the oak's left, and it's looking pretty sickly."

Jane said wistfully as she looked out at the twinkling Christmas lights across the way, "I bet when the flowers were in bloom, this place looked lovely."

Elliot hooted. Jane gave him an acid stare.

"It was pretty isolated, about four miles from the outskirts of the nearest town. It stood about equidistant between Bristol and Oswego. As a matter of fact, it was built at the crossroads of the two main tracks between those two towns and Yorkville and Aurora. Those 'roads'—if you could ever really call them that—have long since disappeared."

"Crossroads, eh?" Elliot again whistled the tune to "The Twilight Zone."

"What's wrong with that?" Jane asked.

"In ancient times, it was considered a magical place."

"Are you telling me that this house was built on tainted soil?" Jane looked around the room anxiously.

"Not tainted, really. Like twilight is a between time—neither night nor day—crossroads were a place between and were associated as often with fairies and elves as with evil."

"Where do you pick up this shit?"

"Dunno," Elliot said. Restless, he looked at Sam. "It's an interesting story, but I doubt this place is haunted despite what the neighbors, or my wife, might say."

Sam turned an inquisitive gaze to Jane. She shrugged. "I've been hearing a few strange noises lately coming from the attic."

"Right, she's as nervous as a cat on a hot tin roof. Sam, are you sure your Auntie Em put Van Clausen's skull in the foundation and not in the attic? Maybe she put the rest of his skeleton up there." Sam laughed uneasily while Elliot continued. "Well, I like this house. I think it's got potential. I love the woodwork. Maybe we'll buy it from you."

"What about your other house?"

"Destroyed beyond recognition, no point really in rebuilding. The insurance, when it comes through, won't be enough at today's prices to get anything comparable. If we're lucky, it will cover the loan with enough left over for a decent down payment on another place. Maybe we can sell the lot and have enough money to fix up this old house. What do you think, Jane?"

Jane wasn't listening. She sat looking out the window, chewing her lip contemplatively.

"Jane?"

"Huh?"

"With the insurance money, don't you think we could fix this house up?"

"Assuming we get the insurance money . . ." Her voice trailed off.

Warming to the topic of renovation, Elliot didn't seem to notice her comment. "We were talking about it just the other day, replacing the old gravity furnace with a forced-air job, maybe a heat—"

Jane interrupted. "But . . ."

He shot her a warning glance. "If we replaced the furnace, then we could put in a new chimney and unstop this one. Presto, instant working fireplace. The woodwork inside is beautiful. It's amazing someone hasn't painted over it by now."

"This place hasn't been lived in much since my aunt's death. People move in, but no one ever stays."

"Well, it's structurally sound. Must have been well built—no matter what you say about the builder—to have withstood the neglect so well. We could tear down the bric-a-brac outside. With a good coat of paint, I bet people wouldn't think it was haunted then."

Sara stood up as the conversation drifted to subjects no longer of interest and slowly climbed the stairs. Critter wandered into the living room unnoticed.

The conversation ebbed and flowed pleasantly. They toasted the New Year with champagne, and Sam left hoping that their lives were on the mend.

As they shook hands at the door, Sam took one last look around the shadowy foyer. This place still gave him the creeps. It would be nice if he could unload it.

Jane turned on Elliot as soon as the door was closed. "What got into you tonight? Buy this house, hell! We never even discussed it."

"We talked about replacing the gravity heater," he said, slurring his words, the bottle of champagne having thickened his tongue.

"Yes, we talked about getting Sam to replace the heater, not doing it ourselves."

"Well, I like this house." He stumbled over the last word, and his voice dropped into unintelligible muttering.

"Well, I don't. Neither does Sara. It's dark, gloomy, drafty. . . ."

His eyes narrowed. Her voice droned on as she listed a series of complaints. *Bitch, bitch, bitch. That's all she ever does—bitch.*

". . . and what about the cockroaches?"

Elliot slammed his fist against the wall. "Shut up! Goddammit!" Jane recoiled at the sudden outburst, but not quickly enough. He seized her arm and savagely pulled her around to face him. "I'm sick of listening to it. All you ever do is complain."

He slapped her. "You sit on your ass all day while I work." He backhanded her. "I've given up everything to support you and that kid of yours." *Slap!* "I bet this house would be a steal." *Slap!* He punctuated each statement with his hand, and as it connected with her cheek, it sent her head crashing against the wall. "And we'll buy this house if I say we should buy this house." He raised his arm to hit her again.

Out of the corner of his eye, Elliot saw a flash of gold at the top of the stairs. He stopped. "Shelley?" he whispered as he recognized the powder-blue overalls.

Jane shook her head to clear it, then turned to follow his gaze. *Nothing there!*

He spun about and ambled up the stairs. "I'm coming, honey."

Jane's mouth dropped open. She was about to call after him and thought better of it. No point in talking to him now. He was crazy. She turned off the foyer light and said in a softly spoken parting retort, "Who'd want this white elephant?"

She clapped her hand over her throbbing mouth. She glanced furtively around the foyer. The house seemed to swallow and digest her words. Jane moved into the living room and unplugged the Christmas-tree lights. Elliot turned off the upstairs hall light, leaving her in ominous darkness. She stood next to the tree for a moment. The silence was pregnant, palpable. She walked quickly toward the stairs.

Sara looked up from what she was doing when they raised their voices. Raggedy Andy looked deflated and forlorn. Next to his body lay a pile of gray ticking. She reached through the hole she had torn in his head and grabbed another handful of stuffing. *They're at it again.*

Elliot shifted uncomfortably in bed. He felt a sharp, stabbing pain in his belly. His stomach roiled and rebelled at that night's abuse. He opened one eye to look at the clock and was confronted with Shelley. She gazed down at him placidly. Elliot rolled over, reaching out to her, and mumbled softly into the pillow, "Just a dream." He fell immediately back into an insensible slumber so he didn't hear her leave and head down the hall to Sara's room, Critter trailing closely behind.

CHAPTER 9

A door closed somewhere in the darkened house, rousing Elliot from a troubled sleep. He awoke bleary-eyed. His mouth tasted stale and metallic from the cigarettes and drinks with which he had hailed the New Year. He awoke with a vague sense of disquiet that came from an unremembered dream. He scowled at the clock trying to recall what had brought him from his slumber. *Oh, yes, a noise.* Elliot pulled his resisting body upright and was rewarded for his efforts with a case of the spins, and the room whirled giddily around him. He cursed softly and waited for the feeling to subside. He stood up and moved silently for the door.

Despite his stealth, the movement registered subliminally in Jane's mind. She rolled over and felt Elliot's side of the bed. *Warm, but empty.* She heard faint, shuffling footsteps in the hall. Primitive, pervasive panic stabbed at her, and she fought her way to consciousness. She sat up, momentarily confused. Critter lay on the floor next to the bed. He too looked up, blinking. His tail hit the bedside table with a cautious thump. Jane turned from him to the dresser, trying to pinpoint her feeling of distress. Just then, the sound of Elliot's muffled cough came to her from down the hall near Sara's room. The stalking fear pounced, and she was out of the bed, fumbling for her robe.

Pulling it around her body, she hurried down the hall. Elliot stood in the doorway to Sara's room. He swayed slowly back and forth as though he was having difficulty maintaining his balance. Jane walked up behind him and waited. Elliot took a hesitant step forward; she reached out and touched his hand, which rested on the wall. He jumped, turning to her in a continuous—if somewhat palsied—motion.

"I heard a noise. Thought I'd better chssheck," he whispered almost apologetically. An embarrassed, prolonged pause followed. Elliot glared at Jane, waiting for her to contradict him.

She cleared her throat. "Uh, me, too. Everything looks okay here." She looked over his shoulder to Sara.

"Yesh," he slurred, "shhleeping peacefully enough. I'd better check downstairs."

Jane nodded and Elliot lurched toward the stairs. She leaned weakly against the door, her hand pressed against her chest. When his head disappeared from her view, she slid slowly to the floor. Shiny beads of perspiration broke along her brow, and she wiped her forehead with her arm. Her heart thundered and raced. She let out a soft exhalation of relief—knowing a dangerous confrontation had been narrowly averted, a crisis prevented.

She wept in the silent hall. It was her fault. She knew that battered children tended to marry batterers. Children of abuse often abused or married those who did. Children of alcoholics married one or became one themselves. The depressing statistics didn't lie, but one could always hope to be the exception rather than the rule—as she had. The hope had died years ago.

Jane lowered her head to her knees and moaned. Did other wives, she wondered, live in terror of the night? She doubted it. In normal families, a husband's nocturnal visit to his daughter was no reason for alarm. A father's love for his child reflected by his watchfulness didn't horrify. In normal families . . . She shook her head, willing the thought away.

She twisted her body so that her torso was moved to an almost impossible angle from her hips. Her shoulder rested on the wooden frame, and she placed her cheek against the door. From here, she could watch her daughter sleep. "Oh, Sara, sweet Sara, you deserve so much more." And the tears of self-disgust and self-loathing that she had tried so often to push away came full force. As though catching Jane's anguish, Sara stirred restlessly upon the bed.

Downstairs, Jane heard Elliot's loud progress

through the house, fueled by rage. He banged into furniture and slammed doors. She waited until she heard him open the study door, and then she stood—pushing herself up along the wall she had previously slid down—to return to bed. Sara was safe, at least for now.

The recently oiled hinges whispered when Elliot opened the door to the study. His chest rose and fell as he struggled to catch his breath. He pressed shaking hands against his temples. Shame engulfed him and his drink-reddened face grew even redder at what he saw as his wife's unexpected and unsolicited humiliation. She taunted him. He had been caught.

Caught? At what, goddammit? Caught at being a conscientious husband and father? Caught at checking out strange noises in the middle of the night? He felt dirtied, slimed, and—guilty, convicted of a crime conceived, but not committed. He stepped into the study, closing the door with such force that the windows shuddered in their frames and a precariously perched book fell to the floor. The noise sent sharp splinters through his already-throbbing head.

He strode across the room, picking up the recalcitrant book and shoving it back into place. The action enhanced the thudding pain. *Goddamn her. How dare she? How dare she do this to me? It was her, always her.* He jammed his fist into the palm of his left hand. *Fucking self-righteous bitch!*

"Prude!" he sneered out loud. He twisted his fist in his palm with a bone-wrenching motion. Elliot dropped his hands to his sides, stabbing out the unsmoked cigarette. His fist twitched with a life of its own, clenching and unclenching at his side. He spun around to face the study door. He'd show her, and he moved swiftly across the room, only to stop himself.

His chest heaved with anger and fury. *Fucking bitch.* Again, he slammed his fist into his palm. *Goddamn cunt!* Slap, and hand hit hand. *How dare she do that to me? By what right?* He squelched the response before it could float up to the realm of consciousness with another twist of his fist against his palm.

Elliot pivoted, stamping to the other end of the room. Again he punched his fist against his hand. *Who the hell did she think she was, anyway? Miss High-'n'-Mighty.* He turned and paced to the study door. Slap! Flesh met flesh. His chest rose and fell convulsively. *Goddamn her!* He turned to race again to the far wall. With each circuit, he paused to perform the same bone-crushing mime and to occasionally murmur the thought expletives. First one direction, then the other.

He stood, panting in front of the bookshelf. Colorful book covers, with titles etched in sharp contrasting ink, swam unseen before his eyes until one, gilt in bright, shiny gold on black, penetrated his unspoken cursing soliloquy. *The Holy Bible.* With a snarl, he pulled it from the shelf and threw it to the floor, kicking it to the far wall. Then he rocked from side to side, groaning feebly. *Oh God, what was happening? It had become so much worse since they m—*

Elliot heard a slight rustle behind him, and the

thought evaporated. He froze, waiting. A soft, cool hand touched his, and he started, looking down. Clear blue eyes peered anxiously into his.

"Daddy?" She shook her head, and shimmering blond hair cascaded down her back in the faint moonlight.

Elliot felt a sob catch in his throat. "Shelley?"

She smiled and the movement lit her face. For Elliot, it lit the entire room. He sank to his knees and held her in a crushing bear hug, burying his face in her thick mane. His body burned, and he felt himself hardening. She stroked his hair, her finger tracing the familiar bald spot on the top of his head. "It's all right, Daddy. It's all right," she whispered soothingly.

He pulled away from her, holding her at arm's length. His eyes devoured her, examining her while he clasped her delicate arms tightly, as though afraid that she would vaporize—vanish like she had so many times before. Shelley stood patiently under his intense scrutiny.

"Oh, Shelley, I've missed you so."

"I know, Daddy." She pulled him to his feet and with slight pressure directed him to the worn easy chair.

"Where have you been?"

She shrugged.

"I should spank you for leaving me like this. Your mother and I have been worried sick."

At the sound of the word *mother*, her face darkened. Elliot noticed her expression and his fury came rushing back to him.

"The bitch," he muttered, and Shelley beamed.

"She doesn't understand. She's never understood," she informed her father. Elliot nodded in mute agreement. "But that's okay, I'm here now." She stood before the chair.

Elliot lifted her gently onto his lap. He played with a strand of her hair. "Yes, you're here now, but where . . ."

Shelley put a finger to his lips to silence him. She kissed him, her tongue lashed out. Elliot's hips thrust upward.

"Daddy!" Shelley said with mock indignation. She climbed down from his lap to station herself beside his chair. He watched her. He poked at the horse symbol on her overalls, and she pulled his head to her shoulder. He felt the rough corduroy against his cheek. "I'll take care of you. You needn't let *her,"* she said the word with disdain, "bother you."

He repeated her words. "Yes, you'll take care of me." What little sanity remained warred with his passion and desire. "But . . ."

"Shush." She unzipped her overalls, took his hand and placed it against her glacial chest. He felt the fragile ribs. His fingers probed and explored until they found her tender nipples. Her lips parted slightly and a little pink tongue darted out which rubbed first over the top lip, then the bottom, wetting them.

"I'm here now, Daddy. I'm your little girl. I'll take care of you."

"Yes, oh yes." He breathed the words softly. She moved closer to the chair, unbuttoning his pajama top. He felt cold fingers slip from his neck to his waist, where their touch burned. She slid to the front of the chair, pulling at his pants and unzipping his fly.

His erection, released from its confines, pulsed as Shelley took it in her hand. Elliot closed his eyes. Part of his mind shrieked at him, screaming, *No, this is madness!* but he was held transfixed. She took him into her mouth. He started to move his hips. *Shelley, Daddy's little girl, is home,* he thought, *and she will take care of me.*

"Ah, ah, ah," he whispered with each ecstatic and erotic thrust. *"Ahhhh!"* He climaxed. With his orgasm came piercing agony and the horrifying realization that Shelley was dead.

His eyes popped open and he looked down. The image blurred, and there was Shelley, her body charred and burned. He tried to push her away. This was answered with dulcet, chiming laughter. Shelley grew larger; her visage became bestial. Her head dropped from its shoulders and fell to the floor with a sickening plop. The head looked up at him and laughed.

He covered his eyes, trying to shut out the image. Shelley vanished. In her place, a little boy knelt, gibbering, before him. Pus dripped and oozed from wounds along his legs and thighs. Noxious fumes rose from a leering mouth. The rank odor of rotting flesh surrounded Elliot. The child licked his lips, hungrily.

The room reeled around him, and he vomited on his own lap. He opened his mouth to scream and the deadly specter smiled, revealing sharp, pointed teeth. Elliot passed out.

* * *

The graying predawn light filtered into the foyer. Jane paused before the study doors. She braced herself for the screeching protest of the sliding doors. They slid silently along the tracks. She sighed, glad that she had oiled them the day before. The sour stench assailed her as soon as the doors were completely open. Her hand went instinctively to cover her nose.

"Oh God," she groaned. Elliot sat in the chair, his legs splayed, his pants around his ankles. Upon his chest were the recognizable remnants of last night's unimaginative Epicurean holiday fare—Cheetos, potato chips, and sour-cream dip. She felt bile rise to her throat. She gagged, revolted. Jane backed away from the door, pushing it shut lest he awaken and discover her there. She moved so quickly that she didn't notice the four fine welts raised along his chest from his neck to his waist.

Jane covered her mouth with the back of her hand. "Oh God," she repeated, but didn't for a moment believe that God listened to her desperate plea. Her legs turned to water as she walked to the stairs. She leaned against the banister. The sight followed her. Elliot wearing his own vomit, pants pulled down to the floor. *What the hell had he done last night?*

With a plaintive cry, she thought of Sara. She raced up the stairs, skidding to a halt in front of the bedroom door. Sara slept soundly. A deflated Raggedy Andy lay discarded at the foot of the bed. Forcing calm she didn't feel, Jane walked to the bed, lifted the covers, searching for a sign. *Nothing.* The girl's pajamas were intact, everything dry. Jane climbed into her daughter's bed and wrapped herself protectively around Sara's sleeping form.

Critter rose from where he slept in Nana's room, circled a couple times, and settled again. Nana watched him as he accomplished this maneuver. The next thing she heard was a muffled sound of footsteps overhead.

CHAPTER 10

Nana sat in front of the bedroom window, looking out over the snow. She shifted as well as her limited mobility would permit in the wheelchair. Despite the pillows, sitting hurt her tailbone; but she was starting to get used to it. True to her word, Jane had gotten Nana up every day just before Sara returned from school for lunch. Jane even tried to work Nana's stiffened joints, gently moving first the knotted fingers, then the sticklike arms, and finally her toothpick legs. Jane would talk as she worked first one limb and then another.

She chattered mindlessly, telling her mother about the day's chores, its inconsequential events and happenings, and in darker moments, about her fears and her dreams. Nana listened hopefully at first and a little wistfully as the weeks progressed. Occasionally, as she listened Nana cried soundlessly, tears rolling down her cheeks. Jane, shaken, would ask repeatedly what was wrong, but her mother couldn't answer. What limited peace had come to the family with Christmas grew threadbare thereafter and disappeared by New Year's. With Christmas break over, the family had drifted apart until they again rotated in their own separate circles of pain.

One day, Jane brought up a letter from her sister, Margaret. Margaret and Jane were the only two left of what should have been a flourishing family. Mark died in Vietnam and James was killed in a motorcycle accident. Jane read the letter out loud. It was full of good news and bubbling enthusiasm. Margaret's husband, Allen, was a full partner in his California accounting firm. Heather, their child, had won some kind of spelling bee while Sean was captain of the Little League football team.

Nana wanted to harrumph at that piece of news. *What good can come of a nine-year-old boy playing football? He'll end up with a broken leg more likely than not.* Gertrude could see the envy in Jane's expression and hear it in her voice as she read the letter. She would have liked to console her daughter, to tell her that somewhere between the lines Margaret and Allen—like she and Elliot—worried about money, their kids, and keeping up with the Joneses. Margaret probably got up in the morning and fussed over the latest wrinkle which had etched itself across her brow and each new gray hair. Jane, however, would not have listened. *The grass was always greener . . .*

Now Nana sat. One of the tapes Elliot had given to her for Christmas played in the background. It didn't register. Instead she listened to Jane as she moved about the house. The "exercise" period over, she could hear Jane as she walked from room to room collecting that day's laundry. Nana's eyes bounced nervously from the closet to the ceiling above her head. She had gotten used to the new room and its appurtenances. At one time someone must have used it as a nursery. A cracked and faded Jack jumped over a perpetually burning candle; Bo Peep frolicked with peeling sheep; and Jack and Jill fell in a ceaseless tumble against a dirty pink background. A dilapidated dresser contained what few clothes Gertrude Goering still owned. The rocker and the bedside table with its box of Pampers made up the rest of the room's sparse furnishings.

Nana paid little heed to the room's or, for that matter, the house's aesthetics. She had other worries and concerns about the house and its tenants. She was preoccupied not so much with what she could see, but with what she couldn't. Nana knew her daughter was bothered by her mother's apparent obsession with the closet, but unlike her daughter, Nana wasn't so quick to dismiss the noises and self-opening doors as the house settling. No, the house was older than she was; surely it should have settled by now. What about Shelley's appearances and the way Sara seemed to have subtly changed—to have become more like her older sister? Nana felt it all had another source—another explanation—and the possibilities frightened her.

She knew she had seen those eyes in the closet, two bright, burning orbs staring back at her. She could neither tell anyone nor explain it to herself, but she knew what she had seen. This was no trick of vision, no senile hallucination. They were there. Even with the door closed, she could sense the presence and its evil intent. What it wanted from a broken-down old woman such as herself, she didn't know. Nana couldn't harm it—whatever it was. She couldn't even alert the others to the presence—only shiver and shake in her bedclothes.

Nana wondered, though, if she were the only one aware of this presence. She felt certain that Sara knew, and she thought that in her heart of hearts Jane suspected, as much as she might try to deny it. Jane had noticed a subtle change in Sara. She had seen the burnt sheets. Nana had watched Jane's eyes as she had done a swift double take, quickly burying the unwanted knowledge deep within her subconscious. Yes, Jane had felt the fear and acknowledged it in some small way.

Nana's eyes darted back to the closet. She was thankful Sara had ceased to terrorize her grandmother with that secret knowledge. The juvenile rebellion, the cruel streak, which marked the initial days after the move, seemed to have dissipated somewhat—or had it? The cruelty was so unlike her, more like her older, more rambunctious sister than Sara. Still, Nana sensed something different about her. Sara remained distant and aloof.

The newfangled stereo blared in the background. *Loud music.* Nana would have chuckled if she could. Jane was more a product of her generation than she was willing to admit. Nana was not unaware of how wild her child had been in her college days, arrested on peace marches, smoking marijuana with the rest of her peers. Her pregnancy and sudden marriage to a "member of the band" was more predictable even to her sheltered, countrified mother than Jane would care to imagine. *Elliot was a nice boy,* she thought. It's too bad that he, like Jane's father before him, had succumbed to the evils of strong drink. Her thoughts were interrupted by a loud exclamation coming from Sara's room.

Jane stood trembling within the cold confines of Sara's closet. She had come in here to make sure no socks, jeans, or sweatshirts had been left on the floor. Sara was generally a neat child, but sometimes she forgot to put things in the bathroom hamper. Yet Jane was unprepared for what she had found. She stared in dismay at the torn doll at her feet, its tattered ticking strewn about the floor. What could have possessed her daughter to tear up Raggedy Andy like that? The question took her back . . .

She stood quaking in rage over the then four-year-old Shelley, and Jane was afraid, afraid of her own anger, afraid to touch the naughty little girl, afraid of what she—Jane in her wrath—might do. So she shook, quivering from head to foot, cords and veins standing out in her neck; her skin flushed.

Shelley cowered at her feet. "I'm sorry, Mommy. I'll fix it. I'll make it better." Had her sense of humor not flown the coop with her ire, Jane might have laughed at this offer and asked how.

The eldest had not taken the birth of her sister well. She considered the small baby a usurper, someone who had stolen away her parents' attention and affection. The first year was pockmarked with infantile revolt, Shelley being intermittently sullen and resentful.

Once, Jane had come into the bedroom to find Shelley holding baby Sara by her feet, threatening to drop her on her head. Jane's fury then had been formidable. It was then she learned not to trust herself. Jane had rescued the infant and spanked Shelley until she was black and blue. Never again had Jane permitted herself to get that angry—until this.

Shelley stood over a toy, Sara's birthday present. Financial reverses had left them strapped. All they could afford for Sara's first birthday was one doll. Thankfully at that age, Sara had been too young to care. She gurgled and drooled happily over the one toy, sticking its stuffed hand in her mouth, chewing on it contentedly. The doll, Raggedy Andy, Shelley had destroyed—its yarn hair ripped out and burned, its stuffing removed through a hole torn in its head.

The Raggedy Andy Jane stood over today had been its replacement. The older vision vanished and the present image coalesced. She shuddered, unable to shake the feeling that she was being watched. She jerked violently over the doll. It felt as though she had lost all muscle control, and it seemed that whoever—or whatever—watched her was wryly amused.

Suddenly, the surrealistic nightmare quality of these past weeks came rushing back to her, no longer repressed. Jane felt faint. She turned and fled from the freezing closet, and the memory. She stopped outside Nana's closed door, head throbbing.

Jane peeked into her mother's room. "How are you doing, Nana? Everything okay?" The tremor in her voice was not lost on Nana. Her eyes flicked in her daughter's direction, and she struggled to turn so she could see Jane's face. "I'm going to go downstairs. I've got a lot of work to do today. I'll be up to check on you later."

Jane closed the door behind her, somehow comforted. Nana was in her wheelchair where Jane had left her, and everything was perfectly normal. She went downstairs to fix herself a drink.

Jane sat in the easy chair, knees pulled up to her chest, and her head propped on her hand, staring out the front window. One drink had turned into two, the second of which sat ignored on the table next to her. She vaguely remembered the washer buzzed, letting her know that the cycle was finished, but she decided the laundry could wait.

Her mind leapfrogged from one memory to another—her unwanted pregnancy, her forced marriage, her remaining daughter, and the loss of the oldest. Her thoughts rambled aimlessly, following no cohesive pattern. Indeed they had only one common thread to tie them together—she felt trapped, enmeshed, and ensnared. Jane felt bound to a life that would continue in the same solitude and helpless desolation forever, from which she had neither the strength nor the desire to escape.

Nana became uncomfortable. She had been up too long. She was tired of sitting in her own filth and wished Jane would come up to put her to bed. From the sun's position in the sky she could tell it was getting late. Sara had come and gone; the school day would end soon. The doorknob behind her started to rattle and twist, and Nana breathed a sigh of relief. *Jane has come.* This turned into a terrified yelp, and she tried to jerk her head around so that she could face the horror full on. It wasn't the doorknob to the hall that had turned; it was the knob on the door which led to the closet.

Jane raised herself from her lethargy. The ice in her third—no fourth—drink had melted. She thought of refreshing it and decided to see to the laundry first. It was after two and Sara would be home from school in little more than an hour. Jane didn't look forward to her daughter's arrival. She walked down the basement stairs; Critter pattered at her heels. He looked at her expectantly while she opened the washer to dump the wet clothes in the dryer. She bent over to pet him. His tail slapped against the mortar-and-brick floor.

She heard a resonant clang behind her. Jane peered about the basement, searching for the source. The cellar was dark, dank, and damp—like a dungeon. Shadows obscured the corners. Debris from several generations of previous tenants decorated its dingy recesses—here a three-legged chair, there a lamp with a frayed cord, elsewhere a broken doll. Someday she would have to clean the place and remove these ghostly remnants.

Jane could see nothing, but she heard the metallic rattle behind her. Curious, she walked around the octopod heater, ducking to miss a long armlike vent.

The blowtorch Elliot had left there rolled from the corner, stopping when it hit her feet. Jane let out her breath in a rush, relieved. She muttered, "Mushrooms, huh? I bet this would be a good place to grow mushrooms. It's great for mold and mildew."

Critter stood up and wagged his tail. "Eh, Critter, you agree?" He panted. She returned to the washer and stuck her hand inside the dark cavity, reaching for the wet clothes. Something dry and fuzzy brushed her hand.

Jane felt a soft prick and something climbed onto her hand. In rapid succession, she recognized the distinct tickling sensation as whatever it was crawled over her skin. The skin on her hand twitched convulsively. Before she had a chance to react, however, this creeping perception was followed by another and yet another.

She yanked her hand from the washer and started to scream. It was covered with black furry spiders. She shook her arm frantically, and they fell to the floor with a faint pattering sound and scattered to the four corners of the basement. She slammed the lid shut on the washer and switched it to the on position.

"Drown those suckers," she murmured under her breath and preceded to stamp on the spiders still within reach.

Without a second glance, she ran up the stairs to the kitchen. Jane stood at the sink, shivering. *Things like that just don't happen except in grade-B horror flicks.* Agitated, her whole body seemed to vibrate with swift, palsied movements. She leaned against the cupboards to steady herself.

Jane wrapped her fingers around the vodka bottle she had left on the counter and lifted it to pour some into a glass, but the spasms were so savage that the clear liquid just dribbled down the sides of the glass to the countertop. She put the bottle down, wringing her hands. Then she pressed them against her forehead and her sides, brushing unseen, imaginary insects away.

"Dammit." She raised the bottle to her lips and took a good healthy swallow. Her ears roared and her throat burned. She coughed and choked, gagging on the vodka in its unadulterated state. Putting the bottle down, she wiped her lips against the back of her hand. She examined it, looking for traces . . . of what?

Calmer now, she poured herself a stiff one. Without moving from her place near the sink, she downed the entire glass. She stared out the kitchen window and then turned to Critter. "Would you like to go outside, fella? I'll take you for a walk. I need to get out of this place." She shuddered.

Critter accompanied her to the foyer and watched as she put on gloves, coat, boots, and a scarf, thinking —as she had so many times before—that it was time to replace the old brown car coat. *It's what, now—five years old?*

Each time Jane had wanted to replace it before, something else had always taken priority—new shoes for Sara, car repairs, or Nana's mounting doctor bills. As she put on the coat, she thought with a touch of defiance that if they could afford a new stereo, then she could damn well afford a new coat. The worn leather gloves needed to be replaced also. The palm on the right glove was torn, and the seams on both were starting to split. *Maybe it's about time for a shopping spree.*

The idea was cheering, and the alcohol had started to take effect, dulling her senses and calming her overwrought nerves. Jane began to hum as she wrapped a gaily checked scarf around her neck. Critter continued to watch the process. As each new article of clothing found its resting place, his excitement mounted. He frolicked about the front hall, barking ecstatically.

"My, my, Critter, you must want to get out of this place as badly as I do. Do you need to piddle?" With the word *piddle,* Jane remembered her mother, who probably needed cleaning and wanted to be put to bed. She looked up the stairs guiltily. It seemed too much trouble to take care of her mother now. Besides, Critter's jubilation had reached manic proportions.

"Come on, boy, let's go for a walk." She walked out the front door. Critter brushed past her, nearly knocking her off her feet. He whizzed down to the yard, rushed up the path, and immediately lifted his leg to spray the mailbox.

"Sorry, Critter, I should have let you out sooner." He looked at her blandly and ran to the corner of the house, stopping again to mark his territory.

She laughed. "Well, I'll say you're full of piss and vinegar today." He bounded around the side of the house, and Jane followed. She turned the corner and examined the old oak. Sam was right, this tree needed to be cut down. She wondered why he hadn't done it before. She didn't like the way that one branch seemed to reach for Sara's window. Jane hoped a storm wouldn't blow it through the glass and into her daughter's room. She supposed it was the last living branch on the dying tree. The others, already broken, were probably more of a danger.

Critter reached the stand of trees behind the house. He paused there, waiting. "Coming, Critter." He moved on at the sound of her voice. The weather was mild, the snow turning to slush. Only the lack of sun kept it from melting completely. The sky was the bleached white of high cloud cover that didn't look promising. *Another storm is on its way.*

Unknowingly, she retraced her daughter's footsteps into the clump of trees. At this time of year, the bare field beyond was clearly visible through the stripped branches, but by summertime, it would be pleasant—green and lush. A good place for Sara to play, away from the street and traffic. Despite the fact that Elm Street ended here in the circle, Jane still worried—perhaps excessively—but she felt no need to apologize to the little voice inside her head that reproached her for overprotectiveness. *Dangers are many and come in often surprising forms, at unexpected times. Losing one daughter is enough.* Jane would protect Sara with her life.

She surveyed the wooded area, remembering summers of her youth where a patch of trees such as this—planted between field and house as a windbreak—became a forest primeval. The recollection of her former childlike flights of fancy brought a smile to her lips. The windbreak had given her a brief respite from the cares of helping on the failing farm. There she could retreat from her harried mother and drunken father, who spent most of his time sleeping it off at the kitchen table, letting his wife and children take over the responsibilities that should have been his.

After her chores for the day were completed, she would wander through Sherwood Forest with Robin Hood and his Merry Men. Later when adolescent romance blossomed along with puberty, the trees became the pristine wilderness of Evangeline and her star-crossed lover. Yes, Jane had had the safety and solace of the small woods behind her house until one day when its shady shelter became a trap; its inviting solitude, a snare.

Jane's face clouded at the thought, bringing with it the unsolicited memory of her father's groping hands and his sweating body on top of hers. *Children of abuse marry* . . . Quickly she pushed both the thought and the memory away to the seldom-explored regions of her mind. *What is it about today that all these morbid memories should surface, almost as though all my terrors and fears were awakened by . . . what?*

The wind picked at her scarf and tore at her hair. She nearly fainted. The ground rushed up to meet her—her wobbly legs unable to support her—and she collapsed against a tree. She wiped a shaky hand along her brow. Another sharp gust blew hollowly through the bare branches. Now completely surrounded by the trees, she thought she heard a soft, low keen so like the sound of a child crying. Jane halted to listen. Her ears—like any mother—were attuned to a child's cry, able to filter out other noises. The wind answered with a mournful howl and dropped, and with it, the sound ceased. The silence that followed was unnerving. She got up and walked on. Critter was just a brown blotch off to the side.

"Critter! Come here, boy." Another blast picked up the words, snatching them from her lips. He sniffed at something of interest and ignored her. The keening started again, becoming at first a wail then a high-pitched shriek.

Inside the gloomy basement, the washer started to do an ungraceful boogie. It bounced and jounced on the cold, hard floor, smashing into the side of the dryer. *Bang! Bang! Bang!* It stopped, and its buzzer started to skree until it too sputtered and died.

Jane thought she noticed something out of the corner of her eye, a figure—was it a child?—huddled in the branches of one tree far off to her left. She saw a flicker of gold. Jane jumped, turning her head in that direction. *Nothing there. Just an overactive imagination.* She was quite alone. Jane called to Critter again, and he left the fascinating shrub and ran toward her in happy leaps. She waited and the gusting wind slowed to a gentle breeze.

Again she thought she saw a figure and the familiar gleam of golden hair out of the corner of her eye. The sorrowful sound of a child weeping pulled at her. She tilted her head to listen. She recognized the voice. "Shelley?"

She moaned. Critter jumped on her with wet and muddy paws. Jane pushed him away and turned in the direction of the sound—not just her head this time, but her entire body so that she faced it head on. A raven sat in the branches. It stared at her, unflinching. The wind played with Jane's hair. She brushed it from her eyes.

Spooked, Jane pulled Critter behind her. "Come on, Critter, let's see what's on the other side of these trees." She turned her back on the great black bird and started toward the far edge of the trees. With a flurry of wings, it flew off. The dog ran ahead of her again, breaking out of the shrubbery as she struggled over some tangled roots. "Whoa, Critter, wait up." He slowed his pace to a trot and did a quick shuffling side step, impatient with the delay.

She came to his side, only then noticing the big black dog that watched them from the center of the field. Unconcerned, it nosed something on the ground. Critter jumped into the field, but Jane seized at his collar with a swift, sharp movement.

"No, Critter, that doesn't look like a dog you want to tangle with. I think we better go home now." She pulled him back the way they had come. The black dog picked something flaccid, flat, and gray up in his mouth, taking off in the opposite direction.

Sara opened the door to the dimly lit foyer. "Mom, I'm home!" she shouted.

"Mom?" No answer. She tugged at her boots and put them on the newspaper by the door.

"Mom, where are you?" She shrugged out of her coat and hung it up in the closet.

"Is anybody home?" She snickered. *That's a silly question. Of course, Nana is here.* Sara went to the kitchen. The digital clock winked at her from the countertop. The brass teakettle gleamed on the stove.

She dragged a chair away from the Formica dinette set, placing it next to the kitchen cupboard.

"Mom?" She said it softly now, experimentally. Satisfied that her mother was nowhere to be found, she climbed onto the chair. It wobbled precariously. She held a steadying hand against the refrigerator, opened the cupboard door, and located the Oreo cookies. Grabbing a handful, Sara jumped down from her perch. She was careful to place the chair back in its original position, walking around the table once, just to make sure. Certain that no clue would reveal her transgression, she turned her interest back to the cookies. With a brisk twist, Sara revealed the white center which she gnawed at contentedly, dumping the chocolate cookie in the garbage. She stared at the cookie, evidence of her "crime," and artfully rearranged the coffee grounds over it.

She noticed the faint outline of her mother through the trees. Critter bounced at Jane's side. Sara made another rapid check of the trash and the table. Reassured, she glanced out the window. Her mother had just exited from the barren grove. She clutched the cookies to her chest and raced up the stairs to her room where she hid them in her bedside table. Catching her breath, she turned and went to her grandmother's room. Nana still sat in her chair, limp. Sara walked around the front of the chair and sat in the window seat.

"Hello, Nana, how are you?" Two blinks.

"Not good, huh?" One blink.

"Want to go to bed?" One blink, a long pause and then another single blink.

"Well, Mom's out walking the dog. I'll tell her you

want to be put up when she gets back." Sara heard the door open and close downstairs. "Meanwhile, do you want to play a game?" Sara pulled Shelley's gift from her pocket. Nana involuntarily pulled back when she saw the book of matches. Sara struck the match. The match burst into a dazzling bright blaze. Sara watched, entranced.

Jane spotted Sara's boots in the hall when she came through the foyer. "Sara!"

Sara looked away from the fire. She moved closer to Nana, holding the flaring match next to her grandmother's cheek. Nana struggled to withdraw from the blistering flame. Its radiant heat parched the already-dry skin. She heard a slight sizzle as a stray strand of hair caught. Her head jerked spasmodically on a useless neck. Sara grinned.

"Don't you think it's pretty?" Nana blinked twice.

"Sara Jane!" The little girl lifted one ear. She heard the underlying anger in her mother's tone and extinguished the match. Spent, she dropped it into Nana's lap as she thought of the cookies. Had she seen Sara through the window? Logic told her no, but her mother's hostility was apparent nonetheless.

"Sara!" Her mother stood at the door, aged car coat unbuttoned. "Sara, didn't you hear me?"

"I was talking to Nana."

"Well, you answer me when I call you, young lady. Come with me, Sara Jane Graves, I want to show you something."

Sara's heart sank. Whenever her mother used her full name, Sara knew she was in for it. She walked to the door. Jane grabbed her hand and pulled her roughly into the next room. Sara's skin twitched. She felt the tear in the palm of her mother's leather glove. Sara tried to extract herself from her mother's tight grasp.

Jane opened the closet door. It banged against the wall, sending a cloud of dry plaster to the floor. She pointed at the floor. Sara's gaze followed her mother's finger. Her eyes widened. On the floor, she saw a tangle of red yarn, Raggedy Andy's empty cloth shell and the scattered gray ticking. Her mouth dropped open and she took an instinctive step backward. Jane caught her and propelled her toward the door. For an instant, Sara thought her mother was going to lock her in the closet and she clung to Jane's hand.

"What is that, young lady?"

"I don't know." Sara began to whimper.

Jane shoved her into the closet. "Why don't you take a real close look at it and tell me?"

Terrified, Sara complied. She squatted next to the doll's remains. Shaking hands reached out first picking up the yarn, then the shell, and lastly the ticking. She let it fall from her fingers. Sara started to cry. "It's Raggedy Andy."

"That's right, it's Raggedy Andy. And how did Raggedy Andy get that way?"

"I don't know."

"Sara." Jane's voice took on a warning quality. Sara peered into her mother's eyes, tears streaming down her face. Her face convulsed.

"I don't know, Mama, really I don't. I liked Raggedy Andy. He was my favorite."

Alarmed, Jane knelt by Sara's side. Her daughter didn't normally lie. Jane gripped her daughter's arms and turned Sara into a position facing her. "Are you sure that you know nothing about this?" She stared into Sara's eyes, looking for the involuntary withdrawal which would tell Jane that she had lied. Sara simply looked back at her, stifling a sob.

"Well, then who did it? It didn't just happen all by itself." Sara remained mute. "Who?" She gave Sara a sharp jerk.

"Shelley! Shelley did it!" Sara shrieked.

With that the fury exploded. Jane's skin flushed. She ground her teeth, her jaw held clenched. She shook Sara. With each stinging jolt, Jane screeched at the horrified child, "She did not! She did not. You lie!" The spittle showered on Sara's upturned face.

Sara screamed back. "She did. She did! Shelley did it!" Jane slapped her daughter across the mouth. Sara's head flopped back like a rag doll. Her teeth snapped, clicking shut with the force of the blow.

"She's dead, goddammit." Jane slapped her again, backhand. "Dead! Don't you understand?" She raised her hand to strike again.

"Noooo!" Sara's voice raised in an anguished wail. Critter started to bark in the hallway. Jane caught herself, realizing what she had done. Shame descended on her in a rush.

"Oh my God, Sara, I'm so sorry. I'm ssso sorry." And she too began to bawl as she bundled her child against her breast. Mother and daughter cried helplessly in each other's arms. Slowly the sobs subsided; Sara's dissolved into retching hiccups. Jane picked Sara up and carried her from the closet.

"Sara, I'm sorry. I shouldn't have done that. Look, I tell you what, I'll fix you up a plate of cookies, if you promise not to tell your father."

Sara threw a furtive glance at the bedside table. "No thanks, Mama, I'm not very hungry," she said sullenly.

"Are you sure?"

"Yes, Mom, I'm sure."

"I'd better go down and fix dinner. Are you going to be okay?"

Sara sniffled and wiped her nose on her sleeve. "Yes, Mom, I'm okay."

CHAPTER 11

Sara sat at her desk. Her fingers traced the outlines of initials carved in its wooden surface by a long-forgotten student. *B.E. & L.F.* The teacher stood in front of the multiplication table, pointer tapping a rhythm against the board.

"Who knows what seven times seven is?"

Hands went up. Sara's was not one of them. Students squirmed uncomfortably in their chairs. Afternoon recess was still thirty minutes away. Some hid their faces fearing Mrs. McGuinness would call on them. Others seemed eager, intent on being the first one chosen. Their hands waved frantically in the air. "Ooh, ooh, I know, I know!"

Sara remained indifferent, caring little what seven times seven would, or could, be. It wouldn't bring her sister back. It wouldn't make her parents stop drinking. Neither would it stop the fights. For Sara, seven times seven held little interest, although she suspected that if she looked in the back of her arithmetic textbook, she would find the answer written somewhere in the enigmatic charts; but Sara was far more interested in who *B.E. & L.F.* were. Where were they now and did they still love each other? If her parents were any guide, probably not.

Mrs. McGuinness's careworn features searched the sea of faces before her and, with a teacher's sadistic sixth sense, called the most fearful. "Tommy Erwin, will you come up here and do the problem, please?"

Sara looked somewhat scornfully at her teacher. Mrs. McGuinness was, as far as Sara was concerned, a relic, a fossil. Her legs were covered with spidery varicosities which showed through the dark hose; her hair was gray tinted with blue, and she wore the type of cologne which Sara associated with old ladies and suffocatingly large breasts like Grandma Graves's.

Please! Ha! Sara thought. *As if Tommy had any choice in the matter.* She turned to Tommy, who sat directly behind her, and felt a secret thrill—Sara had found a friend—no matter that it was a boy. She hadn't expected to make friends in this new school, at least not so soon.

"I—I—I d-d-dunno," he stammered.

"Well, maybe if you spent more time paying attention and less time looking out the window, you would know. Mary?"

"Forty-nine." The girl, whom Tommy called Miss Priss, sent him a scathing look.

"Very good, Mary, and what about . . ." Mrs.

McGuinness's voice became muffled as she turned to the chalkboard, her back to the class.

Tommy stuck his tongue out at Mary and gave Sara a triumphant smile. Sara smiled back at him. He stuck his thumb out and pointed in the direction of the window. Sara looked. Great big wet snowflakes fell in clumps on the playground beyond the wire-mesh glass. He clapped silently. Despite his efforts to hide his actions and his delight, the teacher caught him.

"Tommy! You're asking for trouble. If you don't pay attention, you're going to have to stay inside during recess, writing the multiplication tables. And Sara, I know you're new here, but don't egg him on."

Defeated, Tommy slumped against the back of the chair. Sara sat a little bit straighter and dutifully mumbled, "Yes, Mrs. McGuinness." The half hour stretched interminably before them.

When the bell rang, forty silent students let out a collective sigh of relief. Mrs. McGuinness rapped against her desk. "Everyone bundle up. It looks cold out there."

Tommy fell into step beside Sara. "Almost got it there. Good old Miz Gunnysack." Sara giggled at Tommy's witticism. The name applied. It aptly described the teacher's lumpy, seamed, and wrinkled exterior. Sara glanced back at the cluster of teachers where they stood waiting for their students.

"She'd better not hear you."

"She can't. Besides, who cares, anyway?"

Sara shrugged. She liked Tommy. He had so readily accepted her as part of the gang. Although she strongly suspected that as chubby as he was, he wasn't really a part of the gang himself. They got into their coats and ran out the schoolhouse doors.

"This is great." He went into a running slide, whizzing past her.

"I don't know. Your mom always gives you a ride home. I gotta walk." She scrambled to catch up with him.

"My mom'll give you a ride home."

"Gee whiz, you really think so?"

"Sure. Then you can come over to my house and play."

"Will that big kid David be there?"

"Of course he will, silly. He's my brother."

"Oh yeah, I forgot. He's not very smart, is he?"

"Yeah, he's not real bright—he's in special ed—but he's okay."

"Smart or not, you're lucky to have a brother."

"I am?"

"Yes, I used to have a sister."

Tommy stopped his alternating walk and slide to stare at her. "Used to?"

"She's gone now."

"Gone? Where'd she go?"

"I don't know. She comes back to visit me sometimes, but my mom and dad don't like to have her around."

"Aw, come on. Why not?"

"Well, she looks"—she wrinkled her nose—"funny, and she smells bad."

"Parents can't do that. My brother's kinda dumb, and smells bad!" He whistled. "Wow! You should smell his dirty socks. Whewee!"

Mary Smith pranced by with a group of girls in tow.

Sara's eyes followed her. *She does look like a priss.* Tommy bent over and made a snowball which he let fly. It fell a couple of feet short of his mark, landing just behind Mary and her friends with a thud. The previous peculiar conversation was forgotten in the excitement that followed.

Mary shrieked shrilly at him, "Tommy, I'm gonna tell." She ran off.

The other girls milled about nervously while Tommy danced after Mary, chanting, "Mary, Mary, quite contrary, how does your garden grow?"

Sara nudged him. "You're gonna get in trouble, and they'll keep you after school."

Mary came back, tugging a breathless and flushed Mrs. McGuinness. "Tommy, did you throw a snowball at Mary?"

"I threw a snowball, but not at Mary."

"Sara? Did Tommy throw a snowball at Mary?"

She studied the plump woman before her. "Gee, I don't know, Mrs. McGuinness. Maybe he did, but I guess I wasn't looking," she said shrewdly.

"Girls?" But the other girls had vanished, drifting in a tight little knot toward the swing set. Mrs. McGuinness returned her gaze to Sara and watched her a few moments, eyeing her suspiciously. She looked the child up and down. She could see through the child's innocuous air. Mrs. McGuinness sniffed, remembering the hurried conference held right before Christmas break.

She had been called down to the principal's office after lunch. Not unlike her students, Mrs. McGuinness spent the walk to the office reviewing in her mind any possible misconduct that would have necessitated the unwelcome summons.

When she arrived, she saw a young mother sitting in front of the desk, and her heart did a frantic leap. What student had she punished recently, and had she become over zealous? The principal stood as the older teacher entered the room.

"Mrs. Graves, this is Mrs. McGuinness. She will be Sara's teacher when she starts after Christmas break. And Mrs. McGuinness, this is the mother of the new student. Mrs. Graves has been kind enough to come in and talk to us about her daughter who is—what you might call—kind of a special case."

The young woman also stood, extending her hand. Mrs. McGuinness noted her tired eyes and harried expression. Accepting the woman's limp, damp hand, Mrs. McGuinness shook it, grasping it tightly. Inwardly, she groaned. *Special case* was, in teaching vernacular, a euphemism for *problem child.*

Just what she needed was another special case when it seemed like she already had a class full of them. Still worse, the mother had come in which meant that the mother, if not the child, was going to be a pain in the neck. Mrs. McGuinness sat down.

Dr. Friedman cleared her throat. "Why don't you explain to Mrs. McGuinness what you were telling me?"

The young woman shifted nervously in her chair. She smiled wanly at Mrs. McGuinness. "Please, believe me when I say I don't mean to be a problem for you. My husband is also a teacher, so I sort of know what you go through," Mrs. Graves said as though reading the teacher's thoughts.

The small voice inside Mrs. McGuinness clamored louder. *Oh God, an expert.*

"It's just that I'm concerned about Sara. You see, she's been through so much lately. Her sister died not too long ago, and she's having a hard time adjusting. We all are." Jane looked hopefully at the teacher. Mrs. McGuinness crossed her arms and waited.

"Generally, Sara is a pretty good girl, but recently she's been a little rebellious. I just wanted to let you know so you'd be patient with her. She's not usually like that. It's just that she's having a difficult time accepting her sister's death." Jane fell silent. Her hands wrung the handkerchief in her lap.

Dr. Friedman looked expectantly at Mrs. McGuinness, who continued her cold appraisal of the woman before her, noting the shabby coat and torn gloves. Dr. Friedman scowled and then spoke reassuringly to the mother. "It was nice of you to come in. I wish all our parents were as concerned about their children's education as you are. We've gotten your daughter's records from her previous school. She appears to have been a good student. Of course, Sara has been through a lot and we"—she placed special emphasis on the word *we*—"will keep in mind the recent death in the family when dealing with her, won't we, Mrs. McGuinness?"

Mrs. McGuinness sat up a little straighter. "Of course."

Mrs. Graves let out an explosive sigh. "Oh thank you. Well, I really must be running. We just moved, and I know you are busy, too. I appreciate your time." She gave the teacher a warm smile. "You, Mrs. McGuinness, probably want to get back to your students. Heaven only knows what they have gotten into by now."

She and Dr. Friedman stood and shook hands. "You are always welcome, Mrs. Graves. As I said before, I wish more of our parents paid attention to their children's education." Jane Graves left, and Mrs. McGuinness also stood to take her leave.

Dr. Friedman frowned at her. "You could have been more friendly. That's a very worried mother, and she has a right to be. Sit down, there's more to talk about." Mrs. McGuinness sat. "I not only got Sara's transcripts, I also got her sister's. The other school thought they were important. It would appear there was more of a problem there than Mrs. Graves was willing to admit. Here."

She passed a manila folder across the desk. "I'll let you read about it."

Mrs. McGuinness opened the folder and read. She let out a little gasp and then peered at Dr. Friedman over her glasses. "Why didn't you tell me about this before?"

"I just got them; there hasn't been time."

"And the sister? The child I'm getting in my class."

"As you heard me tell her mother, she appears to have been a very good student. No behavior problems there." She handed the teacher a second folder. "I'll let you keep both files, but you can see that she may—with what she has been through—have some difficulties now. We can discuss this later after you have familiarized yourself with both files."

Dismissed, Mrs. McGuinness walked out the door. Dr. Friedman stared out of the office window, wishing it were any other teacher that would be getting what she knew to be a potential problem. Mrs. McGuinness was a holy terror that had, unfortunately, come with the school. She was a firm believer in the old axiom "spare the rod and spoil the child" and had never adjusted to the state law which denied teachers the right to spank their students. Despite Dr. Friedman's advanced degree and position of authority, Mrs. McGuinness had an air about her which made even the principal feel somehow like an unruly child. She shook her head and returned to the speech she was preparing for that night's PTA.

Mrs. McGuinness stared at Sara's feigned innocence, peering down her hawklike nose at the defiant child. Unlike that young upstart of a principal, Mrs. McGuinness didn't believe in mollycoddling students. Perhaps, if the sister had been appropriately punished for her misbehavior, she would be alive today.

Mrs. McGuinness sniffed again and surveyed the stubborn student before her. She stooped over, grabbing Sara by the shoulders. The teacher's face almost touched the child's as she whispered confidentially. "You know what happens to little girls that lie, don't you?"

With a wide-eyed look, Sara asked, "No, what happens?"

"The Bible says they burn, Sara. Got that? Burn." Aghast, even Mary gasped at the seemingly off-the-wall reference and vehement attack. Sensing it was a losing battle, the teacher snorted her contempt and straightened.

"Never mind. You're getting some bad habits, Sara

Graves. They're going to get you in trouble. Tommy Erwin, no more snowballs—*at all!* I don't care who or what you're throwing them at." Mrs. McGuinness stomped off.

"That was mean." Tommy stared after the teacher. "Thanks. I didn't mean to get you in trouble," he said, turning back toward Sara.

With a careless flip of her hand, Sara replied, "Don't worry. I'll get her."

Tommy shook his head. "How?"

"I don't know yet."

"Aw, forget about it. She's always like that. She hates kids." He changed the subject. "You going to come over to my house after school and play?"

Sara continued to watch Mrs. McGuinness as she huddled with the rest of the teachers. "I don't know if I can. I usually help my mom with my grandmother." The bell rang, and the students shuffled reluctantly back into the building.

Mrs. McGuinness watched the students burst from the classroom after school. She understood and resented their jubilation. Had she been younger, she too would have flown, elated, from the building which long ago had become a prison. Instead, she scowled and hurried to the teachers' lounge, reviewing the incident at recess. It bothered her. Her first confrontation with the new girl was disturbing. She felt that she had lost some kind of battle, that somehow she had been bested. Mrs. McGuinness didn't like being bested. No, she didn't like it at all. She stopped outside the lounge, looking into its dusky interior. Dr.

Friedman was involved in an animated conversation with one of the other teachers. Mrs. McGuinness was in no mood to face Dr. Friedman.

She did a quick about-face and returned to her classroom. As she opened the classroom door to step inside, her nostrils flared. *Smoke!* She looked around the room, searching for its source. A merry blaze licked relentlessly at the papers on her desk. The flames gleefully devoured today's spelling test. Mrs. McGuinness leapt for the pitcher of water she kept off to the side, dumping its contents onto the fire. It went out with an angry hiss. Greasy smoke drifted lazily to the ceiling. Just then the automatic sprinkler system sprung to life—dousing both Mrs. McGuinness and the blackened papers. She started to curse, thinking of the special case.

Outside Sara stood next to Tommy. A long line of cars inched along in the falling snow. He looked occasionally for his mother, but was more interested in catching snowflakes on his tongue. He chased first one clotted flake and then another, turning to show Sara his prize, which more often than not had melted before she could see it. Sara thought his behavior a little undignified so she moved slightly away from him, ignoring him as best she could—unless he called her by name.

A horn honked and Tommy looked up. "There she is. Come on." He clutched Sara's hand and dragged her along behind him. The two children climbed into the car just as the fire alarm sounded in the background.

David Erwin sat in the back seat. He peered at the school with interest. "What's that?"

"Fire drill, I guess." Tommy turned to his mother. "Hi, Mom. This is Sara. I told her you'd give her a ride home."

"Hello, Sara." Mrs. Erwin gave the little girl a perfunctory smile and then frowned at Tommy. "I don't know, dear, not if she lives too far out of our way. You know I have to pick up your father after work and get dinner ready."

"She lives just up the street."

David looked at her dully, but with the words *just up the street* some light snapped on inside his head. "You're the new kid. Mom, she's the new kid that moved into the old haunted house."

"David!"

"Well, it is haunted." He pouted.

"Don't pay him no never-mind, Sara. So you moved into the old Van Clausen place. How do you like it?" Mrs. Erwin asked.

"It's just a house."

"Mom, can I go to Sara's to play? I asked her to come over, but she's gotta help her mom with her grandmother."

"Does your grandmother live with you?"

"Yes."

"It's nice of you to help your mother."

Tommy interrupted. "Well, can I, Mom?"

"Can you what?"

"Can I go over to Sara's house?"

"Now, Tommy, you know I don't . . ." Mrs. Erwin caught Sara's reflection in the mirror. The child stared at her curiously as though gauging her response. Sally Erwin blanched and looked furtively away. "Okay, but you have to be home before dark."

The car pulled into the driveway next to a little tract home on Elm Street. Ceramic elves played among snow-covered evergreens and a plastic deer held a chain in its mouth from which was suspended a plaque which proudly proclaimed the name of the occupants: *The Erwins.* Sara and Tommy jumped out of the car.

Sara stopped to examine the elves, the deer, and a large squirrel. "Gee whiz, that's neat."

"What?"

"All the stuff." She indicated the statuary in the front yard.

"It's bullshit."

Glancing back over her shoulder at Mrs. Erwin, Sara hissed, "Tommy!"

"Well, that's what my dad says. My mom makes that stuff."

Sara patted the deer's plastic nose. "She does?"

"No, not that, the clay junk."

"Oh."

Mrs. Erwin, oblivious to her son's disparaging remarks, pulled a sack from the car. "Now, you remember, Tommy, you be home before it gets dark out. I don't want to have to send your brother over there to get you."

David gave his brother a dirty look. "I wouldn't go, anyway. He could starve for all I care."

Mrs. Erwin dumped the sack in David's hands. "Don't you sass me. You'll do what I tell you to. Now, take this bag of groceries into the house. Sara, you tell your mom to come over for coffee sometime. It must be lonely for her to be in a new neighborhood."

"Yes'm."

Tommy and Sara trudged off. The wind had picked up and they found themselves leaning into it to move ahead. Snow coated the trees, covering them in a thick white blanket.

Sara shouted over the wind, "I guess mothers all do that, don't they?"

"Do what?"

Sara mimicked Tommy's mother. "Don't you sass me!"

Tommy grinned. His ears and nose were turning red. "Yeah, that's what mothers are for."

They continued to struggle against the wind. Snow stung their faces and took their breath away. Tommy paused at the bottom of the stairs at 413 Elm Street. "You really live *here?*"

"Of course, where else would I live? Whazzamatter, you afraid of ghosts?"

"I'm not afraid of anything." He reluctantly mounted the stairs.

Sara bounced up after him, shouting "Boo!" as she landed on each step.

Tommy waved her away. "Aw, quit it."

Sara stopped as they walked in the door. She put a restraining hand on his chest and said, "Wait a second." She peeked cautiously through the door into the living room and then breathed a sigh of relief. *Good.* No telltale cocktail glass adorned the coffeetable.

"Mom, I'm home. I brought a friend with me."

Jane appeared at the head of the stairs, talc container in one hand. "I'm up here with Nana. Hello there. What's your name?"

"I'm Tommy Erwin. I live up the street."

"Nice to meet you, Tommy. You kids go into the kitchen. I'll be down just as soon as I'm finished with your grandmother. I'll fix you both some hot chocolate. Sara, put the teakettle on the burner, won't you?"

"Sure, Mom." Sara pulled Tommy into the kitchen behind her. She grabbed the kettle and put it on the burner. Twisting a knob, it sprang to life, blue flame licking at the kettle's scorched and blackened bottom.

She moved over to the doorway and checked the living room quickly. She put her finger to her lips. "Stay by the door," she ordered imperiously. Sara climbed onto the countertop and pulled some cookies from the cupboard which she passed to Tommy. They heard footsteps in the living room.

"Here, quick! Put 'em in your pockets."

Tommy stuffed the Oreos into his pockets. They sat down at the table opposite each other just as her mother walked into the kitchen.

"How was school today?"

"Okay."

"What did you do?"

"Multiplication," Sara said.

Tommy added an unenthusiastic "bluck."

Jane laughed. "That's what I thought when I was your age." The teakettle let out a shrill whistle. Critter ran into the kitchen. Jane mixed the cocoa and placed it on the table.

"Can Tommy, Critter, and I go upstairs?"

"Sure, but be careful, don't spill." She followed the children into the foyer.

"Goody, I'll show you what I got for Christmas."

Jane smiled at the children as they trooped upstairs, then returned to the kitchen to fix dinner.

Sara stopped outside Nana's door. Tommy looked in; a funny expression crossed his face.

"What's the matter?" she asked.

"Who's that?"

"That's my grandmother."

"She's creepy."

"Well, you'll look creepy, too, when you get to be that old."

"I suppose so." They moved on to Sara's room. Tommy ran to the window. "This is neat. I bet you can see the whole town from here."

"No, I can't. It's in the other direction."

"Well, still it's neat to be so high up here. I bet you could climb down that branch to the ground, and your mom and dad wouldn't even know you were gone."

"Maybe, but I wouldn't want to. I might fall. It would be a long way down."

He peered to the ground below him. "Yeah, it would be. Boy, it sure is snowing. Maybe there won't be any school tomorrow."

"We couldn't be that lucky, not so soon after Christmas. They'd probably make us come in even if it snowed six feet."

He groaned. "Yeah, even if nobody else had to go, I bet that old biddy Miz Gunnysack would be there." They paused, looking at each other. "I'm sorry I got you in trouble today."

Sara put her cocoa on the bedside table and dismissed it with a wave of her hand. "Don't worry about it. I got her."

Tommy raised a questioning brow, but Sara didn't elaborate.

"You still got the cookies?" she asked.

"Sure do. My mom would kill me if I did that."

"So would mine if she caught me." She closed the door to her room and waited. "Well, bring 'em out. We gotta eat them fast before she comes up." They sat on the floor, enjoying their forbidden feast.

The meat loaf baking in the oven, Jane went up the stairs to check on Sara and her little friend. She was pleased that her daughter had managed to make friends so soon. She knew starting in a new school must be difficult. Sara's door was closed. Jane stood in the hall listening. "Oh jeez, what's that?" Tommy pointed at Teddy Ruxpin.

"Something my parents gave me for Christmas," Sara said around a mouthful of Oreos.

"A Teddy Ruxpin, that's for babies."

"I know."

Jane's face fell, hurt.

Sara continued. "But they gave me some good stuff, too. Besides, you know how parents are."

"Yeah, I know, mine gave me a book, *Black Beauty.*" Tommy threw up his hands in disgust. "Would you believe it?"

Jane suppressed a laugh and turned to go, then stayed instead to listen.

"I guess it must be hard sometimes, being parents, I mean," Sara commented thoughtfully. Tommy gave her a puzzled look. "Well, you know, they worry all the time and that kind of junk. By the way, why didn't your mom want you to come over here?"

"Oh, she's heard all the stories."

"What stories?"

"The stories about the house."

"About it being haunted, and stuff like that?"

"Yeah."

"Pah! I don't believe it." She reconsidered and asked curiously, "What do they say?"

"A little kid starved to death here. They found his skeleton in the basement."

"Nah."

"Did too! That's a fact; even my mother talks about it."

"Did she tell you about it?"

"Not me. She thought I was asleep, but I heard her talking to my father when you first moved in. Said the people who built this place locked their kid in the closet and let him starve."

Something stirred in Sara's memory. It spoke with Sam Holloway's voice, but it was all very fuzzy. She cocked her head, listening.

"That's not the only story. The last kid that lived here said he saw someone walking—a little kid who looked more like a skeleton than anything."

"Really?"

"Sure, he wasn't the only one who's seen somethin'. Some kid broke in here once on a dare. He said he saw an old man shuffling around with his head under his arm."

"Uh-uh! I don't believe it."

"Well, you don't have to!"

"He was just making it up. I'm not scared." She fed a cookie to Critter. "If I ran into this headless guy, I'd just tell him to go away. Maybe I'd grab his head away from him and dribble it down the hall like a basketball."

Tommy made a rude noise, blowing cookie crumbs over her and Critter. "Would not!"

She brushed the crumbs from her jumper. "That's gross, Tommy Erwin."

"Well, I don't think you're that brave. If I ran into a ghost, I wouldn't be."

"Maybe not, but I could sic Critter on him."

Outside the door, Jane began to shake. *Starving children and headless men.* She felt faint. She moved soundlessly away from Sara's room, deciding not to wait until Elliot got home before she made herself a drink.

Elliot found his wife seated on the couch and wrapped in a comforter when he arrived home. He looked at the drink in her hand. "That looks good. How about one for old Dad?"

Wordlessly, Jane got up and fixed him a drink. Elliot slapped her on the rump. "How was your day?"

"Not bad. The Sears man came out to fix the washer today."

"Huh? You didn't tell me that it was broken."

"Yes, it blew yesterday. I guess it just slipped my mind."

"I bet that's going to cost a pretty penny."

"No, remember, we got a service contract on it."

"That's good." He took the drink from her hand. "Where's Sara?"

"Upstairs playing. You just missed her little friend. He left a few minutes ago."

"You mean she's making friends already? I'm proud of our little girl. She's pretty resilient."

"Sam was right, you know?" Jane said.

"Right? About what?"

"About the neighbors. Little Tommy told Sara that this place is haunted."

Elliot raised a brow. "Did it bother her?"

"Didn't seem to. She said that she'd just chase any old ghost away."

"See what I mean? Our little girl's got spunk. She's pretty feisty."

"It bothered me, though."

"Why? You should have been expecting it."

"Well, he said the previous residents saw this ghost—a skeletal child." Elliot snickered, but Jane disregarded it and forged ahead. "He also said that some young vandal broke in and saw a grown man. It was headless."

"Like our friend Van Clausen is supposed to be." He chortled and poked Jane in the ribs.

"I don't think it's so funny. He also said that it carried its head under its arm."

"That's a classic image. Are you sure he wasn't thinking of Anne Boleyn?"

"What do you mean?"

"Supposedly, the ghost of Anne Boleyn walks the halls of Windsor Castle—or is that the Tower of London?—head tucked neatly underneath her arm."

"Skeletons buried in castles and the ghost of Anne Boleyn. Where do you pick up this garbage?"

Elliot shrugged. "I don't know. In college maybe, or at school. Things can get pretty boring between classes. Besides, if I'm not mistaken, there's a song about that." He looked at a fixed point up above her head, trying to remember the words or the tune. Brief snatches of a melody came to mind, but he couldn't seem to put a finger on it. "I can't remember the words, but it's something about the same caliber of 'London Bridge Is Falling Down.' "

Jane shook her head. "You're strange, you know that? I tell you about a ghost and you turn music critic. Well, that may explain the so-called headless visitor, but what about a skeletal child?"

"Another classic image, don't you think?"

"I don't know what to think. I know I don't like it—any of it. I'd better check dinner."

Jane moved past him to the kitchen door. Elliot made another playful swipe at her and followed her into the kitchen. "Woo-ee-woo."

She gave him a dirty look. "What are you supposed to be?"

"Why a ghost, of course."

"I'm not impressed." She turned and pulled the meat loaf from the oven.

"You're not really worried about it, are you?"

"Well, Tommy's mother seems to take the stories seriously."

"What do you mean?"

"Tommy overheard his mother and father talking about the Van Clausen story before we moved in, and

I guess she was a little reluctant to let Tommy come over here." She started to set the table.

"What did you say his last name was?"

"I didn't. I believe it was Erwin."

"Erwin? You mean those people who live in that place down the street with all that crap in the front yard?"

Jane laughed. "That's the one."

"I'd wager a guess that Mrs. Erwin has more toys in the attic than in her front yard." He tapped his temple with his index finger.

"I don't know. Sara said she invited me over for coffee. That was nice of her."

"Nice, maybe, but not necessarily bright. Check her out. I bet you find out that I'm right—toys in the attic." Elliot walked up behind her. "I wouldn't worry about it, honey."

She placed the forks next to the plates, looking at him out of the corner of her eye. "You haven't noticed anything unusual happening around here lately, have you?"

"Come on now, Jane. You really are taking this seriously."

She shrugged.

"What do you mean by unusual?"

"I don't know, just strange—out of the ordinary."

Elliot paled at the thought of Shelley's spectral appearance on New Year's—but that was just a drunken hallucination—and then shook his head no. "Well, nothing except for the dreams."

Jane stood up straight and stared at him, wondering what were dreams, and what was reality. "Maybe that's what I'm worried about—that the story about our headless friend and the starving child will start Sara's nightmares up again." Elliot nodded and Jane returned to setting the table. "Would you mind calling Sara? Dinner's almost ready."

CHAPTER 12

Sara sat on the living room floor, watching "Magnum, P.I." Her parents' raised voices came to her from the kitchen. They were fighting again. She reached over and turned up the volume on the television. She neither knew nor cared what this night's dispute was about.

Sara heard a loud slap followed by her mother's indignant cry. The kitchen door flew open and her father burst into the room. He towered over her, breathing heavily. He seemed unaware of Sara's presence. He moved over to the stereo and jabbed at one of its many buttons. The radio sprang to life, blaring the hard-rock strains of the Talking Heads.

Her mother came into the room. "Why, you son of a—" She stopped when she saw Sara looking up at her expectantly. Elliot turned and noticed Sara for the first time. Jane backed away from him and returned to the kitchen.

"Go to your room, Sara."

"But, Dad, I'm watching TV."

He looked from her to the television. "That crap will rot your brain. I thought I told you not to watch that program; it's too violent." Sara stared at him in shocked disbelief. Her mother's shrill laughter floated in from the kitchen. He glared at the door.

"Go on, Sara. I told you to go to your room."

Feeling brave, Sara protested. "Can't I at least finish the program?"

Elliot took a warning step toward her and Sara crawled on all fours toward the hall door. He walked over to the television set and twisted the knob so violently that it came off in his hands. "Damn."

As he bent over to replace it, his lighter fell from his pocket, sliding across the floor. Sara's hand closed over it. She slipped it into her pocket and scurried quietly the rest of the way to the door, triumphant. *Just wait till he tries to light a cigarette. Serves him right.*

He spied her on her hands and knees in the doorway. "Don't you have some homework to do?" He took a threatening step toward her, raising his hand as he did so.

"Yes, Papa."

"Well, then go do it."

Nana lay in the semidarkness. Her heart sank. She cringed, and her insides did a slow, rolling lurch. Sara sat in the rocker. Behind her head the doorknob whirled and spun frantically. Sara ignored it, not seeming to notice the frenzied motion. Instead, she looked at her father's Bic. She examined it, fascinated.

Nana's eyes switched from the knob to Sara who would intermittently spin the striker and recite a singsong, "Purty, purty, purty." The solitary flame flickered and jumped. Its light caught by the crystalline knob was thrown in a myriad of rainbow colors which danced across the walls with each dizzying movement.

Oh no, oh no, Nana thought, *not again.*

Sara turned to Nana and noted the fear. She cocked her head. "What's the matter? Don't you think it's pretty?"

Nana blinked twice. Sara shrugged. "I guess I'd better go do my homework." She moved to the door and exited. The knob stopped reeling the instant she left the room.

Once in her room, Sara plopped down on the throw rug just outside the oblong of light thrown by the window onto the floor. *Tap. Tap. Tap.*

Sara turned to the window. "Oh, rat-a-tat-tat to you, too." She leaned back against her bed, dismissing the idea of homework. Who gave a damn about dumb old multiplication, anyway? During an occasional respite in the branch's rattling, she could hear brief snatches of music coming up from the first floor. Elton John crooned something about madness across the water, and the wind wailed outside her window.

Sara flicked the lighter again, becoming totally absorbed in the flame. *Such a pretty blue-and-yellow light.* She stared at the fine gradation of color, amazed at the changes from blue to purple to red to orange to yellow in such a small space. *It's beautiful.* She smiled, enraptured. Sounds blended into the background and the world outside the circle of light dimmed. All she could hear was the crackle and snap of fire. It roared, echoing throughout her mind.

Jane Graves nursed her drink and her growing animosity in the kitchen. She listened to the soft strains coming in through the door from the living room. The clean dishes sat drying in the rack. She would have liked to go into the other room, but she didn't dare, held in place by resentment and fear.

Jane swore softly, her hands going to the welt which had raised on her cheek, put there by his wedding band. She thought, not without a touch of embittered irony, that this marriage seemed bent on destroying her one way or another.

The uneasy peace which had dulled her senses with fragile, but futile, hope were gone. She got up and fixed herself another drink, taking a cautious peek out the kitchen door. Elliot sat on the couch, his hand waving back and forth in the air to the beat. Jane pulled back into the kitchen before he saw her.

She pressed her throbbing cheek against the cool wall, choking on her sense of outrage and injustice. *The asshole is in there playing conductor and smiling, for Christ's sake.* She sat down, laying her head on the kitchen table. Jane wept when some misbegotten fool began to sing about everlasting love.

Elliot stared at the blank TV screen. The music engulfed and surrounded him, and his fury receded, subsiding in the wake of some tender tune. *Who is this?* he thought. *Ah yes, Fogelberg.* His anger left him in stages until he couldn't remember what they had been arguing about.

Carrying his drink, Elliot got up and headed for bed. He plodded up the stairs, thinking with a twinge of guilt that he should stop in Sara's room and apologize; he had been a little bit hard on her. He stood just outside her door listening to the creaks and groans of the house around him.

As he did, unreasoning dread descended on him like a shroud. He hesitated, not wanting to open the door to Sara's room. Bed and sleep called to him urgently. Elliot argued with himself, telling himself that an apology was not needed. Had he not, after all, been right? Television did rot the juvenile mind, and homework was more important. Yet, he had been overly harsh. In the end, his conscience won. He pushed her door, and it swung open on silent hinges.

Sara sat on the rug playing with his lighter. Her eyes fixed on the dazzling light. Elliot stared at her, horrified. Sara passed her finger slowly through the flame. The glass slipped from his fingers and shattered on the oak floor. Sara looked up, dropping the Bic. It fell harmlessly on the rug, extinguishing itself. Elliot leapt at her.

"What the hell are you doing?" He picked her up and flung her against the far wall. Sara sank to the floor, stunned. She gasped, the wind knocked out of her. Elliot strode to her, grabbing her by the arm. He yanked her to an upright position. "Haven't I told you time and time again not to play with fire?" He swung her around.

"Not me, Daddy, not me. It was Shel—" Elliot cut her off, his hands circling her small neck.

"Haven't I told you? *Haven't I?*" He slammed her against the wall. Still holding her by the throat, he smashed her repeatedly into the hard surface. Plaster fell down around them like snow.

Jane heard the crash followed by a heavy thud and ran from the kitchen. The all-too-familiar sounds came from Sara's room. Jane flew up the stairs. No longer afraid for herself, she had only one thought—one instinct—to protect her daughter from Elliot's wrath.

Jane fell, her knee smashing into the floor. The pain shot through her, but her ears, her thoughts were trained on something else. A regular thumping came from Sara's bedroom. Jane pulled herself upright and stumbled down the hall, dragging her injured leg behind her. She paused momentarily at the door, taking in Elliot's hands around Sara's delicate neck as he slammed her against the wall. Her head snapped forward with the impact.

Jane launched at Elliot, landing on his back. She grabbed his hair with her fingers and pulled, tearing it out at the roots. Her nails raked along his neck and jaw, getting caught in his ear. With a howl of rage and pain, he threw her down, turning from Sara to his wife. Jane slipped to the floor—legs unable to hold her weight. She buckled, again hitting her knee. It sent stabbing pain up her spine to her brain.

Elliot's attention was drawn away from Sara. The child slid liquidly to the floor, her body totally flaccid. Her head drooped, flopping limply to the side.

Elliot stood over Jane, his chest heaving. Eyes wild, he was unaware of his daughter's viscous movement. "How dare you?" he roared. He straddled Jane. "How fucking dare you? Who the hell do you think you are?"

He dropped to the ground, kneeling on her splayed arms. He pinned them to the floor, and he began beating her with his fists. She felt the first blow as it landed on her ear. Small stars burst through her vision. Elliot shrieked at her under the shower of blows. "She was playing with fire! Goddammit. Don't you understand?"

She could only hear from one ear, and Jane realized in some vague and shadowy part of her brain that he had ruptured her eardrum. Another fist connected with her ribs, and she trembled—triumphant—at least he left Sara alone.

The words drifted through the curtain of pain, and she understood what had made him snap. She could comprehend only too well their shared terror. The rain of blows ceased, his rage having spent itself. He stood, giving Jane one final ferocious kick in the ribs. She rolled into a fetal position. He swung from her, back to Sara, gave the motionless child a vicious backhanded slap, and stomped from the room.

Jane crept over to Sara and cradled her unconscious form. "Oh, my baby, my poor, sweet baby, I'm so sorry." She rocked her back and forth, moaning the mournful apology over and over again like a litany. The little girl stirred. Jane crawled onto Sara's bed, pulling her daughter's limp body up behind her. She grabbed the blanket from the foot of the bed and wrapped it around the two of them. Sobbing, she waited for Sara to regain consciousness.

Critter whined softly when the house fell silent. He crept out from where he had cowered during the battle in the protective comfort beneath the Lump's metal bed. He stared mournfully into her eyes. She blinked. He stuck his cold, wet nose into her clawlike hand. She squeezed with what little strength she could muster.

Something moved outside the door. Immediately alert, Critter whipped around, assuming a stiff-legged stance. He growled. Nana stared at the dog. With an innate knowledge most animals seemed to possess, Critter knew. Nana pondered the phenomenon, wondering how she could use his instinctive knowledge.

Critter lowered himself to the floor. Slipping forward with his stomach scraping the ground—much like a cat stalking its prey—Critter crawled, snarling to the door. He stayed there momentarily, listening for further sounds. Nana and the house seemed to hold one collective breath. Critter stood and stepped cautiously into the hall. Once completely out of the room, the door closed. Critter jumped as Nana's, Sara's, and the master bedroom doors slammed shut simultaneously. He spun and scratched at Nana's door. A crash came from below him, and he overcame his fear.

Protect! His family relied on him and now after the fight could do little for themselves. The Man's drunken snores came from the master bedroom, broken sobs came from the Littlest One's room. He slunk down the stairs. *Bang!* Something toppled over in the living room. *Crash!*

The house sprung to life around him. Fed by the violence, it gained strength. Again in a belly-scraping posture, he slithered into the living room. He felt the sudden rush of air as something whizzed past his head. *Whoosh!* Courage deserted him as an album hit the door next to his ear.

Another album went careening through the air. Critter ducked and spun. Tail tucked between his legs, he hit the decks, racing for the stairs. The wax-slick floor sent him skidding into the bottom step. He scampered clumsily up to the second floor. Normal caution thrown to the wind, he stumbled into the Evil Spot as he headed for the relative safety of Nana's room.

He howled as it caught him. Critter froze. The Evil held him. He yelped. *It's got Critter! It's got Critter!* he thought, his fear telegraphing through the closed door into Nana's room, where she began to thrash upon the bed. The danger surrounded him. *Protect!* A bass voice echoed disdainful laughter in his mind. The dog dropped bonelessly to the ground. His legs and head writhed convulsively. Sara cried out once from her mother's arms. The house grew quiet while Critter jittered in a distorted horizontal dance on the floor near the vent.

"Sara, hold still." Jane sat on the toilet. Sara squirmed as Jane gently dabbed makeup on the large purpling bruise below her left eye.

"Ouch!"

Jane applied more foundation to her finger and softly patted it on the tender skin.

Sara pushed her mother's hand away. "That hurts."

"It's not the makeup that hurts, honey."

"I don't care. It *still* hurts."

"I know it hurts, but I'm almost finished." She leaned back to survey her work. "That's one helluva shiner you have."

Sara stared back at her mother, her eyes holding an unvoiced accusation.

"I know he shouldn't have done it, Sara, but you've got to try and understand." Sara didn't say a word. "He was scared, Sara, afraid for you. He saw you with that lighter and he just . . ."—Jane groped for the right words—"went a little crazy. You know how your father is." She noticed her daughter examining the cut on her cheek, and she winced, glad that Sara couldn't see the bruises on her arms and ribs. "You shouldn't have been playing with fire, and you know that."

"But . . ." Sara was about to tell her mother that she hadn't been playing with fire and decided against it. It wouldn't do any good, anyway; her mother wouldn't believe her.

Jane smiled sadly at her daughter, relieved that Sara had broken the tight-lipped silence. "I know that it's hard for you to see that. After all, we're big people. We're your parents, and we're supposed to know everything. We're not supposed to get scared, but we do. When you grow up, Sara, you'll understand that adults aren't much more than big kids—pretending to know and understand things that they really don't know or understand."

Sara watched her mother.

"I just wanted you to try and understand so you wouldn't be too mad at your father. He loves you as best he can, Sara, and he doesn't want to see you get hurt." Jane watched her daughter try and assimilate this information. Sara's expression remained puzzled.

With a sigh, Jane struggled to explain. "I know that that doesn't make much sense to you because he hurt you, but remember how I told you about good and bad, about how doing some things were worse than others." Jane snapped her fingers in sudden inspiration. "Like white lies."

"You mean, like you telling Mrs. Gibbons that you liked her hat when you really thought it looked funny."

"Yes, like that."

"Yeah," she said uncertainly, and Jane could tell that her daughter couldn't grasp the association.

"Well, there's hurt and there's *hurt.* Big and little hurts, you might call them. If you stub your toe, that hurts; but if you fall down the stairs, that hurts worse. Do you see what I mean?"

"I don't know," Sara mused.

"Well, I know your daddy hurt you last night, but if you had started a fire, you could have been hurt a lot worse. Like Shelley, you could have died."

"No!"

Jane blinked, brought up short. She didn't know if Sara thought that she was somehow immune or if she still refused to acknowledge her sister's death. She decided not to pursue the issue. "You probably don't see that because you didn't start a fire, but trust me. A fire would hurt you far more than your father ever could." Jane paused, and Sara caught her mother's soft, barely breathed "I think." Sara waited for her mother to continue.

"In a way—not a good way, mind you, but I'll be honest with you—what your dad did last night was awful—but your father was trying to do what he thought was best for you. He was trying to protect you."

"Mama, why is Dad so afraid?"

"Because we don't want to lose you like we lost Shelley."

Sara wanted to tell her mother that they hadn't lost Shelley. She wanted to tell her that Shelley was still here, only afraid to show herself, afraid that Dad would do to her just what he had done to Sara the night before. Jane stared out the window to the street below, chewing her lip.

"Shelley used to—" Sara stopped, unsure what to say.

"Yes, I know, Sara, Shelley used to start fires and Daddy would punish her for it." She shied from the memory.

"How come?"

"How come he punished her? Or how come she started fires?"

Sara shrugged.

"Well, he would punish her for the same reason he lit in to you like he did last night. Only it didn't work and now she's gone. And Shelley started fires like she did in the house . . ."

Her voice died off. She looked at the tire tracks in the streets and from there to the quiet houses beyond. How did one explain pyromania to a child? "The doctors said she started fires because she was angry, because she was mad at your father and me."

Jane uttered a strangulated sound, choking on the last statement. When she next spoke it was in a voice scarcely above a whisper. "It's called acting out. Someday I'll explain it to you, but for now you'd better get going. You're going to be late as it is. I've written a note for you so you won't get in trouble with your teacher."

Jane stood in the bathroom watching her daughter as she made her way up the road. Sara jumped from rut to rut. Jane started to unlock the window so she could yell at her and tell her to get out of the street. Before she could, Sara climbed up a particularly large snowbank and then slid down on her rear to the sidewalk on the other side. Jane chuckled to herself. Elliot was right, Sara was pretty resilient. She had to be.

Jane turned from the window so she didn't see when Sara swerved into the Erwins' yard. Reassured, Jane went down the hall to Nana's room. She moved mechanically through the morning's ministrations. "Nana, I'm not going to get you up in the chair yet. I've got to go out for a little while."

Nana didn't blink; she didn't stir. She only peered up at her daughter, never taking her eyes off the cut on Jane's cheek and the red mark that surrounded it.

Jane felt uncomfortable under her mother's scrutiny. She pulled away from Nana so she was just outside of her mother's field of vision.

"I'll be back as soon as I can."

Jane stopped in the foyer. An album lay on the floor. She picked it up and walked into the living room to put it away. Unjacketed albums littered the floor. Had

Elliot come down last night? The end table was overturned. She quickly straightened the mess, her mind too preoccupied to wonder about its cause.

Critter stood at the head of the stairs, watching. As she pulled her coat on in the front hall, he ran down the stairs. She silenced the jumping mongrel with a gentle rebuff. "No, you've got to stay here."

Jane extracted her gloves from her pocket, checked her purse to make sure she had enough money, and slipped out the door before Critter could squeeze past. The bright sunlight glinted off the snow.

Hurriedly, she made her way up the street, limping slightly. She stopped in front of the Erwins' house, taking in the cheerful menagerie. One elf, however, lay broken. A frozen smile turned to the sky, fragmented limbs lay disconnected from the body. Other colorful elves peeked—witnesses to its destruction—out of the shrubbery. A clay squirrel sat eternally poised on its haunches, and the deer silenced forever with a chain gag from which hung suspended a wooden plaque with the Erwins' name.

She pondered the shattered elf and shook her head. Gathering her courage, she marched up to the door. What person, who so adorned her yard, could be intimidating? Jane thought to herself. She rang the bell, and a stocky woman with bleached blond hair answered the door.

"Hello, I'm Jane Graves. I just moved in up the street."

"Oh, you're Sara's mother." Mrs. Erwin frowned down at the broken statue. "Damn! I'm sorry. It's just"—she indicated the clay shards—"the neighborhood kids can be so destructive." She backed away from the door, eyeing the gouge along Jane's cheekbone.

Jane fingered the scratch self-consciously. "I bumped into the cupboard door last night. I can be a real clod sometimes. Between my bumping into things and Sara's falling down the stairs last night, I'm afraid we all look a little worse for wear."

"I do that kind of thing all the time in my workshop—knock into things, trip over boxes. And the kids are always falling over something or other, aren't they? It's a wonder they survive to adulthood." She opened the door wider and stepped away from it. "You must be freezing. Why don't you come in and have a cup of coffee?"

"Yes, I'd love some. I can't stay long, though. I take care of my mother, and I don't like to leave her alone. I was on my way to the store and wanted to stop by and introduce myself." Jane followed Mrs. Erwin to the kitchen.

"Yes, Sara told me that your mother stayed with you. That must be quite a handful. Tell me, is she able to care for herself at all?" She bustled around the kitchen. She pulled two coffee cups from the strainer and dried them, poured coffee in each, then grabbed some pastries out of the bread box and offered one to Jane.

Jane declined the proffered pastries. "No, I'm afraid not. She's been pretty well bedridden for a couple of years now." Mrs. Erwin picked up an éclair and sat at the table, gesturing to a chair with her free hand. "Actually, I wanted to thank you, Mrs. Erwin."

"Pah! Thank me, what for? And please don't be formal; call me Sally."

"Sally, then. Thanks for letting Tommy come over and play."

"But why thank me?"

"For a couple of reasons. I'm delighted to have Sara make friends so soon. It's difficult for her since . . . well, she's such a solitary child. Here we are in a new neighborhood, and all." Sally Erwin nodded sagely. Jane noted that bad news traveled fast. She wondered who else in the neighborhood knew.

"Besides, I've heard the stories they tell about the house. Sam Holloway warned us. Some people might think twice before they let their son or their daughter come over to that house."

Sally took another enormous bite of éclair. Custard squirted out each side. Jane warmed her hands on the hot coffee cup. Mrs. Erwin swallowed the mouthful, licked the sticky filling from her fingers, and replied, "I admit, I did think twice about it, but it's just children's tales, I'm sure."

Jane laughed. "I haven't run into any ghosts." She looked nervously away from Mrs. Erwin. "At least no headless gentleman, anyway."

Sally looked momentarily disturbed and then laughed also.

Jane rushed on before Sally had a chance to speak. "I was wondering if I could ask a favor. I know I don't know you that well, but . . ."

"Well, that depends, of course, on the favor."

"Would it be all right if I send Sara over here after school? I mean, if it wouldn't be too much trouble."

"Trouble? If I know my Tommy, he'll probably drag her home from school, anyway. Sara seems like a delightful child, very polite. She's always welcome."

"Oh, thank you so much. You see her father and I haven't had much time to ourselves since the move and—" She cut her sentence off, giving Mrs. Erwin a wistful smile which she hoped would be construed as an implied confidence. It worked.

"Ah! No problem. I was young once." She snorted. "Now I'm just as happy if the boys' father leaves me alone. Maybe she should stay for dinner."

"I don't think that will be necessary."

"I'll cook a little extra just the same. You give a call when you're ready for her to come home. So nice to see a couple still have some romance left in their marriage." Jane blushed and Mrs. Erwin reached for a doughnut. "What do you think of our neighborhood?"

"I've lived in this town for a few years, but not this side of it. So far, I haven't had much of a chance to get out. First, there was the move, then Christmas, and I've got Mother to take care of and all. With that and not having a car, I'm afraid I haven't seen much of it. Besides shopping for Christmas and groceries, this is the first time I've been out. By the way, can you tell me if there's a hardware store near here?"

"Oh, about a mile away."

"I didn't know it was that far. I should probably get going."

Sally waved Jane back down. "Sit, sit. You haven't even finished your coffee. I'll give you a ride."

"I couldn't impose any more than I already have."

"You're not imposing. It's nice to get a break from

the housework." She smiled and went on to tell Jane about her ceramics workshop. She twittered, explaining her hobby in more detail than Jane could absorb. Jane tried to listen, but kept looking at the clock over Sally's shoulder. Sally finished the doughnut and coffee, not noticing that Jane's had grown cold. "I know you have to get back home. I'll show you where the hardware store is. There's a little strip center not far from here that has everything—a grocery store, a couple of boutiques, and a hobby shop. That's where I pick up my supplies."

Sara looked through the mesh glass at the class beyond the door. Students bent over third-grade readers. She walked into the room, pausing uncertainly in the doorway. Mrs. McGuinness glared at her, waiting until Belinda Johnson finished reading her portion of the text.

"Sara Graves, so nice of you to join us," she said. Her voice dripped sarcasm.

Sara shifted from one foot to the other. "My mom wrote me a note." She held it up like a shield and a talisman.

"Oh, she did, did she?" Mrs. McGuinness pursed her lips. She had been right, this child and her mother were going to be problems.

"Class, continue reading. I'll be back in a second." She moved to the back of the class. She grasped Sara's shoulder and dragged her unceremoniously through the door to the hall. Sara handed her the note. Mrs. McGuinness studied the young girl, noting the poorly covered bruise under her eye. Then she read the letter.

Sara contemplated the regular rows of gray lockers

that lined the hall to either side of the classroom door. Mrs. McGuinness turned to her. "Yes, you have a note, but that's not good enough."

Sara stared down at the ground. She traced the outline of a tile on the floor with her toe and said nothing.

"I guess it will have to do for now, though, won't it?"

Relieved, Sara pulled awkwardly at the door. Mrs. McGuinness stopped her. She bent close, and Sara recognized the same sick smile she had seen on her face before. "I know all about you, Sara. I know it was you that left me that little present." The teacher seized her shoulder and shook her. "Wasn't it? Now you've got a black eye. What did you do to deserve that, eh, little girl?" Sara cringed. Retreating from the teacher's gaze, she tried to back away.

Mrs. McGuinness spun the child around and shoved her toward the door. "Go take your seat."

Sara escaped into the classroom. Mrs. McGuinness strode to the front of the class. "Sara!" Sara froze, one leg lifted over the wooden seat. Everyone in the room turned to stare at her.

"You tell your mother that from now on I expect you here on time. There will be no special treatment in this class. We can't have you wandering in anytime you'd—" The teacher caught herself. "—at all hours, now, can we?"

Sara looked confused. "No, ma'am."

"All right, you may take your seat."

"Yes'm." She climbed into her chair.

Mrs. McGuinness shot Sara a look of gloating triumph. "Who wants to read the next selection?" A few isolated hands popped up in various parts of the room.

Tommy punched Sara in the shoulder. She flinched, swinging around halfway so she could see him out of the corner of her eye. Tommy gave her the thumbs-up sign and winked at her.

Jane was glad when the effervescent Sally Erwin dropped her off at her door. The woman's irrepressible good spirits were depressing. She had insisted on giving Jane a tour of the strip mall—what there was of it. After stopping at the hardware store and picking up a present for Sara, Jane had waited impatiently, anxious to be home. Sally, however, had dithered around the hobby shop, pointing out items of little or no interest.

Leaning against the front door, Jane exhaled a long drawn-out sigh of relief. "Whew! Critter, I thought that woman was going to talk my ear off." Critter responded eagerly by jumping on her chest. Jane flinched, angrily pushing him away, and walked through the foyer to the living room. The gloomy old house had never looked quite as good to her as it did right now. At least the tenebrous atmosphere fit her mood. The Christmas-tree lights blinked defiant cheer.

It was time to take the tree down. She put her package on the coffee table, grabbed the cord and pulled. Sparks flew and arced as the cord came apart in her hand, a portion of it remaining in the wall. The bulbs popped, starting at the top of the tree until reaching the bottom of the strand. Critter turned tail and ran while Jane dropped her section of the cord and protected her eyes, covering them with her hand. What was left of the wire wiggled and snaked along the floor.

"Damn." She ran to the kitchen to get a pot holder. The entire rack came down from the wall as she pulled at one. Ignoring the mess, she went back to the living room where she seized what remained of the cord and yanked it from the wall. She stamped on the smoldering rug. Then she sat on the couch with a sigh of relief. Critter crept back into the room and whined.

"It's okay now, fella." She hesitated and added a guarded "I think. Shit." She returned to the kitchen to survey the wreckage there. The hole in the plaster would have to be fixed. Jane picked up the rest of the pot holders, stacking them neatly on the counter.

"It seems, Critter," she said to the dog who stood guardedly at the door, "that this place is bent on self-destructing."

Jane took off her coat. She got the toolbox from the basement and began to change the lock on one of the kitchen drawers. Critter, losing interest, left her to her own devices. Once the lock was changed, Jane nailed the rack back on the wall near the stove. The hole itself would have to wait until later; she didn't have the spackling compound to fix it now.

With this chore done, Jane went back into the living room. The lights were unsalvageable, but the tree was intact. She was thankful that she and Elliot had opted for an artificial Christmas tree years ago. With any luck, she would have it put away before Sara came home for lunch.

Jane fixed herself a Bloody Mary, letting it soothe her jangled nerves while she worked. She made Sara's lunch, did the laundry, and got Nana up. One drink followed another. She had made up her mind to talk to Elliot, but Jane feared the consequences, so she silenced the nagging terror with a liquid lobotomy.

That afternoon when Sara came home from school, Jane sent her over to Mrs. Erwin's, warning her not to come home until she was called. Sara eyed her mother suspiciously. Sara didn't know what her mom had in mind, but Sara could smell the vodka, and she could smell trouble. *Something is up.*

CHAPTER 13

Jane was waiting for Elliot when he got home. He disregarded her angry stare and headed for the liquor cabinet. She sat silently as he fixed himself a drink. He plopped down on one of the kitchen chairs. "All right, out with it. I know you're going to bitch me out so we might as well get it over with."

Jane began quiet, her voice calm and level despite her fury. She felt angrier still that he somehow had managed to steal part of her fire. "What you did last night was unforgivable, and now you make it sound like I'm being unreasonable."

"Look, the kid was playing with matches."

"She wasn't playing with matches. She was playing with your goddamn lighter."

"Matches, lighter, what difference does it make?"

"That doesn't justify beating the living shit out of your daughter. Good God, Elliot, do you know what you were doing to her? You throttled her. Her neck is bruised where you held her while smashing her against the wall."

"Hey, I'm sorry." He avoided her eyes, examining his hands as though no longer a part of his body. "Okay, I admit it, I got carried away. With what has happened, can you blame me?"

"Carried away! Hell! Yes, Elliot, I can and do blame you. You know beatings don't work. Remember, you tried it with Shelley. What good did it do? She's dead now. Are you proud of that? I'm not."

He glared at her. Jane returned it with a rude gesture. Elliot raised a threatening hand, stopping himself, and sighed in resignation.

"Go ahead, Jane, rub salt in an open wound. You know how I felt about Shelley. I loved her."

Jane stood up. "You had a funny way of showing it. So what do you want from me? Sympathy? I'm supposed to feel sorry for you. Well, I don't, buster. We're all wounded here, walking wounded, and Sara's the worst of all. You never did to Shelley what you did to Sara last night."

Contrite, Elliot looked into his glass. "I already said I'm sorry. I just went a little crazy. What the hell am I supposed to do? Let her burn the place down?"

"No, not if it can be avoided, but I'd rather this place burn to the ground than have you batter my only daughter." A loud thud came from somewhere below them. In her anger, Jane let it pass, unheeded. She could feel her pulse surging in her temples—it bounded, explosively. The veins on her neck stood out as she tried to calm herself.

"I don't know what the right thing to do is, but you

are never, *never*, going to do what you did last night again, I can tell you that."

"Oh ho! What's this? A threat?"

"No, not a threat, Elliot, a promise. Do you know you gave Sara a black eye?"

Elliot looked up at her, chagrined. He rubbed his hands together. His palms were damp and clammy.

Jane didn't let up. "Well, you did. When you left her, she was unconscious. Do you know what that means? Do you?" she shrieked at him. "You beat her senseless, you bastard!"

Jane saw his remorse, his shame. Tears formed in his eyes. She repressed the feelings of pity—concentrating instead on the years of accumulated resentment mixed with terror—and went on. "You could have killed her. You could have killed your own daughter."

Elliot spoke in a subdued whisper. "Where is she?"

"She's over at a neighbor's house. I figured she had been through enough, she didn't have to listen to this."

"Look." He reached for her across the table, weeping. She pulled away from his questing hand. "Honey, I'm sorry."

"Sorry's not good enough, Elliot, not anymore."

The apology unaccepted, Elliot became belligerent. He slammed his glass down on the table—no longer repentant. The amber liquid splashed over the side. Jane instinctively shrank away from him. "I told you I'm sorry. What else do you want from me? Blood?"

With as much bluff as she could muster, she returned his ire with a steady and defiant gaze. "If that's what it takes, Elliot. I don't care if you beat the crap out of me; I'm going to finish what I've got to say."

In a total about-face, he moaned softly, "Look, I can't take back what happened last night. It's too late."

"No, you can't take that back, but you can keep it from happening again. I don't care what she's doing. I don't bloody well care if she poured gasoline on the living room floor and is throwing lit matches into the puddle. You don't touch her, don't lay a finger on her. You don't do a fucking thing. Just call me, I'll take care of it."

He stared at her. His mouth dropped open. "Do you understand me, Elliot?"

Defeated, he gave in. "I understand."

"You'll call me?"

"I'll call you. At least I'll try."

"You call—don't try—because, so help me God, if you ever do that to my daughter again, I'll kill you." She regarded him coldly.

Shocked into silence, Elliot held back the retort he was about to make. Jane's eyes inadvertently went to the line of scratches below his ear. Between the three of them, they looked like they had been through a battle, and they had. Each bore scars.

Jane felt suddenly ashamed. Mortification and humiliation followed quickly on the heels of shame. How had this happened? How had their family disintegrated to this? She wanted to take back what she had said. She feared her own violence. Jane stifled the emotion before it had a chance to fully surface, but he must have noticed her softening because he gave her a sidelong look.

"And how do you plan on doing that, dear, sweet wife?" Elliot purred at her. Jane stood up and retreated to the kitchen sink. She knew that deceptively sweet tone, and it held more danger than any shout or curse.

Resolve fixed, her eyes narrowed, and she didn't answer, only turned to the one locked drawer in the kitchen that held the twenty-two caliber revolver. Following her gaze, Elliot smiled maliciously. "And how do you know I won't hide it?"

"You can't get to it. I changed the lock today. You couldn't open that drawer if you tried. I put all the matches in there, too, so Sara can't get at them."

Elliot fell silent, looking from her to the drawer. Then he stood up. "I've got some papers to grade. Don't worry about dinner. I'm not very hungry."

He sniffed, arrogant, insolent. He gave her a long, hard look, expecting her to quail before him. He toyed with his drink. She could see the implied "just wait" mirrored in his eyes, and she suppressed the fit of tremors she felt coming.

He pivoted, saying to her over his shoulder, "I lost my appetite."

Jane stopped him as he was about to leave the room. "Wait." She held out his lighter. "This is yours. Do you think you can hang on to it?"

He stared at the lighter and grabbed it from her.

"By the way, tantrums won't do you any good, either."

"What the hell's that supposed to mean?"

"You know what I mean, the albums."

His eyes swept her up and down. "I haven't the

foggiest idea what you're talking about. You're nuts." He stormed out of the kitchen.

Sara and Tommy were watching television in the Erwins' den when Jane's call came. Mrs. Erwin walked into the room and stood between them and the television, blocking their view. Tommy adjusted his position so he could still see Scooby Doo and Scrappy between her legs.

"Sara, it's your mother."

Sara dutifully got up and headed for the hall phone.

"Tommy, go wash your hands and get ready for supper."

Tommy began to plead. "Aw, Mom, this is the best part."

"They're all the best part." Sally turned and watched Scooby Doo chase after the hamburger which some ingenious white-sheeted ghost held out as bait before the hungry hound. The canine slipped and slid after the enticing prize which hung from a line on the end of a fishing rod. "Doesn't look very interesting to me. Go on, your father and David are hungry. They don't want to wait for you and Scooby Doo."

She turned and called after Sara. "Oh, Sara, don't forget to tell your mother that you are welcome to stay for supper."

Sara picked up the receiver. "Hello?"

"Sara, this is Mom. It's okay to come home now."

"Is it?" She paused uncertainly. "Uh, Mrs. Erwin invited me over for supper. Can I stay? They're having fried chicken."

"No, honey, we've inconvenienced the Erwins

enough for today. Besides, I've got dinner ready for you here. How does spaghetti sound to you?"

"Okay, I guess."

Jane Graves missed the disappointment in her daughter's tone. "I'm going to be upstairs putting Nana to bed. You come up there and join me. Your father's in the study. I don't want you bothering him, okay?"

"Yes, Mom."

Tommy waited, his hands stuffed in his pockets. "Can you stay?"

"Nope, I gotta go."

"Too bad. I'll save you a piece of chicken if David doesn't make too big of a pig of himself."

David, who had just entered the hallway, poked his brother in the ribs. "Who's the pig? Oink! Oink!"

Not about to be outdone, Tommy grunted back at David. They circled each other, grunting. Sally emerged from the den. "What's going on here?"

"Mom, David's picking on me 'n' Sara again."

"David, leave your little brother alone. I've got to check on dinner."

David scowled. Tommy ignored him. "I'll bring it to school tomorrow," he told Sara. "You can eat it for lunch."

"Naw, don't bother." She got her coat from the closet. "I'll be leaving now, Mrs. Erwin. Thanks for having me over."

Sally hurried out of the kitchen, dishtowel in hand. "It was a pleasure, Sara." Sara put her hand on the door. "Wait a second, isn't your mother coming over to pick you up?"

"No."

"Well, you can't go out alone. It's after dark."

"It's all right. It's not very far. I just live up the street."

"I know where you live, Sara, and I don't care. I won't have a child your age running around the streets after dark. I can't imagine what your mother must be thinking, letting you go out alone at this time."

Defensively, Sara said, "She's putting Nana to bed, and my father's got papers to grade."

"I'm sorry, Sara. I'm sure your mother has her reasons, but I still won't let you walk home by yourself. David, you put on your coat and take Sara home."

"I will not. If I'm not good enough to play with them, I don't see why I gotta walk her home." David pointed an accusing finger at Sara.

"What's the matter?" Tommy jeered. "Ya' scared?" He began to dance around his older brother. "Scaredy-cat! Scaredy-cat!"

"Tommy Erwin, you quiet down." Mrs. Erwin rolled her eyes toward the ceiling. She looked down at Sara and shook her head. "You two are going to be the death of me. Between one hyperactive little boy and a dim-witted older brother, I don't know what I'm going to do."

She made a funny face and threw Sara a look of exasperation. "Now, both of you go put on your coats.

"What do you think I should do with them, Sara?" she asked as Tommy and his brother disappeared to the back of the house.

Sara didn't know what hyperactive meant, but she put on her most serious expression and said, "I don't know, ma'am."

Sally laughed. "You're a treasure, Sara." Mrs. Erwin stooped over the little girl and examined her face. "That is a nasty bruise you have there. Got it falling down the stairs, huh?"

Sara backed away from the large woman's gaze, feeling a minute of total panic. What had her mother told Mrs. Erwin? Sara took the woman's comment as a clue. "Yes."

"You should be more careful and watch where you are going. I bet you don't end up with as many lumps, bumps, and bruises as my two do. I hope your mother knows how lucky she is to have a little girl. I've always wanted a girl, but I got those instead." She indicated her sons with a quick toss of her black-rooted blond hair toward the back of the house. "Just be glad that you're not a mother yourself, yet."

Sara squared her shoulders. "I'm not going to be a mother."

"What are you going to be? A father?"

"Nope, I'm not gonna have kids."

"You sound awfully sure of yourself."

"I am. My sister told me."

"Your sister? When did she tell you that?"

"A couple of weeks ago, I guess."

"A couple of weeks ago?" Sally frowned. "Well, how do you know she's right?"

"My sister's always right. She knows these things." Baffled, Sally studied the little girl before her as Tommy ran into the front hall from the den with his older brother bringing up the rear.

"I'm ready. How about you, Sara?"

"Yep."

"David?"

He snarled and took a swing at his younger brother.

"David, you behave yourself," Mrs. Erwin admonished. "Now, you two boys take Sara home and come right back. I don't want you dawdling along the way."

She let them out the front door. Her husband wandered into the hall. "That's odd." she said to him.

"What's odd?"

"Sara said her sister told her she wouldn't have any children, but her sister's dead."

"You probably misunderstood, that's all."

"Perhaps," she mused. "But she seemed so insistent. As a matter of fact, Sara said that her sister told her only a couple of weeks ago, but the sister died before Christmas." Sally shook her head.

"You know kids, now that her sister's gone, maybe she's made up an imaginary sister the way David used to have an imaginary friend."

"You're probably right. Poor child."

Unconcerned, Fred Erwin picked up his newspaper from the hall table. "Will they be back soon? I'm starved."

Sally poked her husband's expanding belly. "You're always starved." She headed for the kitchen.

Fred shook open his paper, grumbling, "You ain't exactly svelte yourself."

Tommy and Sara ran along the darkened street hand in hand. David followed in silence. He looked anxiously about him.

"What's wrong, David?" Tommy jeered at his older brother.

Sara dropped Tommy's pudgy hand and ran around behind the teenager. *"Boo!"*

David jumped. She started to dance a frolicsome jig at his side. "Nyah, nyah, David's sceered." And Tommy picked up the chorus. David took a swing at Sara, stumbled and fell. Sara kicked snow in his face.

Tommy pushed her down. "Quit that! That's not fair."

Sara sat up. "You just be careful, Tommy Erwin, or I'll get back at you like I did Miz Gunnysack."

Tommy helped his brother up. "I don't care what you do to that old bat, but you leave my brother alone. He can't help it if he's slow."

David brushed the snow from his pants. "Am not! You take that back!"

Tommy glared first at David and then at Sara. "Aw, who cares, anyway? Come on, David, let's go home." He walked briskly away from them as they stood and stared at him.

David scratched his head, perplexed. Sara stood up and ran after Tommy. "Tommy, I'm sorry, but you make fun of him, too."

The small boy stared back at his older brother who hadn't seemed to have caught on to the topic of conversation. "Yeah, I know I do."

"Friends?" She held out her hand. He stuffed his hands in his pockets and shuffled in the snow. "Pleeease?"

Ignoring her outstretched hand, he growled, "Okay, friends. Come on, David, let's go home." The two boys headed for the Erwins' house. Sara stood under the streetlight and watched them enter the front door. She kicked at the snow and turned to walk the rest of the way home.

* * *

Sara walked into Nana's room just as her mother finished feeding her. Jane handed the dirty bowl to Sara who eyed the remains of the Franco-American SpaghettiOs. Yuck! Her mother had made her come home for *this?*

"I'm glad you're home, Sara. How's Tommy today?"

"Okay. How's Dad?"

Her mother shrugged. "Okay, but don't disturb him. He's got his papers to grade, you know." Sara nodded sagely.

"Let's go downstairs and eat." Jane caught Sara's look of dismay. She laughed. "Don't worry, Sara, we get the real thing, but I can't feed spaghetti to Nana." Jane made loud slurping noises. Sara snickered. "Come on, kiddo, let's go."

Jane filled a large kettle with water. "It'll take a few minutes. I didn't want to start the noodles until you were home or else we would have ended up with spaghetti lump."

"Yuck!" Sara shuffled aimlessly around the kitchen. She stopped in front of the garbage can and looked in. "Wow. What's this?" She lifted the strand of shattered Christmas lights. The cord was blackened and fused in places. Most of the delicate bulbs had burst, leaving jagged edges. A few others had melted into a caricature of the tiny tulips they had once resembled.

"Those were the Christmas-tree lights."

"What happened?" She lowered the molten black mass back into the can.

"They burned up. It was pretty spectacular, with sparks flying all over the place."

Sara leaned over the can. "A lot of stuff seems to be breaking, doesn't it?"

"You noticed that, too, huh?"

Sara turned to her mother, watching her profile as she stood over the steaming pot. Jane dropped the spaghetti into the kettle. Sara walked over to the counter and pointed at the food processor. "What about this?"

Jane looked up, confused. "What about what?"

"That." She pointed again. "Has it broke?"

Jane frowned. "Broken, dear."

"Broken."

"Not yet. It better not; it's new, so don't jinx it."

She stirred the spaghetti. Satisfied that the noodles were properly separated, Jane put the lid on the pan and went to sit at the table. "Come here, Sara." She patted her lap. Sara went and stood before her mother. "Come on, climb up."

Sara looked at her mother's lap doubtfully. "I thought you said I was too big."

"Too big to sit there all of the time, but not some of the time." Sara climbed on. "Ooph! You are getting big, though." Jane rolled the collar back on Sara's shirt and examined the necklace of bruises. "Does it hurt much?"

"Not too bad."

"I got a surprise for you. Mrs. Erwin took me to that little mall today, and I picked up a present for you."

"What? What?" Sara started to wiggle in Jane's lap.

"Hold still a second. It's not going anywhere." She spit on her thumb and gently rubbed away the makeup under Sara's eye.

Sara squirmed. "Mom! That's . . ."

"I know, that's *gross!*" Jane made a funny face and Sara laughed. "I just wanted to check your eye. All checked. I think you'll live. Go on, get down. Your surprise is in the pantry." Sara scrambled down from her mother's lap. "Whew, I feel sixty pounds lighter."

"Aw, Mom."

"Well, go ahead. Get it out of the pantry. It's in a bag marked 'Toys-'n'-Things.' "

Sara opened the pantry door and pulled the bag out. She glanced over her shoulder and gave her mother a questioning look.

"That's okay. Open it." Sara opened the bag and a brand-new Raggedy Andy stared out at her. She dropped the package.

"What's the matter, Sara? It's to replace your other one. Don't you like it or are you getting too old for that sort of thing, too?"

"No, it's just that . . ." Sara paused. "What if something happens to it?"

"Nothing's going to happen to it if you take good care of it."

"But . . ."

"Now, Sara, I don't want to hear any more about it," Jane said crossly.

Sara extracted Raggedy Andy from the sack. She hugged the doll. "It's neat, Mom. Thanks." Sara plopped down on the floor. Critter got up from his warm spot near the stove, stretched, yawned, and gave the doll an experimental sniff.

"You're welcome, Sara. After what you've been through, you deserve it. You deserve a lot more than that, but that's all I could afford with the cookie-jar money."

Sara held on to Raggedy Andy by his arms and began to dance him around the floor. Jane smiled. The lid on the kettle began to rattle and shake. Water spewed over the edge of the pan, dousing the flame on the gas stove. Jane leapt up and turned off the gas burner.

"I bet the noodles are done."

Sara stood. "I'll go get Dad."

"No!" Sara froze. "I'm sorry, honey. I didn't mean to yell like that. It's just that your father said he didn't want to be interrupted, not even for dinner. Why don't you go wash your hands while I dish everything up."

Jane moved noiselessly through the unlit house. She stopped before the locked kitchen drawer and looked apprehensively over her shoulder. Even the sounds of Elliot's snores from the study did not console her. She had been fooled more than once by this feint. When he wanted something badly enough, he exhibited a certain cunning and inebriate stealth. She had learned not to trust him.

She checked again. Nothing, not even the colorful Christmas lights blinked at her now that the tree was down. She dug in the pocket of the floral duster and came out with the key. Another quick look, and she unlocked the drawer.

The blue-black muzzle of the twenty-two caliber revolver gleamed dully in the subdued light. Jane wrapped her fingers around the wooden stock, pulling it from the drawer. She held it against her body. She found the feel of its cold metal oddly reassuring. With one eye still on the kitchen door, she grabbed the additional shells and dropped the plastic case in her pocket. Quickly she locked the drawer and headed back for her bedroom.

Jane wasn't exactly sure why she wanted the gun by her side that night. She didn't expect a recurrence of last night's events, but she did expect Elliot to try and rifle the drawer. Critter was waiting for her when she returned to the master bedroom.

"Hello, Critter. You don't seem to like sleeping with Sara anymore. How come?" He tilted his head, lifting one black-tipped ear. Jane listened to the noises coming from the attic. She scratched his snout. "Well, I'll be glad to have you here tonight."

She turned on the lamp and sat down to load the gun, occasionally eyeing the ceiling. *Skitter, skitter, bump,* it answered back to her. Farther in the background, she could hear the steady rapping of the branch on Sara's bedroom window.

Jane spun the cylinder, put on the safety, and tucked the loaded revolver under her pillow. Critter jumped up on the bed. She patted the top of his head. "You be careful, puppy dog. It would be a hell of a note if we shot ourselves during the night, wouldn't it?" Unimpressed, he circled around and lay down.

Jane pulled a *Woman's Day* from her stack of magazines and started to read. A few moments later, she threw it down in disgust. Critter lifted his head from the bed and peered at her.

"Don't worry, Critter. I'm not mad at you. I don't

know why I keep buying that damn magazine. You'd think to read it that American women did nothing more than flit around a happy home, compare quality on disposable diapers, bake cookies, and knit little doilies."

Critter yawned.

"My sentiment exactly. I should start reading those cheap detective magazines. At least those would be funny." She picked up the magazine again. She had to do something to keep herself awake. Jane chose an article on how to save a failing marriage, interrupting the dog's sleep with periodic exclamations of scorn and hoots of disgust. Eventually, she dozed.

Thud! Suddenly awake and afraid, Jane bolted from the bed. Critter growled. *Bang!* The sound came from directly overhead. Jane walked out to the hall, pulling the dust mop from the hall closet. She returned to the bedroom. *Thump!* She poked at the ceiling with the mop handle. She had to stand on the bed to reach it.

"Stop it. *Stop it!*" She banged on the ceiling. "I don't care who you are or what you want in this house. Leave us alone!" Jane stood there, feeling a little bit ludicrous. Dead silence. The skin on the back of her neck crawled, and she felt a prickling sensation of panic. The quiet seemed more intimidating than the continuous noise.

"Well, it worked, didn't it, Critter?" She leaned the dust mop against the wall, sat in front of the vanity, and waited. Nothing. Jane turned to her reflection in the mirror, checking for any new lines or gray hairs. She picked up the hairbrush and began to brush her long blond hair, counting the strokes. The repetitive movements lulled her, calming her so that she didn't notice when the sounds in the attic began again.

". . . ninety-nine, one hundred." The hairbrush slid from nerveless fingers and fell clattering to the floor. Mouth agape, the astounded woman stared at herself in the mirror—both of them. She gasped, whirling around. Except for Critter, the room was empty. She turned slowly back to the mirror, holding her breath. Still, there *she* stood, two steps behind herself—complete with floral duster. Jane reached out with shaking hands and touched the reflected double in the mirror. The second Jane smiled sadly at the original, shook her head, and vanished.

She got up from the stool and checked the mirror again. The room looked normal. Only one image of herself—dazed, ashen, and gray—gazed back at her. Dusty brocade wallpaper revealed ghostly light squares where pictures hung no more. Critter slept blissfully on the bed. His feet twitched while he chased some imaginary rabbit. Jane headed for the stairs to fix herself a drink to help her sleep.

Nana listened to the sound of muffled footsteps overhead and the thrashing which came from her closet. *It* was getting restless. Otherwise, the house was quiet as though *it*—like Nana—waited for something to happen. Critter left the master bedroom and paced the hall, whining nervously. Nana lay motionless.

Shelley came, marionette in hand, as Nana knew she would. She stood in the doorway in her powder-blue dungarees. Nana tried to turn her head so she could get a better look. She had grown used to

Shelley's visits, no longer fearing them. The child did not rest, and why should she? Hers was an unquiet grave.

The apparition moved noiselessly to the closet which had grown ominously silent. She dropped her toy into the chair and dragged the rocker away from the door. Sweat broke out on Nana's upper lip, and she kicked helplessly at the sheets.

"Shhh." Momentarily shocked by her own successful attempt at speech, Nana forgot the specter and the terror that lay beyond the door. Then, alert again, Nana saw the small hand close around the knob. "Sh-Shah-Shah-Sh . . ." she hissed.

The little girl turned and Nana saw the rounded, gentle features twisted into a sneer. *No, not Shelley—but Sara!* The hand closed around the doorknob and yanked the door open. Two red eyes stared out at her, and Nana thought she saw a mouth. It drooled. Nana's heart fluttered in her chest like a leaf in the wind.

Sara walked over to the bed. Nana's eyes flitted from Sara's face to the embroidered emblem on the pocket of the overalls to the marionette. *But where . . . how?*

Sara leaned over the bed. Her child's hand closed easily over the emaciated woman's delicate throat. She squeezed, cutting off the air. "Nana," she whispered, "the beast is loose." Nana looked over Sara's shoulder to the open closet door which revealed the creature within. Sara's hand relaxed its hold on the old woman's neck. Strangulated noises came from Nana's throat. Sara let go completely.

Nana got the fleeting impression that the child's face wavered and blurred. The red embers from the closet burned in Sara's eyes. Sara laughed, her voice deepening. The glowing orbs came to rest on the strings of the puppet in her hands. "What would happen, old woman, if I were to wrap these"—she lifted the marionette—"around your neck? Would you dance for me?"

Nana shifted in her bed, and the impression was gone. Sara stood before her, and the two kindled coals blinked in the closet. "Night, night, Nana." Sara kissed the dry cheek. Nana shuddered—revolted at her granddaughter's touch—and Sara skipped gaily back down the hall.

CHAPTER 14

Jane awoke the next morning with a horrible hangover. She lay on the sagging bed and opened one eye. Lazily, she inspected the dusty brocade wallpaper. In an earlier era, it must have been sumptuous, but now—covered with fingerprints and peeling from the walls—it told of faded glory, of a house with more past than future. Its once-golden opulence seemed somehow profane.

The small window revealed a sodden, gray late-morning sky. It suited Jane's melancholy, and she peeked cautiously at the clock. *Ten.* "Damn!" Sara would be late for school again. She heaved herself into an upright position. Her head spun and her stomach did a slow rolling lurch as she sat up in bed. "Oh, God!" she muttered under her breath, sinking back to the pillows.

Steeling herself against the repercussions, she got up, yelling, "Sara! Oh."

The shout dissolved into a groan. Jane stood unsteadily next to the bed. Softer this time, she said, "Sara?" Critter loped into the room. Holding her head, Jane stumbled down the hall to her daughter's room. It was empty, the bed made.

Jane moved to the stair. She couldn't believe this pain was self-inflicted. Jane shouldn't have fixed herself that "one last drink"—ostensibly to help herself sleep—but she had been totally unnerved after seeing her double.

She started down to the first floor, checking the muddied newspaper next to the door. Sara's boots were gone. She must have gotten herself ready for school somehow. With a sigh, Jane headed for the kitchen. She found Elliot's note on the kitchen table.

You were out cold this morning. I decided to let you sleep. Don't worry about Sara, I gave her a ride to school.

Love,
Elliot

P.S. You must have really tied one on last night.

She stared at the note. "Screw you, buddy," she murmured. "I bet you ain't feelin' too whoopee yourself today."

Something nagged at her. Jane walked over to the coffeepot, wondering what it was that bothered her. "Oh Jesus, the gun." She turned swiftly to race for the door, but her head protested the rapid movement and her still-sore knee complained at the unexpected activity.

With as much composure as she could muster, Jane walked sedately to the door. The sense of urgency ebbed. If he had gotten the gun, then he had gotten the gun. There wasn't much she could do about it now.

Jane mounted the stairs, climbing with stiff-necked rigidity. She went into the bedroom, put her hand under the pillow, and pulled out the revolver. She checked the safety again, unable to believe that she had slept with it. She was damn lucky she hadn't shot herself—or the mirror—after seeing the second reflection. She shivered at the thought.

Critter stood outside the bedroom door, watching her. "Don't you have anything better to do, dog, than follow me around the house? Shoo!" He withdrew, steering clear of the cold spot next to the register.

Jane went into Nana's room. The rocker had been pulled away from its place in front of the closet, and the door was slightly cracked. Nana stared at it. Jane ignored it and walked over to the bed.

"Good morning, Mother." Nana made gurgling noises in her throat. Jane turned to look at the closet. "Come on, Mom, aren't you a little old for such foolishness? What do you expect, the boogeyman to come jumping out at you?"

Nana blinked once.

"Christ, I'm in no mood for this." Jane started to bathe her mother and strip the bed. "I don't know what it is about you and that damn closet, but it's getting ridiculous. It can stay open for all I care. I'm tired of tripping over the rocker, anyway."

She rolled Nana over on her side so that she faced the wall. "There! That better? Now you don't have to look at it." Jane bent to get the dirty linens. Her head swam. "I'll go get your breakfast."

Once back in the kitchen, Jane threw Elliot's note away, feeling somewhat ashamed that he had been unable to awaken her this morning. She boiled water for Nana's oatmeal, trying to decide what she was going to make for dinner tonight. She remembered a new recipe she had seen in *Woman's Day* the previous night. It required a lot of dicing and chopping. She looked at the food processor. She would give it its virgin run.

Jane returned to Nana's room and dug a clean robe out of the closet which seemed to have lost its chill today. She didn't notice that the rocking chair had shifted from its former position. She located the purple robe and put it on her mother. Jane got Nana up, setting her in the chair so she could brush her mother's hair.

"That's better. You look positively stunning today. Purple must be your color." The biting sarcasm in Jane's tone didn't escape unnoticed. Nana blinked two times. Jane observed neither the action nor her mother's angry glare of reproach. She fed Nana the oatmeal silently, occasionally contemplating the open closet door. Jane put on the tape, *All Creatures Great and Small,* and closed the closet door. As she stood with her hand on the knob, Jane thought she could feel the menace and hatred. It seeped into her soul. She shook her head. It didn't seem to come from within the closet, rather it came from without. She shuddered, pulled the rocker over, and wedged its back firmly under the handle.

With Nana clean and up, Jane was ready to start the day—slowly. She got the revolver from where it lay on the bed and carried it gingerly back to the kitchen. Yesterday's brashness and the nonchalance she exhibited in front of Elliot were gone. Jane no longer felt the bravado that had enabled her to stand up to her husband the night before. It had been replaced by panic.

She unlocked and opened the drawer. She gently placed the gun and bullets inside, pushing them toward the back. Jane stopped, stifling a gasp. She swore softly and bent to examine the wood. *Chisel marks.* Elliot had tried to pry it open. What else had he done in his nightly perambulations? The thought and its possible implications sickened her.

She gripped the gun, hugging it to her breast. She looked desperately around the room. It felt hard and unwieldy, providing cold comfort. Where was she going to hide the thing? If the drawer was still locked this morning, chances are that he had been unsuccessful, but that didn't guarantee that he wouldn't succeed next time. She started toward the pantry and halted. *No, that will be the first place he'll look once he knows it isn't in the drawer.*

A small, bitter smile played around her lips. She didn't need it down here, anyway. She climbed the stairs and went into Nana's room. She looked first at the bedside table and then at the bureau. Her eyes settled on the barricaded closet door.

Jane held the gun with a single index finger stuck

through the trigger guard. It swung back and forth like a pendulum. She showed it to her mother. "You don't mind if I keep this in here, do you?"

Nana blinked.

Jane turned her back on Nana and went over to the closet. Nana blinked twice, stopped, and blinked twice again, but Jane couldn't see her mother's frenzied reaction. Jane threw open the closet door. Nana began to choke. Jane quickly shoved the revolver onto the back shelf and exited, shivering. The chill was back again.

She blocked the door. Moving swiftly to Nana's side, she patted the old woman on the back. "Don't worry, Nana. It's safe in there, and I promise I won't forget about it. In a couple of days, I'll find some other place to keep it, but for now I want it well hidden. I don't want Elliot to get his hands on it, and he won't think to look in here."

Nana gasped for air and moaned. Jane turned the chair around so Nana faced her. "You're not getting a cold again, are you?"

Two blinks.

"Well, I'd better start the laundry. I'll check back with you later." Jane walked down the hall and into Sara's room. She pulled the covers back and ran her hand over the sheets. She let out an explosive sigh of relief. With her head still throbbing, she started to strip the bed.

Nana faced the closet. The tape clicked off, that side finished. In the silence that followed, Nana could have sworn she heard the rumbling laughter coming from the closet. It floated around her and echoed off the walls, profane mirth.

It was back again.

By noon, Jane felt much better. At least, she knew she was going to make it through the day. She warmed up leftover spaghetti for Sara. The front door opened and closed. "Mom, I'm home."

"I'm in the kitchen, Sara."

Sara came in to find her mother standing next to the sink. "What's to eat?"

"Oh, I just reheated last night's spaghetti."

Sara squirmed uncomfortably. "Again."

Jane chuckled. "You want some soup? I can chop up the spaghetti in the food processor and feed it to Nana. She won't complain."

Sara brightened. "You really don't mind?"

"Now why should I mind? I'll put on some soup."

"Can I watch TV?" Sara asked.

"Sure, just don't make a mess in the living room."

Sara went to turn on the television. The sound of voices drifted into the kitchen. Jane opened a can of soup. She dumped the spaghetti into the processor and dug out the instruction manual from the junk drawer. She inspected the blade and the locking mechanism. It grinned at her, the blade forming an evil half-smile like the perverted leer of a comedy-tragedy mask.

She studied the various speeds, chose one, and turned it on. It sprang to life with a vicious growl. Damn, it was noisy enough to wake the dead.

She checked the manual again. *Is it supposed to make that much noise?* Jane laughed at herself. Now where did she expect to find that little tidbit in the manual? The processor began to sputter and shake. It skipped along the countertop. The sauce spewed from the top, splattering bloodred splotches against the wall.

Sara watched "The Rifleman" in the other room, jumping slightly when the food processor started. It churned for a while, and then she heard her mother cursing loudly in the kitchen.

Jane sniffed. The smell of ozone and burning rubber was unmistakable. She grabbed the cord, screaming as molten black insulation stuck to her hand. Jane opened the spigot and put her hand under the cold water. The processor continued its skittering dance along the countertop. The soup boiled over the confines of the pan, extinguishing the flame.

When her mother screamed, Sara ran into the kitchen. Spaghetti slopped over the sides of the processor, oozing onto the floor. Jane held her hand under the faucet and shouted to her daughter. "Turn off the burner, Sara."

Sara twisted the knob on the stove and went to yank the food processor's cord from the wall. *"No!* I'll get it." Jane wrapped her good hand in a towel and managed to extract the plug from the wall plate. The room grew quiet except for the sound of running water.

"Jesus."

"What happened?"

"I don't know. The food processor broke." Jane saw the fear in her daughter's eyes and tried to make light of the situation. "You didn't put a hex on this thing last night, did you?"

Sara gave her mother a wide-eyed look and shook her head no. Her thumb went instinctively into her mouth.

Her mother glowered at Sara. "Now, stop it. I was only kidding." She wrapped a paper towel around her injured hand. "Come on, kiddo, help me clean this up. No, never mind, your soup's hot. Why don't you eat?"

With angry, saltatorial movements, Jane poured the contents into the bowl. "It's a little scorched, but it's edible." While Sara watched, Jane cleaned the counter and the wall. She got the mop from the pantry and washed the mess from the floor.

"Well, that was exciting. How'd you like that? Adventures in good eating."

Sara nodded silently as Jane dressed her burn.

"I wonder if there's enough left to feed Mother." She approached the food processor cautiously, double-checking to make sure it was unplugged. She touched it experimentally as though expecting it to spring to life again and looked inside. It grinned back at her. Jane grimaced as she dumped the spaghetti into a bowl, and it came out in a thick lump. "Well, Nana won't have any problem chewing this; that's for sure. I wonder how she'll like spaghetti slop."

She slammed the plastic container down on the counter. "So much for dinner." Sara stared at her. "Go on and finish your lunch," Jane said irritably. "I've got to feed your grandmother."

Jane sat in the recliner, staring out the window. Night came later each day as winter eased toward spring. The warm day had melted much of the snow, but nighttime's freeze coated everything with ice. Sara played upstairs, and Nana was tucked safely into bed.

Elliot's portion of dinner was cold, left unattended in the dining room. He was long overdue, and Jane was worried. He usually wasn't late unless he went out drinking after work. That plus the icy roads made a dangerous combination.

She looked at her watch. Eight o'clock. The album Jane had put on was over and the turntable shut off with a faint click. Jane got up, flipping through the albums—Grateful Dead; Crosby, Stills, Nash and Young; The Bee Gees. She couldn't make up her mind. Nothing sounded good to her. She switched the stereo to tuner and turned on the radio. Her daughter's footsteps sounded on the stairs.

"Dad home yet?"

"No, Sara, not yet."

Sara frowned. "Where do you think he could be?"

"Hard to tell. Probably out drinking with his buddies."

Sara sighed. Jane looked sadly at her daughter. She was too young to have to worry like this. "I'm sure he's all right, Sara. Go back upstairs and put on your pj's. I'll call you when he gets home."

"Okay, Mama." She went back out into the foyer, paused, and turned back to her mother. "You okay, Mom?"

"I'm just fine. Now, scoot." Jane thought about fixing herself a drink, but this morning's hangover was still fresh in her mind. Besides, she had a feeling that she was going to need to have her wits about her tonight.

She curled up in the chair, trying to concentrate on

her book. The words swam, blurring and running together. She rubbed her eyes. Finally, she gave up and stared out the window again. The crescent moon rose over the neighbor's house across the way, and the DJ cheerfully announced that today's warming trend was going to last, at least through tomorrow.

". . . looks like we'll get rid of all that nasty old snow out there, but it's icy tonight, and the roads are slick. If you have to go out tonight, you be sure and drive carefully."

Thanks, she thought. *I needed that.* The phone rang. Jane leaped up and ran into the kitchen. She skidded to a halt in front of the phone, picking it up on the third ring.

"Hello, Mrs. Graves?"

"Yes, this is Mrs. Graves."

"This is Audry."

Jane pulled the phone away from her ear and looked at the receiver, mouthing the words, "Audry who?"

"You don't know me, but I own Audry's Place, that little bar on Fourth Street."

"Yes?"

"Your husband's here, and I'm afraid he's had . . . ah . . . a few too many. I don't think he should be driving tonight. Is it possible for you to come pick him up?"

Exasperated, Jane snapped into the phone, "With what? My broomstick? I don't have a car."

"I'm sorry, Mrs. Graves. I didn't know that."

"Don't apologize. I'm the one who should apologize. I'm sorry, I shouldn't have snapped at you. I'm just a little frustrated. I do appreciate your calling me rather than turning him loose in the car. I've been worried sick about him."

"I could put him in a cab."

"No, I'll take a cab to your place. He'll need the car to get to work tomorrow. Tell him I'm on my way." She reconsidered. "No, better yet, don't tell him anything, just keep him there. Fix him another drink if you have to."

"Don't worry, I won't let him go anywhere. I don't know about another drink, though; he can hardly hold his head up as it is. I'll be expecting you. Good-bye."

"Oh, uh, Audry?"

"Yes?"

"Thanks again for calling."

"No problem. Please hurry, though, he's getting a little antsy. My license will get pulled if he causes a ruckus." Jane hung up the phone.

"Mama?" Jane turned to see Sara standing in the living room.

"Yes, honey?"

"Was that Daddy?"

"Not quite, it was a friend. Daddy needs a ride home." Jane thumbed through the phone book, looking for the number of the local taxi service. "I'm going to have to go get him. He can't drive."

"Is he sick?"

"I guess you could say that," she said absent-mindedly.

"Oh." Sara gave her mother a knowing look which was lost on her as she scanned the book searching for the phone number.

"Look, you don't mind if I leave you alone with

Nana for a bit? It shouldn't take very long. I'm going to take a taxi there and then drive myself and your daddy right back."

"I don't suppose," Sara said unenthusiastically.

Jane dialed the number. She gave the dispatcher her address and hung up. "If you want me to, I can call the Erwins. Maybe that big kid, what's his name?"

"David."

"Maybe David can come over and sit with you."

"Aw, David's nothing but a big dummy. Besides he's a scaredy-cat, even Tommy thinks so. He wouldn't come. He's afraid of this place."

Jane nodded silently. She dug through her wallet and her purse, checking her funds. She looked up. "I'm sorry, Sara, I wasn't listening. What did you say? Do you want me to call the Erwins?"

"No, Mom, I'll be okay."

"Well, Nana's bedded down for the night. She shouldn't need anything, and I won't be long." Jane went to the front closet and pulled her coat off a hook. "You need anything while I'm out?"

"Nope."

"I tell you what. You and I can have hot chocolate and cookies when I get back."

A horn sounded outside. "That must be the taxi. That was quick." She bent and kissed Sara. "Thanks, you're a doll." She walked out to the cab, telling the driver her destination as she climbed into the back seat.

Sara moved up to the front door and pressed her nose against the glass. "Bye, Momma," she whispered. She waved at the departing cab. Her mother, who was leaning over the front seat talking to the cabbie, didn't seem to notice.

Sara turned back to the foyer. "It's okay, Shelley. You can come out now. We're alone." Critter whined and stuck his head under Sara's outstretched hand. She ignored him. "Shelley?" No answer. The lights flickered and dimmed.

The branch tapped incessantly against the window. The cold sliver of a moon peeked through the gnarled tree limb. Sara lay curled into a tight little ball on the bed, thumb in her mouth. Critter had wrapped himself protectively around her.

She could hear strange noises coming from Nana's room, and she didn't like it. Something raged inside Nana's closet. *Bang, bang!* Critter raised his head at each sound, emitting a soft rumbling growl from deep within his chest.

The stairs creaked spontaneously. Sara burrowed deeper into Critter's warm brown fur. Shelley hadn't come. *It* wouldn't let her come. Something kept her away.

Sara heard a loud crash out in the hall near Nana's room, followed by another closer to her door. She knew she should check Nana, but she couldn't. Her breath caught in her throat and adrenaline surged into her bloodstream as she thought of having to go into Nana's room. Whatever it was, *it* was there, and *it* waited, ready to pounce on Sara as soon as she walked in the door.

The house seemed to wheeze around her, the room itself expanding and contracting with each harsh breath. Sara heard another thud which sounded like it came from downstairs. *It* was loose in the house, and *it* knew she was alone. *It* reveled in her solitude and isolation. She sat up. "Shelley?" she said hopefully.

The house answered back with sepulchral laughter. Sara dove back down into the bed, hugging Critter tightly, who had started to bark. Behind her the doorknob on her closet began to rattle and turn.

Oh no, it's here. It left Nana's room and it's in my room. It's coming to get me. Sara backed against the wall and started to cry.

Critter jumped up, vigilant, hackles raised and stiff-legged ready to attack. The fur on the back of his neck started to crawl. He let out a timorous yelp. Something beat against the door. Digging in, he growled. He was going to protect the Littlest One from the Thing. The knob spun crazily.

Jane pulled up in front of the darkened house. Every light was out. She checked her watch. It was too early for Sara to have gone to bed. She helped Elliot from the car. They struggled up the stairs. He cursed and took a few ill-aimed swings at her.

"Sara!" Jane, supporting her drunken husband, stood in the pitch-black foyer. "Sara? Are you all right?"

With a sob of relief, Sara ran to the door as Critter faced the thing in the closet. Sara flung the door open. The knob stilled and Critter relaxed his stance.

"Mama?"

The lights flared, flooding the house with sudden illumination. Jane almost dropped Elliot. "Christ!"

Elliot mumbled something incoherent, and Jane steered him toward the study.

"Sara, what happened to the lights?" Sara didn't answer. "Oh, never mind, let me get your father tucked in, and I'll make us some hot chocolate."

Her daughter appeared at the head of the stairs, but Jane was so busy with the staggering, stumbling Elliot, she didn't notice the terror in the little girl's eyes.

Nana started at every sound. The night's turmoil left her alert and watchful. She was fully aware of every noise and bump. She had listened to the *thing* storm and seethe in her closet. She felt a rush of relief when *it* left—followed quickly by horrified alarm as she realized that *it* was, indeed, loose in the house—its power grown.

She had heard the thudding and the crashes which had come from beyond her room. *The beast is loose in the house.* She had watched as the lights had flickered, dimmed, and then gone out—only to come to life again with her daughter's arrival home.

Then Nana had *known.* She had known what *it* wanted. No, *it* wasn't interested in a broken-down, desiccated old woman, more dead than alive. *It* desired life; *it* wanted—Sara—poor, sweet little Sara.

With that revelation, Nana also knew that Sara had not, despite appearances, come into her room during the night. It was something else—something that spoke through Sara—controlled Sara. Sara herself had no control. She was as much a captive as Nana was.

Only Nana understood. How? She didn't know. She

couldn't explain. Gertrude Goering had never claimed any special gift of sight. Perhaps as death drew nearer, Nana was allowed to see its inner workings, to know that for some, death was not repose, it was unquiet, driven with an unhallowed envy of the living. Until tonight her understanding had been partial; but now. . . .

Nana's eyes rested on the appliquéd Jill, caught in her eternal tumble. She realized whatever the threat had been before, it was now doubled. *The beast is loose in the house.* She thought and thought, trying to come up with some way to let Jane know before . . . before . . .

The closet door began to rattle and quake. Something smashed against it with a vengeance. "Jah-jah-jah." Her daughter's name caught in her throat.

Slam, slam, slam. The creature—whatever it was—threw itself at the door which separated it from her. With all the strength she had left, Nana turned to face the monster head on. *Slam!* The door shuddered under the last thrust and the chair gave a little bit, sliding across the floor.

Surely, she thought, *someone must hear.* "Jah—" *Slam!* Her daughter's name died on her lips as the door burst open. The back of the old oak rocker snapped, folding in half. Its supports cracked as though it were made of toothpicks. The starved, fiery red eyes glared incongruously from the body of a little boy. She heard Sara cry out in her sleep, and it came—slavering.

Rank, stale air surrounded Nana, and she found she couldn't breathe. Soft, slithering noises covered the quiet weeping that came from Sara's room. A child's face held a drooling mouth which hovered above her head, and *Oh, my God, the demon eyes.* Nana started to gag. She fought to remain conscious; she fought to retain control over her faculties.

She fought and lost. She felt something give inside her head and felt a sharp, stabbing pain behind her eyes. Oblivion overcame her as she faced the hounds of hell. Blackness covered her. The last thing Nana remembered was a snarling, snapping mouth with sharp yellow teeth and a fiend's burning eyes.

Sara thrashed in her bed. Shelley had come. At long last, she was here. Sara would have greeted her sister joyously, but Shelley was not alone. The *thing* came with her. As Sara watched, she saw that it was a child a little younger than herself—a little boy with haggard face and hollow eyes. She backed away from her sister, pressing her back against the headboard. Its legs were covered with open, oozing sores. A gaping hole was where its stomach should have been.

"Sara, Sara. I'm here, Sara, and I brought a friend." Shelley fastened her perpetually weeping eye on her sister. Behind Shelley, Sara saw *it. It* was slimy. *Its* skin gleamed in the pale moonlight, dripping malevolence. *Its* eyes glowed with hunger. They fixed on Sara balefully.

Sara whimpered. "It's no friend."

Shelley took a step closer to the bed, cocking a blistered, reddened head. "What do you mean, Sara? He is too my friend. Who do you think I play with when you're not around? I play with William. Who do you think called me back home to you?" She took another step and the *thing* slid noiselessly along beside her.

"No, Shelley, don't. Make it go away!"

"Uh-uh, Sara. He's hungry, sooo very hungry and he wants you. I want you."

Sara crawled to the foot of the bed, her voice choked in a puling, muted cry. In a single, swift motion, Shelley was on top of her. Clawlike hands held her fast. Shelley's touch burned. Sara twisted, trying to escape her sister's grasp. Shelley kept her pinned as the grotesque little boy slithered toward the bed.

"Shelleeey!" Sara wailed.

Her sister's laughter echoed around her. Then the *thing* wrapped itself around Shelley to merge with her. It and Shelley became one, holding Sara in an obscene embrace.

CHAPTER 15

A crackling, popping roar interrupted Marilyn McGuinness's drug-induced slumber. She clawed her way angrily from a dream where she was still young and beautiful. The one-time Marilyn had loved and been loved. This woman, then known by the name of Simmons, had just received her teacher's certificate and enjoyed the pupils she taught. She was buxom, even-tempered, and kind.

The current Marilyn McGuinness—changed by bitterness and age—fought the fogged, drugged sleep into a waking nightmare of orange-red light. Dazed, she sought to throw off the covers, shielding her eyes from the glare. The brackish, burning fumes set her coughing. Flames flickered and crept up the curtains, devouring wall and wallpaper as it continued its pitiless progress. The federal blue pattern turned red, purple, and brown. The small plastic clock grew limp, melting like a cheap imitation of a Dalí painting. It was only then that she noticed the time, three o'clock. Pictures fell shattering to the floor as the heat dissolved the metal hooks that held them in place. Her frowning father scowled at her from cracked glass and warped frame. Then in a flash, he and his photo were gone.

The roof above her head exploded in a demonic frenzy. Sparks showered down upon her head, and the bedspread caught. Her hair sizzled, curling with a snakelike motion. Frantic, Marilyn beat at her own head. She turned, only to find herself tied into her bed by the sheets. *That child,* she thought, and she could almost hear the high-pitched peal of laughter.

Suddenly, she was free, freed by the fire that turned the confining bedclothes to ash. The tattered flannel gown flared, and its synthetic threads melded with a hiss, adhering to the flesh on her legs. McGuinness screamed. The fire formed walls all around her. She spun, arms beating helplessly in an attempt to smother the flames, but the action served only to fan them. They danced giddily up her torso, stroking her breasts in a fiery caress. Another spark caught and her blue-gray hair turned crimson as she ran shrieking from the room into the roaring inferno beyond.

Jane stood on the porch and watched Sara walk up the street to school. The radio announcer had promised an unseasonably warm day, and it would appear that he was right. Sara unzipped her bright yellow jacket. Her red mittens dangled from the clips which held them to the jacket sleeves. Jane waved as Sara turned around to look at her. Sara waved back.

She looked so small and vulnerable. Jane felt the cold finger of fear trace its way down her back. She shuddered involuntarily. She wondered what would greet her daughter today at school since she hadn't bothered with the formality of makeup this morning. It seemed pointless since Elliot had sent her to school yesterday—black eye and all. She had examined the bruise and was pleased to note that it was fading nicely.

Up the street, Mrs. Erwin held the car door open for Sara who climbed in without a backward glance. Jane walked over to the thermostat—nearly forty degrees—and it was still early yet. She went back into the house. It looked drab and dreary after the sun's brilliant radiance.

Once Mrs. Erwin's station wagon had disappeared up the street, Jane let Critter out. He capered and frolicked around the front yard, chasing birds away from his turf with self-important ferocity. Jane smiled at him, then turned looking up the stairs. She had to get Nana up, but wasn't ready to face that chore yet. She got a sweater from the hall closet and went to refill her coffee. She'd have just one more cup before she got to Nana.

Jane took the mug and last night's forgotten book to the front porch. She brushed the step, checking for residual water. It was dry. Critter ran up the stairs, tail wagging in large, sweeping circles. He gave Jane a wet, sloppy kiss. She wiped her face.

"Go away, dog, you bother me." He didn't seem to

care; he was off again, nosing around some shrubbery which apparently offered a particularly fascinating scent. Jane opened the book, but she couldn't seem to concentrate. *Yes, it's going to be a beautiful day. Too bad Elliot can't enjoy it.* She snickered vindictively.

But she doubted he could enjoy anything today. He had looked decidedly ill when she got him up this morning. She felt a stab of pity when she looked into his bloodshot eyes. Her eyes had probably looked like that the day before. He moaned and the sympathy flew to the wind to be replaced by glee. Served him right for making her leave Sara and Nana alone.

Critter had wandered across the cul-de-sac and was contentedly taking a dump on the neighbor's lawn. She shielded her eyes against the sun. "Critter!"

He looked up at her unconcerned and finished his business. With a certain canine dignity, he dug around a few times and came back to the front porch to sit next to Jane, his tongue lolling inelegantly.

"Jeez, mutt, can't you do that in the vacant lot? We've got one on either side of the house. Now I'm going to have to clean it up before the neighbors get home." She peered around the side of the house to make sure the driveway was empty. "To quote Sara, you're gross."

She picked up the coffee and took a tentative sip. It was cool enough to drink. Critter stuck his nose against the rim of the mug and sniffed. Deciding it was nothing for him, he padded down the stairs to the front yard again. Jane continued to sip the coffee. It was so peaceful, she wished the morning would never end. She returned to her book.

A horn sent her sprawling; her coffee spilled, and

she dropped the book which bumped down the stairs into a puddle. Jane looked up. It was Sally Erwin. Controlling her temper, Jane bit back a sharp comment and waved. "Beautiful day, isn't it?"

Sally overlooked Jane's comment. She was brimming with news. "Have you heard?" Jane regarded her curiously.

"Oh, of course, you couldn't have. You haven't left the house."

Jane waited.

"A teacher's house burned down last night."

Jane felt her heart sink. "Which one?"

"I'm not sure. Everything was in total chaos when I got there to drop Tommy and Sara off. Isn't that awful?"

"Yes." That cold finger of fear found its mark. The icy hand closed around Jane's heart. *Could it be . . .* She shook her head as doubt mixed with relief. *No, of course not, Sara was home last night.*

Sally didn't notice the tremor in Jane's voice. She plunged on. "Probably was smoking in bed. People are so careless nowadays." She rubbed a beefy hand across her brow. "Whew, it's too hot to be wearing this winter coat. I bet it's warm enough today that I can work in my ceramics workshop. I'm going to do some firing. Want to come over and see how it's done?"

Jane grimaced. The idea of listening to Sally's chatter didn't appeal to her. "I don't know. I really can't leave Nana for very long."

"Well, how about a cup of coffee?" Sally eyed the tipped mug on the edge of the porch.

"Not now." Jane looked at her watch. "I'm running

a little late this morning. I haven't even gotten my mother up yet. I usually have her dressed by now."

"Oh, well, maybe later. By the way, I hope you didn't mind my giving Sara a ride today."

"No, not at all. I'm sure she appreciated it."

"Oh, yes, and she said thank you, too. I wish my boys were that polite. Will never happen, though. Tommy was acting a little strangely today. Did Sara say anything to you about their having a fight?"

"No, not at all."

"Oh, well, it's probably nothing. I gotta run. Stop by later if you have a chance. Tootles." She honked again as a form of final farewell.

She watched Mrs. Erwin drive the tan Plymouth wagon slowly up the street. *Tootles?* Jane went to collect the mug and the soaked book. "Crap."

Elliot was right. Sally didn't seem to be playing with a full deck. *Tootles, for God's sake. The pot's cracked.* She giggled at the unintended pun. Jane spread the book out on the porch rail, exposing it to the full sun where she hoped it could dry.

"Critter, time to go in." He gave the soaked earth in the front yard two sharp sweeps with his hind legs as if in defiant comment and pranced up the stairs, snoot up in the air.

"Well, the same to you, fella." She opened the front door to let him in and checked the thermostat again. Forty-two degrees. It had gone up two degrees in the short time she had been out. Promising herself that she would sit outside later, Jane went back into the house. She had chores to do. She took her cup into the kitchen and returned to the living room.

She looked at the stairs, thinking about Nana, but

was for some reason reluctant to face her mother. Instead, she walked through the kitchen and down the basement stairs. She flicked on the light. The bare, cobweb-covered bulb fought weakly against the enveloping gloom. It bathed everything in a sickly yellow cast.

Jane rolled up her sleeves. It would take no time at all to pick up the junk from here and haul it down to the street. She started gathering the dilapidated chair and lamp with the frayed cord. She took load after load to the curb. Soon she found it was necessary to shed her sweater. It seemed the more garbage Jane disposed of, the more she discovered. The larger pieces hid old newspapers and torn clothes. She looked at her watch. This was going to take longer than she had expected, and she couldn't put off taking care of Nana any longer. The cleaning would have to wait. She could finish it this afternoon.

Jane trudged up the stairs toward the kitchen. As she got to the landing, she heard the sound of movement coming from the basement below. She swung around. "Critter?" He padded out from the kitchen. Jane stood for a moment listening, no sounds came to her. *It must have been my imagination.*

She shrugged and went on to Nana's room. She hadn't noticed earlier that morning the door was closed. She wondered who had closed it. Generally, Jane left it partially cracked so she could look in periodically. She turned the knob and pushed against the door. It immediately banged into something on the other side. Jane pushed harder. Whatever blocked the door resisted her gently exerted pressure.

"Nana?"

Something gave and the door creaked open. Jane walked into the room. The rocker, its back broken, folded at the joint, stood in the middle of the floor. The supports were shattered, and jagged pieces of wood pointed toward the ceiling. Splintered wood was scattered across the floor in a trail that led to Nana's bed.

The closet door was wide open. Nana lay flat on her back. Jane hurried over to the bed. That was definitely *not* the position Jane had left her mother in the night before. She looked down at her mother who returned her look with a glassy-eyed stare.

"Oh my God." Jane waved her hand before her mother's eyes. She didn't blink. Jane gasped. Bending closer, she looked down at her mother's abdomen, searching for the telltale rise and fall of her chest. She saw nothing, no movement at all.

"Oh God, oh God," Jane moaned as she stumbled from the room, weeping. She ran for the phone in the master bedroom and dialed the number which she had memorized long ago.

"Hello. Doctor's office," a nasal voice informed her.

"Hello, is Dr. Gunthar there? This is Jane Graves. I've got to talk to him. It's an emergency."

"Just a minute, I'll check."

Jane wanted to scream, *You dumb, fucking bitch, don't you know if your boss is in the office?* She waited impatiently, drumming her fingers against the hard surface of the bedside table.

"Hello, Mrs. Graves? This is Dr. Gunthar."

"Oh, doctor, it's Mother." Jane started to sob.

Taken aback by her hysteria, the doctor paused slightly, waiting before he spoke. "Now, calm down, Jane. Start at the beginning. Just remember, there's nothing so wrong that we can't handle it. Should I send an ambulance over?"

"I don't think so. I think it's too late for that. Oh God," she stopped, trying to catch her breath. "Dr. Gunthar, I think she's dead."

"Did you check for a pulse?"

"No, I didn't do that, but she's not breathing. I'm sure of that."

"Her breathing may be so shallow that you can't see it, and if she's not breathing—well—these things happen, Jane, you've got to know that. Your mother was old and not well. We both know she couldn't last forever."

"Oh, but doctor." Jane dissolved into tears.

"Look, Jane, get ahold of yourself. There are things I need you to do. First, calm down; don't panic. Getting yourself all upset isn't going to do anybody any good. Go downstairs; pour yourself a cup of coffee, whatever you have to do. Then, when you think you can face it, get a hand mirror. You've got one of those, don't you?" He didn't wait for a reply. "If you don't, use a compact. Any portable mirror will do. Place it under her nose and mouth. If she's breathing, it'll show. The mirror will steam up.

"If she is, check her pulse. Check her wrists and if you can't feel a pulse there, check under her jaw near her ear. If you still can't find it, try her heart. Even if you find it the first time, check all three places. We need to know how good her circulation is, so don't skip any one of them. Once you've found it, count it a full minute. Notice if there are any irregularities. Remember, the wrist, the jaw, and her heart for a full minute. Got that? I'll want a full report when I get there."

"And if she's not?" Her voice sounded small.

"If she's not, do whatever you feel most comfortable with. Sit with her if you want to, or get the hell out of there; but don't call the funeral home yet. I might remind you that only a doctor can pronounce someone dead. I'll be over as soon as I can." He hung up.

Jane stared at the phone a few minutes, forcing herself to be calm. She pulled a compact from her purse and went back to Nana's room. She placed the mirror under Nana's nose; a small semicircle of mist appeared at its rim.

"Oh, thank God." Feeling steadier, Jane felt Nana's wrist for a pulse. It was weak and thready, but present. She counted, her eyes on her watch. *Ninety-eight beats.* Then she searched near the jawline, and finally found the spot. The beat was stronger there. Again she counted. Next the heart. The pulse varied. Jane counted a full hundred and six beats at the heart, slightly less at the jaw. It seemed to skip every four to six beats. She wrote the information down.

Jane blanched, shrinking from Nana's fixed stare. "Mama, you gave me quite a start." She began to straighten the sheet and then stopped, confused. Perhaps she should just leave her alone. She knew in certain instances you shouldn't move "the patient." She searched her memory, trying to remember when. Broken backs? Were there other times? She couldn't remember, so Jane left Nana tangled in the sheets, deciding that it was better to be safe than sorry.

She leaned against the bedside table, looking down at her mother and pondered her horrified stare. She noted the dilated pupils. Tears rose to her eyes and she willed them away. "Poor Mama, life hasn't given you a very fair shake, has it?"

The emaciated figure who lay in the bed before Jane was far removed from the hardy, bustling, strong woman that had managed to run a farm and raise four children alone. Often in the past, Jane marveled: *Is this really the same woman?* But she knew that it was—her mother who had been crippled and broken upon the unrelenting wheel of fate.

Jane patted Nana's limp hand and stroked her hair. She turned her head, brushing away the teardrops which refused to be suppressed. But a single, stray tear fell on the pillow, and Jane found herself looking again into the empty eyes.

She sighed. To take her mind off cruel fortune and the irony and frailty of life, she turned to survey the room—the open closet and the chair's shattered back. *What the hell had happened to the rocker?* She abruptly remembered the gun and ran into the closet. It was there. She looked around her. Heavy footsteps sounded on the stair. Jane started. She waited, wondering who—or what—visited her now. She heard Dr. Gunthar call her name.

"I'm up here, in Nana's room, toward the back of the house." She walked out of the closet as Dr. Gunthar came in the door.

"Well, how's our patient?"

"She's alive."

"See, I told you so. You were worrying needlessly."

"Hardly needlessly, doctor. Take a look at her."

The doctor moved over to the bed. "Hmmm . . ."

"What?"

"Scat, woman, you're making me nervous. You know, I don't normally make house calls; your husband's really going to squawk when he gets the bill." Jane followed him, making no comment.

"Lost your sense of humor, I see."

"That's my mother there." Jane began to cry again.

Dr. Gunthar patted her shoulder awkwardly. "There, there. Do you have any coffee?" Jane nodded yes. "Then go pour yourself a cup."

"I don't want any."

"Then pour me a cup. Anything to get you out from underfoot."

"Yes, sir," she replied meekly and left the room.

Dr. Gunthar shook his head and turned to the wreck of human life upon the bed. "Doesn't that little girl know when you get to be our age, death can be a comfort?" Nana just stared at the ceiling. He took a light from his bag and checked her eyes—first one and then the other. He poked and prodded, testing her reflexes.

Jane returned with two steaming cups. "I made some fresh."

"You've collected yourself, I see." He straightened, pocketing the stethoscope. "I believe she's had another stroke."

"Does she need to go into the hospital?"

"No, you can probably take care of her here as well as they can, and save yourself some money, too."

"The money doesn't matter."

"I know, Jane, but they really can't do anything for her in a hospital that you can't do for her right here in your own home, and I think once she comes out of it—and I believe she will come out of it, at least partially—she'll be comforted to know she's with the people she loves."

Jane moved over and stood next to the bed. She looked at her mother's unblinking gaze and shuddered. "It's too bad. I was getting her up every day, and it seemed to be working. She was getting better all the time. She was doing well until this."

"Mom, I'm home." Sara's piping voice penetrated from downstairs.

Jane turned to the doctor. "Is it that late already?"

The doctor paused from putting the medical paraphernalia in the bag. "Time flies."

"I'm up here, Sara."

Sara walked up the stairs. She stopped when she saw the doctor and his bag. "Is Nana sick?"

"Yes, baby. Nana's sick."

Sara walked over to the bed and peered down at Nana. "Is she going away?"

Dr. Gunthar turned to face the child. "No, Sara, we're not going to take your grandmother away." He knelt by her side. "Look up at your mother, Sara."

Obediently, Sara looked at her mother. "It looks like you had a pretty nasty bruise there. How'd you get it?" An expression of fear flitted across the little girl's face. "Sara, where'd you get it?"

"I fell down the stairs."

"And landed on your eye?" Sara squirmed. "You

wouldn't tell old Dr. Gunthar a fib, would you?" Sara looked cautiously up at Jane. "Or is that what your mother told you to say?"

Sara squared her shoulders. "My mother didn't tell me to say nothing."

"Anything." Her mother corrected her automatically.

"Anything—and that's the truth."

"Okay, Sara, you go downstairs now. I want to talk to your mother alone."

Jane fluttered nervously around the room, picking up the larger splintered woodchips from the floor and compulsively straightening the covers on the bed.

Dr. Gunthar noted this and raised a brow of inquiry. "Jane, what happened?"

She looked down at her mother and put her hand over her mother's eyes. Nana's blank stare totally unnerved her. "I don't know what you mean."

"Jane, let's not be coy."

She turned to face the doctor. "She fell, that's all."

"And you fell, too, I suppose." He pointed to the cut under her eye.

"Let's just say that we're a little bit accident-prone."

"Let's not." He indicated the chair. "Is this an accident, too?"

"I don't know what happened there."

"What's going on, Jane? I've been treating your family for years. Don't lie to me."

Jane gave in. "It's nothing. Well, it's just that with Shelley, Nana, and everything, it's been kind of hard on Elliot—on all of us. He tries to provide for us, but he's under a lot of pressure. I mean, with Sara's not adjusting well to her sister's death."

"Does she still refuse to acknowledge it?" Jane shook her head in assent. "That's not uncommon. Children cope differently than we do."

"She's been . . . well, rebellious, and Elliot, he just gets a little carried away."

"It looks like he got more than just carried away, Jane. I should report this, you know."

"Oh, doctor, please don't. I mean, what good would it do? As I said, this has been a difficult time. Don't make it any worse than it already is."

Dr. Gunthar relented. "All right, I won't report it this time. I may regret it, but I'll look the other way. If I ever see another bruise like that on Sara, though, I will report it. Do you understand?"

"Yes, doctor."

"Look, I've got to run. I've got a waiting room full of old ladies with bowel problems. It seems that the regularity of this entire community rests on my shoulders. Promise me, Jane, if anything like this"—he motioned from the chair to the cut under her eye—"ever happens again, you'll call me. You don't have to put up with abuse."

She nodded silently, unsure—if given the chance—whether or not she could.

The doctor walked out of the room and down the stairs. Jane trailed behind him. Sara watched them. Dr. Gunthar stooped over her and chucked her under the chin. "You take good care of your mama and Nana, won't you, Sara?"

Sara looked at him, noticing the obvious omission

of her father's name. "Yes, sir, I will." She shook her head solemnly.

"I'm sure you will."

"I'll be off. Remember, Jane, call me if you need me." He left.

Sara took her mother's hand and they watched him get into his car. "Are we in trouble, Mama?"

Jane looked down at her daughter, startled. Sara had an uncanny way of picking up things. "Were you listening at the door?"

"No, ma'am. Are we?"

"In trouble? I think so, honey. I think we are." Sara wrapped her arms around her mother's waist and hugged her. Jane wept quietly as the doctor drove away.

CHAPTER 16

When Jane returned to the basement the following day, she felt none of yesterday's curiosity—only dread. The previous day she had felt that the cellar was a story to be told, a mystery to be unraveled. She had wondered how many families had lived in this house in the years since Emma Van Clausen's demise. How many people had left shoes without mates, noshed-on teething rings, battered pans, and chipped cups? Where had they gone? How long had they stayed and what had driven them away? It seemed that generations had come and gone, yet Jane knew that less than a generation's time had passed. The mystery, she thought then, would have to wait until she changed and cleaned her mother. It was postponed longer than she had expected in the intervening crisis.

Critter came down the stairs with her. He, it appeared, was even less anxious for her to continue the task than she was. He whimpered and worried at the cuffs of her trousers. Skittish, Critter repeatedly tugged at her sleeve until she pushed him away in anger. "Skat!" Rebuffed, he padded up the stairs. He flopped down on the landing with an exaggerated sigh, resting his head on his paws. Soulful brown eyes followed her every movement.

Jane peered into the murky recesses, pondering what other forlorn and forgotten items she might find there. She had already discovered dated newspapers which she had meant to read, but had thrown away instead. In a surge of rebellion and procrastination, Jane decided to go upstairs and dig them out of the garbage—to find out what had happened X number of years ago on some miscellaneous date—but conscience and self-discipline got the better of her. That plus the innate knowledge that this morning's coffee grounds had probably been dumped on top of them.

She pushed up her sleeves and made her way around the octopod furnace vents which stretched across the basement. Something moved behind her. She looked to the top of the stairs. Critter lay quietly on the landing. He stared back at her with a perplexed expression. Jane snorted and walked on. She glanced apprehensively over her shoulder, each step taking her farther from the light.

Her foot struck something hard and small. It slid across the floor, catching the insipid jaundiced illumination and reflecting it back at her. It cast the light in a myriad of rainbow colors. She followed it to its new position, squatting down to pick it up. A hand mirror with a large crack down its center revealed two identical Janes. Repelled, she stared at the twin images of the gaunt, hollow-cheeked woman. Her skin looked gray, her eyes cloudy and bloodshot. She shivered.

She fingered the crack and then dumped the small looking glass in the large plastic garbage sack she had brought down with her. Scraps of cloth and paper littered the floor. In turn, she bent and picked up each item. Jane started in one corner—the brighter one, not completely overshadowed by the gargantuan draft furnace—and duck-walked toward its opposite. *Bam!* The sound came from the far side of the basement.

"Critter?" Jane said. Her voice quivered.

A growl came back to her from beyond the heater's bulk and opposite the original thud. She heard Critter's nails clicking against the wooden stair. She turned first toward Critter and then toward the source of the sound. She blinked. Jane could have sworn she saw two small, glowing eyes, staring back at her. Rats? Jane would have to set traps. She continued her squatting walk.

Critter came up behind her, his cold nose touching the back of her neck. She jumped. "Jesus Christ, Critter, you scared the hell out of me." Critter whined. Another movement and Jane spun around in time to see a small child's toy fly across the basement, landing not inches away from her.

She shook her head. Something else whizzed past her ear, and she dove for the corner as an old windup alarm clock hit the wall behind her and shattered. Critter, barking wildly, whirled swiftly back and forth —first in the direction from which the items came, then to where they landed. A cracked plate smacked him sharply in the nose, and he yelped. Tucking his tail between his legs, Critter ran for the stairs.

Jane—reflexes dulled by the unreality of what she saw, or worse, didn't see—again attempted to pierce the darkness, looking for some sort of logical explanation. She searched the inky recesses . . . for what? A gremlin or a goblin. Something struck her arm. The pain riveted her in place. She was hit again, and then she followed Critter to the kitchen. Jane slammed the basement door shut behind her and locked it. Critter snuffed around the door and growled.

Jane poured herself a drink, moved to put the vodka away, and put it on the table instead. She stood at the sink and gulped down the first drink, trembling. Feeling a little better, she sat at the kitchen table. Jane rolled the empty glass between her hands and tried to piece what had happened together. It was like a large jigsaw puzzle from which a portion was missing. What was missing? *Sanity, of course.*

Who would believe it? She could see herself stirring the mashed potatoes tonight. Elliot would ask her about her day and she'd just casually mention: "Nothing unusual. Things just started flying around the house by themselves, that's all." And he'd say: "That's nice, dear." She laughed weakly. Picking up the vodka, Jane poured herself two fingers, then added a third.

She called softly to Critter. "Did we really see what I think we saw?" He yawned. "Sure, easy for you to say." Jane added the Bloody Mary mix to her generous allotment of vodka. After a couple of healthy swigs, she held out her hand; it fluttered like a bird in a cage. *That's me, steady as the Rock of Gibraltar. No sweat.* She snapped her fingers in the air. *Things flying around—it happens all the time.*

Maybe after another drink or two she'd be ready to check on Nana, but for the time being she wanted to stay in the kitchen with its bright Formica table, digital clock, and everything firmly planted in present-day reality. Jane thought of the self-destructing food processor and the coffee maker. Then she remembered the cockroaches and decided to check Nana now.

She moved quietly through the house. Even the day's brilliant sunshine couldn't chase away the house's dismal gloom. Jane knocked gently against Nana's cracked door. "Mama? You all right?"

She opened the door. Elliot had put two clamps on the rocker to hold its back in place while the glue dried. Jane tested its strength. It shifted slightly under her weight. *A handyman, Elliot is not.*

Jane walked across the floor to Nana's bedside, sticking a hand under the covers to see if the sheets were dry. By some lucky fluke, they were. She breathed a sigh of relief. Laundry or no, nothing would coerce her to go back into that basement until she was three sheets to the wind. Jane chuckled at the thought.

Nana, however, didn't look amused. She didn't look anything. Her eyes exhibited none of the furtive, continuous movement Jane had seen before. It was as if her brain had died, and Jane supposed that it had. *Isn't that what made a stroke, a stroke?*

She wondered what kept her mother alive. Jane stooped low over the bed, searching for some sign of life besides the shallow, stertorous breathing. Nothing, just that same blank stare. She rubbed the top of her mother's head in an unconscious display of affection. "I'll be back in a little bit, Mom, with something to eat." Jane went back the way she came, pausing to examine the shiny new doorknob and lock on the closet door.

She opened it and felt none of the chill she had noticed in previous visits. The back shelf was empty, the gun having been replaced in the locked drawer downstairs. For some reason with everything else that had happened recently, it seemed a moot point. A quick death at gunpoint seemed preferable to this dizzying, spinning descent into madness.

Jane headed down the stairs, the list of chores diminishing with each downward step. As she came closer to the first floor, cleaning the basement, doing the laundry and the dishes lost its urgency. Maybe she should get falling-down drunk by the time Sara got home for lunch.

With that in mind, Jane went into the kitchen and made two peanut butter and jelly sandwiches. She placed one on a plate with cookies and chips which she covered with cellophane and left out for Sara. The other, once wrapped, she put in the refrigerator for Nana. Clutching the vodka and the mix, Jane switched to the living room couch so that she would be better able to put what seemed like a dandy master plan into effect.

Sara arrived home at lunchtime to find her mother out cold on the sofa. While not a common phenomenon, it was not altogether unprecedented. In times past after a particularly brutal battle, the two girls would return from school only to find their mother sleeping it off in the living room.

Sara sighed and went into the kitchen to get the lunch she knew she would find there. She shredded the sandwich and fed the pieces to Critter, grumbling, "She doesn't care. She doesn't care at all." Sara extracted the cookies from the rest of her lunch and pulled the Oreo box from the cupboard. *Cookies for lunch.* She hummed tunelessly as she nibbled at the white filling.

Her eyes turned to the plate, and Sara glared at the chips. *I could starve for all she cared.* She brought a tiny clenched fist down on the plate of chips, smashing them. The crumbs scattered across the table and onto the kitchen floor. Her mother snoozed on in the living room. Critter lapped happily at the debris. Once he had finished cleaning the floor, he stood up on his hind legs and licked the table clean. Only a few crumbs remained on the plate. These Sara put in Critter's bowl.

Two hours later, Jane woke up to the intense sound of buzzing. Her tongue felt furry and thick. Critter scratched frantically at the door. "I'm comin', I'm comin'. Hol' you horshes, dawg," Jane slurred. She lurched unsteadily to her feet. Jane wobbled in front of the couch, temporarily disoriented by the unexpected noise, and blinked at the brilliant sunlight which filtered inside from outdoors. The steady, monotonous thrum grew louder, and the world reeled crazily about her. Stupefied, Jane let the incessant drone lull her. She started toward the foyer where Critter continued his agitated yapping. "Comin'." She found herself moving through a thick black humming cloud.

She felt a sharp sting on the side of her face, followed quickly by another and another. She slapped herself. "Ouch!" Her hand came away from her cheek, covered with several small black splotches. She stared in shocked disbelief at the smashed remains of the black-and-yellow insects on her palm.

Fucking bees! Jane looked around the room. A few bees buzzed lazily in the sun which came in through the window. The soft, somnambulant sound brought to mind a slow, sultry summer afternoon. *But it's February.* Baffled, her eyes made a wide sweep of the living room, stopping at the fireplace. The ebony swarm flew from its confines.

But the chimney's not even hooked up, she thought wildly. The bees zeroed in on her and zoomed in for the kill. Jane flailed helplessly. Her arms windmilled ineffectively against their growing numbers, and she flung herself at the door to the foyer. The bees trailed behind her, swarming angrily.

Critter yelped, howled, and began to dig at the front door again. She yanked it open. It banged against the wall. She and Critter made a clumsy exit from the house. The bees followed. Jane flattened herself against the porch wall, holding the screen door like a shield between herself and the bees. Even in her hung-over state, she had the presence of mind to check the thermostat. *Fifty-five degrees.*

Critter groveled at her feet. "Bees in February? I don't believe it." The frightened dog didn't seem to care about the situation's lack of credibility, the statistical probabilities, or the season. He only pressed himself against her legs and whimpered.

"Oh my God, Nana!" Jane forgot her swelling stings and her rising terror. She thrust the cowering dog out of her way and raced back into the house. Jane took the stairs two at a time. She burst into Nana's room and set the chair to rocking furiously. *Nothing, not so much as a buzz.*

With more caution, Jane made her way to her bedroom, grabbed her floppy strawhat and a scarf. She draped the scarf over her head and put on the hat. She returned to the hall, pulling the broom from the upstairs hall closet. She went down the stairs a step at a time, pausing briefly to look around. *Step, stop. Step, stop.* The scarf flapped around her face. *Step, stop.* She lifted the gauzy cloth like a veil in order to take another cautious peek. That and her strange gait reminded her of a bizarre burlesque of the wedding march. She collapsed in hysterical laughter on the landing. "With this broom, I thee wed."

She guffawed. She heard a single thump. Critter watched her, puzzled. "Here comes the bride, Critter."

Critter, still skeptical, stood at the front door, cocked his head, and twitched his tail slightly. Jane took another look at him and whooped. He panted. Her shoulders shook, and she gulped for air. She laughed until the tears rolled down her cheeks.

"Big" . . . *gasp* . . . "brave" . . . *gasp* . . . "watchdog," she wheezed. Critter trotted up the stairs to where she sat on the landing and stuck his snout under the scarf which only made her laugh harder. Unable to understand the joke, he just chewed on the flimsy scarf. "Go away," she twittered and shooed him off.

Once she had gotten herself under control, Jane went to the kitchen to get the bug spray. Shielded with the hat and scarf and armed with the broom and insecticide, she made a circuit of the entire first floor—no longer caring how ridiculous she must have looked. *No bees.* To be on the safe side, Jane locked Critter out of the living room. Holding the scarf over her mouth and nose, she sprayed the insecticide up what was left of the chimney and in the fireplace. Its fumes made her cough and sputter.

Jane had gotten her hangover to manageable levels by the time Sara arrived from school. She eyed her mother and the glass on the coffee table suspiciously as she walked in the door. "Anything happen today?"

"Nothing out of the ordinary, right, Critter?" her mother said. She stroked his scraggly head and giggled.

Sara wrinkled her nose. *Still drunk.*

Jane patted her daughter a little shakily. "It's so nice out; why don't you go outside and play?"

"Sure." Sara went back to the front porch. Critter followed, and Sara took a good swift kick at him. He scooted away. "Damn!" She looked over her shoulder at her mother who peered owlishly at a book, pretending to read.

Sara jumped stiff-legged down the stairs, step by step. She shed her jacket and left it on the front sidewalk. The sun beat down. Up the street, she could see Tommy and David go into their house. Tommy waved. Sara looked sullenly down at her feet. She didn't want Tommy coming over now. Her shadow stretched before her, yawning and long.

She jumped, trying to catch it. It evaded her, moving as she moved. She jumped again. She became totally absorbed in this new game of capture the shadow, following her shadow down the sidewalk and onto the driveway, forgetting about her mother and Tommy.

Jane watched her daughter from her living room. *Hop. Hop. Hop.* Sara had bounced all the way down to the street, turned and headed for the driveway. Jane didn't understand it, but there did seem to be some kind of reason behind this random skipping cavort. Curious, she went to the porch.

Sara continued to jump around. *Pounce. Pounce.* Jane joined her daughter on the driveway.

"Sara, what in heaven's name are you doing?"

"Playing capture the shadow."

"You look ridiculous, like Critter when he's trying to catch his own tail."

Sara stopped—feeling confused, hurt, and mad all at the same time. What did it matter to her mother what she was doing or how she looked? Mom was drunk, anyway. A sly expression crossed her face, and she gave her mother a sidelong glance.

"Maybe I can't catch my own shadow, but I can capture yours." Sara leapt directly on the portion of her mother's shadow that was Jane's head and she trampled it ferociously. She stamped and kicked at the phantom skull.

Disturbed, Jane backed away. "I'm sorry I bothered you. Go ahead with what you were doing." She withdrew to the safe haven of the front porch and contemplated her daughter.

Sara stuffed her hands in her pockets and peered up and down the street. She ambled up the walk, losing interest in her game. It wasn't fun anymore.

Jane went inside to cook dinner and decided on Hamburger Helper. She examined her reflection in a small mirror she had tacked to the kitchen wall. The stings were nothing more than small red bumps—no longer painful—but that didn't matter. Jane decided she had been through enough for today. Hamburger Helper was about as fancy as she would get.

Elliot arrived just as Sara returned from washing her hands for supper. He kissed Sara's cheek and playfully patted Jane's rump. Jane moved away. He didn't notice. "So how was your day today, Jane?"

"Okay."

"Anything exciting happen?"

Jane looked from Sara to the dog. "No." *Elliot wouldn't believe me, anyway.*

"How was your day?"

"Same old thing. Mentally abused a few students with excerpts of Berlioz's *Symphonie Fantastique.* Put them right to sleep."

"Hmm."

"Anything wrong? You seem kind of preoccupied." He poured two drinks and took one over to her.

Jane shook her head no, and turned to look at her daughter. "Nothing's wrong. Nothing at all."

CHAPTER 17

The warm spell continued, and Saturday was another beautiful day. Most of the snow had melted, exposing drab brown winter grass. Once mountainous snowbanks were now gray and dirtied molehills, and a reminder that winter was only held at bay—not gone. The field behind the house had become a sea of thick black sludge. The children hit the streets. Released from school's prison, they celebrated the third consecutive day of sunshine. Jane, like the children, felt no ambition to work and no desire to stay in the house. The place oppressed her. She collected Critter and went for a walk, leaving Elliot and Sara to their own devices.

Jane followed Critter's erratic path as he marked his territory—first to the mailbox, then to the dying oak, and lastly on an aimless meander through the vacant lots. She grabbed him as he was about to traipse into the neighbor's yard, pulled him back into the cul-de-sac and steered him up Elm. He moved in a slow, easy trot. Jane brought up the rear. Critter stopped occasionally, giving a tree or a shrub a disinterested sniff.

She too paused and turned to look back at 413 Elm's grotesque exterior. The shades were pulled down against the morning sun. The twin windows stood equidistant to the front door, like lifeless, lidded eyes around a nose. The gingerbread trim appeared to be hair—bangs over a square forehead. The slightly bowed and warped porch completed the effect. The house looked like a face which was twisted into a perpetual sneer. It frowned—dark and disapproving—down upon its neighbors.

The gabled roof towered above the cheery, more modern tract homes around it, completely overshadowing them. Next to the house, the skeletal, gnarled tree stood—a dying testament to its poisonous influence. Jane thought she saw the curtains in Nana's room move and dismissed the notion before it completely surfaced. Sara was watching Saturday-morning cartoons, and Elliot had holed up in the study.

She wondered again if she should tell Elliot about yesterday's strange events, but what good would it do? Even if he did believe her, what could he do? Nail garlic over the windows, or get a priest to bless the place. *Ha! What priest would bless that house? Holy water would probably curdle in that peculiar domicile.*

She mused. Things moving about on their own and bees swarming in February, what sane person would believe that? Jane wasn't sure she believed it herself, despite the fact that she had seen it. Critter loped on, unconcerned. Every once and a while, she would call him to task when he chased exuberantly after a cat or one of the neighborhood children.

Tommy waved at her from across the street. He separated from a group of excited children and ran up to her, breathless. "Can Sara come out and play?"

Jane smiled at him. "I don't see why not. I'm glad to see you two are on speaking terms. Why don't you go to the house and ask her yourself?"

He peered suspiciously at the house, his look mirroring her thoughts. "Go ahead, Tommy. I think the ghost is gone on vacation for the day."

Surprised, Tommy stared up at her. "You mean there is one?"

Absorbed as she was with watching the other children, she didn't notice the tremor in his voice. "Mmm, don't we all have some skeletons in our closet?"

"Huh?"

"Forgive me, Tommy, I wasn't paying attention. What are the children so interested in over there?"

"Amy Wilfred's cat had kittens, and she's giving them away."

"Ah." She moved across the street, leaving Tommy to make his own decision. Jane bent over the box, holding onto Critter's collar.

"Hey, lady," a zealous pigtailed saleslady hailed her. "You want a kitten?"

"No, I'm afraid not. They're cute, though." Jane peered down at the girl's carton of wriggling, mewing merchandise. The mother cat lay under the tumbling litter, purring contentedly and blinking in the brilliant sun.

"Are you sure? If I don't give them all away, my dad

says they gotta go to the pound, and you know what they do to them there."

"Yes, I know, but I don't think my dad would let me have one, either." Jane winked at the child, and Critter squirmed to get a closer look.

Baffled, the girl shrugged and turned to the next new face. "Hey, you want a kitten?"

Jane tugged at Critter's collar, pulling him away from the group, and they started up the street. They went to the corner and turned down Maple. She noticed Tommy walking up the stairs to the front door. *Good, it's nice that Sara has someone to play with.*

Jane's mood lightened the farther away they got from home. They wandered aimlessly around the neighborhood, later returning to Elm Street. The young saleswoman must have found a better spot to hawk her wares, for she and her potential customers were nowhere in sight. Soon Jane was parallel to their house and still reluctant to go inside.

Critter looked curiously at her and then at the house. He headed for the stand of trees. Jane trailed along behind, happy for the diversion. The field beyond the trees was ankle-deep in mud. Jane grabbed Critter just before he was about to dive into the middle of the mire. He backed off and then moved along the boundary, staying within the windbreak. Jane struggled over fallen branches, tangled roots, and underbrush, unable to keep up with her four-footed companion. She came upon an uprooted tree and scrambled over the top.

Critter stood on the other side, erect and stiff, the fur raised on his back and shoulders. Ten feet away a lumbering black Labrador mimicked his stance. It growled and showed frighteningly long yellow teeth. Jane thought inanely of dog-biscuit commercials which advertised clean teeth.

"Critter." Jane tried to call him back, while the Labrador took a menacing step forward. Critter barked. As though the sound unleashed some kind of devil within, the other dog lunged, becoming a black blur with flashing sharp fangs. It landed on top of Critter, and Jane started to shout.

She jumped down from her perch on the uprooted tree trunk, frantically trying to decide what to do. Jane skirted the mass of snarling black-and-brown fur and leapt to the side as the two dogs came crashing into her.

She aimed a kick at the black Lab's flank. Stunned, its concentration broken, it stopped. Critter backed off, panting. Blood dripped from a large scratch above his eyes.

The Lab blinked and looked around for the source of the interruption. It saw Jane and sprung. Suddenly seventy pounds of snarling, growling beast crashed down on her, and she was fighting for her life. She seized the animal's throat, pushing the slobbering, snapping jaws away from her neck. The next thing she knew, Critter had joined the fray, and the black dog turned away from her. She crawled away from the fight and into some bushes. She watched helplessly as the dogs rolled along the wet ground.

Critter's growling turned to yelps, then to anguished howls of confusion and pain. Jane put her hands over her eyes unable to watch anymore, and then as quickly as it began, it was over. The Lab limped off in the direction of the house, leaving Critter a wasted heap of torn brown fur. Jane moved swiftly on all fours to Critter's side. He licked her hand weakly, his tail gave two small thumps, and he lay still. She looked in the direction of the house and realized that the Lab was gone. It had vanished, simply disappeared.

Weeping, she pulled the beloved family pet onto her lap and struggled to her feet. She half stumbled, half walked to the edge of the field. Her feet immediately sank in the bog, but it seemed preferable to confronting the uprooted tree and the tangled underbrush with her heavy burden. She moved slowly, carefully. Her tears were dried by the gentle breeze. Critter roused himself and licked her face. Jane lowered him gently to the ground.

"Good boy, can you walk?" Critter just looked up at her. "Come on, fella, stand up." After much persuasion, he did—promptly plopping down again on shaky haunches.

"Thank God, you're all right." Critter whimpered in response. "Yes, and thank you, too, Critter. I think you may have saved my life. Okay, try it again. We'll go slow." He stood unsteadily. Blood dripped into his eye. Jane pulled her sweater off to wipe it away.

"Come on, Critter. Come on, good old boy." Critter curled his upper lip with his best imitation of a human smile.

"You think you can walk? You're too damn big to carry very far. After this, I think I'm going to put you on a diet." She urged him on, sporadically cajoling the bedraggled beast and later cheering his efforts.

They plodded haltingly home, moving a few feet, then stopping and resting. The morning sun was high in the sky when they finally stood at the base of the back stairs.

"Elliot! Elliot," she called. A few moments later, he appeared on the back porch.

"Jesus Christ, what happened?"

"Dog fight."

He walked down the steps and gave her a playful peck on her mud-spattered cheek. "You fighting with Critter again?" He lifted the dog with an "ooph" and added with forced levity, "I told you, Jane, you gotta learn to share your doggy biscuits."

He carried Critter through the porch and into the kitchen. Elliot dropped to his knees and gently placed the injured dog on the floor.

Running toward the phone, she called over her shoulder. "I'll call the vet."

"I don't think it'll be necessary," Elliot said. "Let's just wash him up."

"What if that damn Lab had rabies? It attacked me, too, you know."

"Okay, go wash up and change. I'll load Critter into the car. You can tell me what happened on the way to the vet."

A few minutes later, Jane returned to the kitchen, wiping mud from her sweater. "Where's Critter?"

"In the car. I called the vet; he's expecting us."

"What about Sara?"

"She's at that Tommy Erwin's house. We'll stop and tell her where we're going. She can come back to look after Nana while we're gone."

Reluctantly, Sara returned to the house. Critter had looked bad. He looked just awful.

"Dumb ol' dog," she muttered. She resented having to leave Tommy's house to come home and take care of Nana. She climbed the stairs slowly. Her arm extended, she slapped at the banister supports as she passed. She ignored Nana's door and went into her room. Sara opened the closet door and pulled Raggedy Andy from a shelf.

Then she went to the kitchen where she dug the ice cream from the freezer. Sitting on the floor, Sara helped herself. Her parents would be mad if they found out. *Who cares?* The sticky chocolate dripped down her chin and splattered on the linoleum. She hit Raggedy Andy. "You're making a mess!" She made a funny face, rose and cleaned up the tiles.

Holding Raggedy Andy by the heel, she mounted the stairs. His head bounced on each step. Once on the second floor, she turned toward Nana's room. Sara dragged the rocker over to Nana's bedside. She looked down at her grandmother. Nana stared blankly at the ceiling.

"Nana?" she said softly. Nothing, no movement, no responding blink.

"Nana?" she said a little more firmly. Nana just lay motionless. Sara bent over the bed so her face was only inches away from her grandmother's. Her hands searched her pockets until she found the matches she had picked up at Tommy's house.

"Nana, are you in there? Can you hear me?" Nana continued to stare at the ceiling. Sara turned her head, looking where her grandmother's eyes seemed to be focused. Paint peeled from its cracked surface.

"Nana." Sara's voice took on a singsong lilt. "Oh, Nana?" Sara turned back to her, grinning wickedly.

She lit a match and held it within the old woman's field of vision. Sara shook it out and dropped it on the floor. She lit another and placed it next to the old woman's cheek, looking deeply into her grandmother's eyes. No blink, no response, but then Sara registered a slight dilation and contraction of the pupils.

Sara recognized fear. Nana knew what Sara was doing, and she knew what was up there directly above her head—Shelley's toy box. Sara glared down at her grandmother. Yes, she knew all right. She knew about the house, but then the house knew about Nana, too. It knew what to do. Nana knew about Shelley, and perhaps, Nana knew about Sara also; but Sara—she smiled at the thought—knew about Nana. The match burned Sara's fingers. She swore loudly as she dropped the match.

Sara would make sure Nana choked on that knowledge. Her hand closed around a pillow. She pulled the soggy, sodden cushion from between Nana's legs. Sara's head swung around when she heard the crunch of the Nova's wheels in the driveway. She stopped. *Later,* she thought, *I'll get to you later.*

Sara moved away from the bed, scooping the spent matches from the floor. She went to sit in the window seat, pocketing the book of matches.

"You want me to sing you a lullaby?" Sara asked. Not waiting for a response, she started to sing:

The old gray mare,
Ain't what she used to be (thwock!),
Ain't what she used to be (thwock!),
Ain't what she used to be (thwock!)
Many long years ago.

"Sara, we're home." Jane's voice drifted up from downstairs.

She gave Raggedy Andy another resounding *thwock!*

"Coming, Mother!" Sara left the door open behind her, and Nana started to quake upon the bed.

Sara leaned over the railing on the first landing. "How's Critter?"

Jane came out from the kitchen and looked at her daughter. "A little sore, but he'll live. How does steak sound for supper? If your daddy can dig the grill out from the garage, we'll have a barbecue. Might as well take advantage of the good weather while it lasts."

"Yum!"

Her father's voice came from the kitchen. "I heard that snide crack about the grill. Are you implying I need to clean the garage?" He walked into the foyer and hugged Jane. Sara came the rest of the way down the stairs.

"Actually, I thought I had done pretty well. I found the toolbox and the blowtorch when I needed it, didn't I?"

Jane rolled her eyes toward the ceiling. "Yes, dear, but it would be nice if we could park the car in there just once before we move."

"Ah, that means I have plenty of time."

Jane whispered, "I hope not," as he exited through the living room.

Sara peered into her mother's face. "Is something wrong?"

Jane gave Sara a tired smile. "No, dear."

Elliot shouted to them over his shoulder. "One grill

coming up. If I'm not back in an hour, send a search party."

"Can I go help, Daddy?"

"Sure, but don't get lost in that maze of boxes."

Jane and Sara went into the kitchen. Her father had donned his "Dad's the chef" apron and was sorting through utensils in one of the drawers. "Jane, where's the long-handled spatula?"

"I think it's with the grill."

"Oh, oh, we're in trouble."

Sara sat down with Critter, delighted that everyone seemed in such good spirits. A large bandage was wrapped around his head, pinning down one ear. Another dressing had been placed on his right foreleg. "Poor Critter."

Elliot turned to his daughter. "I think he looks pretty good. All he needs is a couple of other dogs with a drum and a fife."

"Huh?"

"Never mind, honey, it's a joke." He stabbed at the air with a fork. "Onward. Jane"—he grasped his wife tightly around her waist—"I'll be back with my grill or on it." He held the fork before himself and ran from the kitchen.

"What does he mean, Mama?"

"He's just trying to be funny, Sara."

"Is he?"

"Is he what?"

"Funny."

Jane laughed. "If he's not funny, you are? You said you were going to help him."

Sara followed her father out the door and into the garage. "Can me and Raggedy Andy come, too?"

"Sure. The more, the merrier." The two paused to survey the stacks of boxes. Her father let out a long, loud sigh. "What a mess!"

Sara wandered aimlessly, peeking curiously first into one box and then another. "If you see the spatula, let out a hoot." He started rooting through boxes. He looked up. "Eureka! The grill." He pointed to a corner behind a jumble of cartons. "If your mother's right, the utensils and charcoal lighter fluid should be close by. Try that box."

Sara pulled the lid off the carton and stared inside. "Nope."

Elliot moved over to her side and lifted it from the stack, opening the one below. "Here they are. We did pretty well. We haven't even been out here five minutes, and your mother thought we couldn't do it. We make a pretty good team, eh, pumpkin?" He prodded Sara's flank.

"Sure." Sara giggled and twitched away from him. He clutched her sides and started to tickle her.

She screeched, "Stop it, that tickles."

Elliot dropped his arms. "It was supposed to, Shelley."

He hugged her while Sara struggled from his tight grip.

"Daddyyy, I'm not . . ."

He paused and then lifted her chin with his index finger, examining the bruise under her eye. "Sara, I mean." It had turned a sickly green-and-yellow hue. "Look, Sara, I'm sorry."

"About what?"

He indicated her eye. "About that."

Embarrassed, she shuffled uncomfortably under his gaze. "It's, uh, okay."

Jane came into the garage, interrupting their conversation and rescuing them from the momentary uneasiness. "Elliot, I fixed you a drink."

Sara grimaced and turned away in disgust. "Thanks, love," he said. "We found the grill over in the corner."

"That's pretty good. I was just getting ready to box a lunch for the two of you and tie a keg around Critter's neck in case you got lost."

"Can you help, hon? Grab that side, and I'll get this one. Sara, you bring the spatula and the lighter"—he looked at Jane—"fluid here to me."

"Sure, Dad."

He set the grill up in the driveway. Critter limped out to the back porch. Sara sat with him on the top step, Raggedy Andy on her lap. They both watched as Elliot filled the grill with charcoal and lit it. Mesmerized, Sara descended the back steps until she stood beside the grill. She watched the flames dance and leap in fiery ecstasy.

Elliot stared at her and felt a twinge of fear stirring just below the edges of consciousness. He wiped sweat from his brow and moved over to the stair.

"S-S . . ." He never completed what he had started to say. Jane walked out from the kitchen, steak platter in her hand. The spell broken, Sara joined Critter and her mother on the porch. Elliot picked up his drink, toasting them.

"We'll have to let the grill heat up a bit."

"Should I refrigerate these while we wait?"

"It wouldn't hurt."

Sara stood on her tiptoes and looked at the platter. "Hey, there's four steaks there."

"Yep, the small one's for Critter."

"For Critter?" she said, amazed.

Elliot scooped Sara up, throwing her over his shoulder like a sack of potatoes and carried her into the kitchen. "Yes, for Critter. He's hero of the day. Didn't you know that? He saved your mom's life." He set Sara down.

"He did?"

"Sure did. You go get a sweater for yourself and bring me my jacket—it's getting a little chilly out—then I'll tell you all about it."

Sara obediently did as she was bidden. Elliot picked up the doll she had left behind.

He called out to the hall. "Raggedy Andy looks a little different, Sara. What'd you do to him?"

Sara returned to the kitchen, and threw a cautious glance at her mother, who shook her head in warning.

"I dunno," she said sullenly.

Jane intervened. "I washed him. He probably looks a little cleaner, that's all."

Jane cut small pieces of steak for Critter, feeding him between her own bites. She had, with a bit of intoxicated inspiration and mischief, tied a napkin around his neck as a bib. He looked mighty pleased with himself.

"Don't feed him at the table, Jane, you'll start him begging."

"No, I won't. Besides, he deserves to eat with the

big folks just this once." Elliot grumbled something in acid response.

"What's that?" She glowered at him. "Look, just because I told you that I want to buy a new coat, what's wrong with that? I haven't gotten a new one for years. If we can afford a new stereo, we can afford a coat for me, right, Sara?" Sara dug herself a little bit deeper into the chair, trying to make herself as small as possible.

Elliot didn't notice. "The stereo wasn't only for me, it was for both of us. Don't tell me you don't enjoy it, too?"

"I didn't say that. I said, if we can afford a stereo, then we can afford a coat."

Sara climbed down from her chair. "I'm finished now. Can I be excused?"

Jane nodded, and Elliot ignored her. "And all I said is"—he pointed at Jane with his steak knife, and she cringed—"that with the vet bill and the house call the other day, let's wait. Between your mother and the goddamn mongrel, we'll be through what's left of the insurance money in no time."

"I'll be in Nana's room," Sara informed her parents, but nobody was listening. She moved out into the foyer, dragging Raggedy Andy behind her. She peered back over her shoulder to see if her parents were watching and then drop-kicked the doll to the first landing. They were just squabbling now, but the blows would start soon.

Nana listened to the raised voices downstairs. She heard the quiet thud when Raggedy Andy landed outside her door. She trembled at the sound of Sara's footsteps in the hall.

"Nana, I'm back." Sara poked her head in the door. She came over to the bed. "You want to play?"

Nana looked at the little girl, her eyes shining in terror. She made no attempt to hide her horror. One blink, two.

"So you are there. I thought so." Sara sat in the rocker. "And you know, don't you?" One blink.

"What are you going to do about it, old woman?" The normally soft, childlike voice turned hard and gravelly.

Nana turned her head, eyes wide open. She studied the child before her. It didn't sound like Sara anymore. The *other* was there, inside her. Nana closed her eyes and started to pray. She prayed for guidance; she prayed for strength; and she prayed for the impossible to happen.

A slight sound brought her out of her hurried entreaty. Sara stood over the bed, her hand on the pillow she had laid carelessly off to the side earlier that afternoon. "Eh, old woman? What are you going to do?" the alien voice taunted, the tone mocking. Nana could only stare at the child.

"You're afraid. You should be." It laughed, deep, husky laughter. "I like that. Don't you know your fear feeds me?"

Nana quivered, willing her mind to be silent. *Feeds it. Yes, it would.* Nana began to pray again, imploring the heavens for something—something, she didn't know what.

Pillow in hand, Sara walked over to the window seat. "That won't help you, either, old woman. Don't you know your God's not listening?" She turned around to face Nana, her outline silhouetted in the moonlight.

Nana's rasping voice rose in prayer:

Our Father who art in heaven,
Hallowed be thy name . . .

Sara snarled, leaping for the bed. *The old woman spoke.* That wasn't supposed to happen; she couldn't speak. Her spring was met with a shriek of rage from the decrepit form upon the urine-soaked mattress. Jane and Elliot looked up from their argument at the bizarre, haunting howl.

"Good God, what's that?" Jane said.

"I don't know. It came from upstairs."

The cry was met by an unearthly, inhuman screech, and downstairs Jane and Elliot stood up simultaneously. Elliot's chair fell to the floor with a bang. They both sped for the dining-room door, racing through the living room and into the foyer. Elliot bounded up the stairs with Jane following closely on his heels. Critter sat whining at the bottom of the steps.

Another strident screech directed them to Nana's room. They ran to the door. Elliot flipped the switch, and the room flooded with light. The sight that confronted them held them spellbound. Astounded, they both stood frozen in place.

Nana had somehow managed to get out of bed and was on top of Sara. Her spiderlike, contorted limbs were further bent into unrealistic and impossible angles. Gnarled fingers tore at the little girl who snarled beneath her with animal sounds. Nana's long-silenced vocal chords emitted a continuous scream that ripped at Elliot's and Jane's already overwrought nerves. Sara fought the demented woman with a vengeance. Her hands encircled Nana's neck in a stranglehold, and she squeezed, throttling her. Nana's breath came in ragged gasps.

"Jesus Christ." Awaking to the nightmare, Elliot came round first. He ran, but his movements seemed agonizingly slow as though he were wading through thick molasses. He struggled to get to the center of the room where the siege continued. Finally he reached them. He tried to pull Nana off his daughter, and the child bit him while she loosened her hold on Nana's neck to swing viciously at him.

He strengthened his grip on Nana's shoulder and yanked her off his daughter. Nana went limp in his hand, coming away easily, without resistance. Sara let go of her. He dragged them apart. Nana rolled lifelessly in his grasp, like a rag doll. She gazed with empty eyes at the ceiling. He put his hand over her heart. Nothing. It was still, no beat, not so much as a flutter. Elliot turned and looked at Jane where she remained, still spellbound in the doorway. He felt scalding hot tears splash on his face. "My God, Jane, she's dead."

Critter let out a mournful yowl from the hall below. This seemed to release Jane from her trance and she pointed to her compact on the bedside table. "Hold it under her nose to see if she's still breathing."

He stretched to reach it, doing as he had been told. He shook his head. "No, nothing, nothing at all."

Jane entered the room and flopped down on the rocker, ignoring the clamp which stuck her in the back. "Oh my God, it was Nana. It was Nana all along."

"What do you mean?"

"Well, if she could move, that would explain the strange things that have been happening, wouldn't it?"

Elliot looked down at Jane's mother. Nana's eyes were fixed on him. He could read the rebuke there. He saw Nana's dying denial of his wife's implied accusation. He put his thumb and index finger on each lid. His shoulders sagged, and he gently closed her eyes. He stared at Nana, silent for a while. Blood dripped languidly from her nose and mouth.

His gaze turned to Sara where she had retreated to the corner of the room. She stood, dumbfounded, looking from Elliot to Nana, her thumb planted firmly in her mouth. Elliot got the disconcerting feeling that something wasn't quite right. Somehow her innocence seemed fake. Her eyes revealed triumph and something else again—glee. He lowered Nana's limp form slowly to the floor and said, "I wouldn't be so sure of that."

CHAPTER 18

Elliot sat at the old battered desk. A worn easy chair, the music stand, the sax in its case, and walls lined with makeshift shelves of concrete blocks and two-by-fours provided the rest of the study's mismatched decor. Elliot leaned over an antiquated manual Royal typewriter, intermittently hitting keys and cursing.

"Goddammit!" He reached for the correction tape, backspaced, and hit a key. His index finger circled over the keyboard until he spied the right one, which he gave a savage tap. "Success." He surveyed his work. The paper looked tattered and abused, its surface covered with lumps of white-out, occasional *X*'s, and a few smudges. He rubbed his eyes. He didn't know which was worse, his handwriting or this poor excuse for typing.

A sound from the foyer brought him out of his

reverie. Jane had returned from the funeral home. Elliot looked up from the old portable as she walked into the study.

"How goes the test?" she asked.

"Not well. I'm having a hard time concentrating, not to mention typing. How about you?"

Jane settled in the easy chair on the opposite side of the desk. She waved her hand in a noncommittal gesture. "It was depressing. I picked out one of the cheaper coffins. I don't think she would mind, she was always a pretty thrifty woman." Jane began to cry.

Elliot moved around the desk and squatted in front of his wife. He patted her hand awkwardly. "I'm sorry, Jane. At least we know that we did the best we could."

Jane nodded, wiping her nose with a handkerchief. "Did you call Margaret?"

"Yes, she'll be able to come. She's taking the kids out of school. She doesn't know if Allen will make it, though. The first quarter is his busy time of year. Tax time, you know, and for many companies the end of the fiscal year."

"The funeral's set for Tuesday. The wake's tomorrow. I gave him her best dress." She let out a strangulated sob. "Elliot, she's going to just swim in that thing. I'm so afraid she'll look just plain ridiculous. She lost so much weight since the last time she wore it. She used to be a pretty big woman."

"We're probably lucky she lost the weight, though, with you having to haul her in and out of the chair all the time. Besides, the funeral director can do something about that. They've got tricks for that sort of thing."

"He said he'd try to pin it up. I think, though, I'd rather have the services closed-coffin. I don't think I can face her, her limbs all twisted up and her made up like a French whore. She was such a staunch God-fearing Lutheran, I think she'd rather die than be seen with all that—what did she used to call it?—war paint. Besides, what will Margaret think to see her like that?"

"I wouldn't worry about Margaret." Elliot stood up. His knees popped. He winced. "Christ, I'm getting old."

He leaned back against the desk. "You know, a closed coffin is a good idea. I always thought an open casket was kind of barbaric, anyway, with everyone standing around hemming and hawing and saying 'she looks so natural.'" He rolled his eyes toward the ceiling.

"Not to change the subject, but I dug out her insurance papers."

"Will the money cover the cost of the funeral?"

"Oh, definitely, more than. Your mother had a twenty-five-thousand-dollar policy when she moved in with us, and right after she moved in, I took out a second policy on her for the same amount. I talked to her about it then and she agreed. We decided to get it then before her health deteriorated so badly that she could no longer qualify. You're the beneficiary." He waited for the information to sink in. Jane stared blankly at a fixed point above his head, unmoved.

"You know your mother loved you very much. I know you blame her for what's been happening here recently, but don't judge her too harshly. She did love you, Jane. She never told you in so many words, but she told me while she could still talk. She wanted to make sure you were well taken care of since you, at least, were willing to go a little out of your way to help her—not like Margaret. Besides, there's the money left from the farm and the original policy to split between the two of you."

"Good old Elliot, always a pragmatist."

He snapped, "Someone has got to be." Noticing her hurt expression, he hurried on. "But you missed the point. I know you loved your mother, and I just wanted you to know how much she loved you and appreciated what you have done for her."

Jane looked up at Elliot and gave him an apathetic smile. "What we've done for her. Remember that—we. Most husbands would have had her put in a nursing home a long time ago."

"Well, you did most of the work."

"Perhaps." Jane got up listlessly. "I guess I better see to dinner."

"Don't worry about dinner. Let's go out tonight."

"What about your test?"

"I can finish it up shortly. My main problem—besides typing—is that I can't decide if I should spell Bach, B-A-C-H or B-O-C-K. I'm afraid if I spell it correctly the entire class will flunk."

"And how do you plan to spell Beethoven? B-A-Y . . . or B-A-T-E . . . ?"

"How about B-A-I-T . . . ?"

Jane chuckled. "Spell it B-A-C-H. If they flunk, it serves them right." She stopped in the doorway. "Where's Sara?"

"Upstairs, I think."

"How's she taking all this?"

"Okay, I guess." Elliot stared out the window, troubled.

"Strange, wasn't it? I mean how this happened. I still don't understand. How could she move like that? How could she get out of bed after all these years?"

Elliot raised a thoughtful brow. "Who knows?"

"You didn't tell Margaret, did you?"

"No, of course not."

"How are we going to explain the scratches?"

"You mean on Sara's face? What about the black eye?" He looked sadly down at his hands.

"We can tell her the dog did it, jumped up and knocked her down, I suppose."

"Critter doesn't look like he's capable of doing that."

"You're right." Jane sighed, leaning against the doorjamb for support. "Jesus, this family's in fine shape."

Elliot returned to his desk. He examined the page before him while Jane headed for Sara's room. Muttering an expletive, he continued his hunt-and-peck version of typing.

Sara sat on the bed, her thumb in her mouth. She held Raggedy Andy tightly against her chest and listened to her mother's footsteps in the hall. Jane opened the door and looked down at her daughter's florid, tearstained face. She gently pulled Sara's thumb from her mouth.

"Mommy, I'm sorry."

"About what, dear?"

"About Nana."

"You didn't do anything. At least, I don't think you

did. I'm sorry she hurt you. Old people get a little crazy sometimes, like I told you before. The older people get, the worse it is. They've even got a name for it."

"Yeah?" she asked disinterestedly.

"Yes, it's called senile psychosis—only I didn't realize that Nana had gotten that way or I would have put her in a home."

"But she was in a home."

"I mean a nursing home."

"Oh."

Jane sat down on the bed. "You don't look well, Sara. Are you sure you're feeling all right?" Jane placed her hand against her daughter's forehead to check her temperature. "You're burning up."

"Oh no," Sara wailed. "I've been a bad girl, and now I'm burning up."

Jane gave her daughter a perplexed look. "Honey, now why would you say that?"

Sara sniffled. "Mrs. McGuinness told me."

"Told you what?"

"Told me that bad little girls burn."

"What? She told you that!"

"Uh-huh."

"Why, that bitch!"

Sara flinched.

"I'm sorry, Sara, I know I shouldn't cuss, but that makes me mad. That was a mean thing to say. I'm going to talk to her and the principal about it Monday. She won't ever say anything like that to you again. I promise." Jane brushed Sara's silky hair away from her face and didn't notice her daughter's fleeting smile.

"You can't talk to her, anyway. She's in the hospital," Sara said.

"Mrs. McGuinness is in the hospital? Why?" The question died on her lips as Jane remembered Sally telling her about the fire.

"Sara, you don't know anything about . . ." Jane studied her daughter's face—looking into the child's anguished and fevered eyes—and dismissed the query before it was completely voiced. How could she even think such a thing? She glanced self-consciously toward the door.

"Never mind, kiddo. Look, you get into your pj's. I've got something to discuss with your father. He was going to take us out to eat, and I think it would be better if we stayed home."

Sara groaned. "I spoiled everything."

"No, you didn't. We'll get Chinese carry-out instead. How does that sound? Wouldn't you like egg rolls and chop suey? And who knows, maybe I can talk your father into bringing the TV upstairs. He'll complain and say he's going to get a hernia, but if I ask him real nice, I bet he'll do it. Then you can watch TV."

"Yes, Mama."

Jane picked up the tray from Sara's bedside table. Sara seemed perfectly contented as she watched "Murder She Wrote." Jane stopped in the door. "As soon as your program's over, you turn off the light and get some sleep."

Whooo! An eerie hoot floated through the room.

"What was that, Sara?"

"I didn't say anything, Mama."

Jane stepped back into the room, looking around, mystified. "Well, I'll be darned." She put the tray on the dresser top.

"What?" Sara stopped watching TV and turned to face her mother.

"Look." Jane pointed to the window. "You don't see one of those every day."

Sara looked. A bundle of brown-and-gray feathers sat on the quiescent tree limb, weighing it down. Two glowing golden eyes blinked from a horned head.

"What is it?"

"It's an owl."

"It looks scary. It's got horns."

"Yes, it's what they call a great horned owl, Sara. Isn't that imaginative?" Jane quipped. She walked over to the window and tapped on the pane.

Whoo.

Jane grinned. "You fool. Silly bird."

She rapped the glass again with her index finger. The bird took off in a flurry of whirring wings. "Oh well."

She turned back to Sara, who sat trembling on the bed. "What's the matter, you cold?" She tested Sara's forehead. "Get under the covers, and remember what I told you. Once your program's over, you turn off the TV and get some sleep."

Jane carried the tray into the living room. "We saw an owl sitting on the branch outside of Sara's room." Elliot looked up from his book. "And don't you go telling me it's an evil omen. I know all about that old wives' tale."

"So I won't tell you."

"Look, I'm going to put this away." She lifted the tray. "And then I'm going to bed myself. I'm bushed."

"Sure, I'll be up in a bit."

A few minutes later, Jane returned to the living room. She kissed Elliot good night and went up the stairs. Critter limped along behind her. Elliot put his book down and headed for the kitchen to fix himself a drink.

Sara stood shivering outside Tommy Erwin's garage. She patted her jacket pocket. *Good, it's still there.* She paused to listen for any sounds of life emanating from the Erwins' house. Silence, nothing but the growl of a car motor which came from the street. She held her breath and waited a few more minutes to make sure no one was going to come out and discover her.

She put her hand on the doorknob. Her heart did a quick two-step in her chest. *What if it's locked?* Or worse still, what if Tommy Erwin's mother had found the kitten in the garage? Sara tried the door. The knob turned easily in her hand. She slipped inside and away from the chilling wind.

"Mew."

Sara leaned against the door, waiting for her eyes to adjust to the darkness.

"Mew," the kitten said again from the other side of the Erwins' station wagon.

"Here, kitty, kitty." She wondered if Tommy had thought of a name for it yet. She wondered too how he had managed to hide the cat this long, or how he was planning to explain its presence.

"Kitty, kitty. Come here, kitty, kitty." She pushed

herself away from the door and walked around the car, feeling ahead of her with her foot before each step. She didn't want to trip over something and wake somebody up. A sheen of sweat covered her forehead, and her eyes glittered feverishly.

She continued her cautious circuit until she stepped into something soft. Sara looked down. She stood with her foot in a saucer full of half-dried macaroni and cheese.

"Yuck." She extracted her foot, shaking off the sticky remains. Evidently, Tommy didn't know a whole lot about what little kitties liked to eat. The cat pounced on Sara's foot as she set it down on the floor next to the saucer.

"There you are, pretty kitty. I brought something for you." Sara pulled out a small jar of warm milk from her pocket. She hoped it was still good. She had gotten it from the kitchen today while her mother was at the funeral home and her daddy was busy in the study.

She sniffed; it smelled okay. Sara poured some over the macaroni and cheese. The kitten lapped it up greedily. Sara stroked the soft fur with cold-stiffened fingers. "You're so soft." In the dim light she could just barely make out the kitten's gray-and-black stripes.

"Is that good?" She continued to pet the kitten who stepped into the center of the saucer to drink.

"Are you a boy kitty or a girl kitty?" Sara sat on the cold cement floor and waited patiently for the kitten to finish its feast. Presently, the cat stepped back. It lifted its forepaw and delicately cleaned it, licking up the last of the milk from between soft pads.

"All done?" The cat wrapped itself around her ankles and purred contentedly. "Do you want to play? I'm going to take you to my house so we can play."

She picked up the cat, who protested with a loud meow. "Sh-sh-sh!" Sara put her finger to her lips. "You'll wake everyone up." She snuck out of the garage and started up Elm Street toward home.

Elliot finished his drink, returning to the kitchen. Looking at the pile of dirty dishes, he decided to surprise Jane. *What with her mother dying and Sara sick, she needs a break.*

Soft jazz came through the swinging door from the living room. He stood at the kitchen sink up to his elbows in dishwater. He hummed along with the tune, his toe tapping in time to the music. He rinsed a plate and put it in the strainer next to the sink. Changing the lyrics, he sang exuberantly, "This is the way we wash the dishes, wash the dishes."

Over his bellowing rendition, he didn't hear Sara when she closed the screen door on the back porch. She put the kitten down. "I wish you could stay here, kitty, but you can't. My mom and dad wouldn't like it." She scowled. "There's a lot of things they don't like."

She bent over and reached for the cat. The kitten swatted at the mitten which hung from the sleeve of her jacket. "You like that, huh?" She dangled the tantalizing plaything in front of the cat, who arched its back and hissed. It did a small dance, backing away from the mitten and then pounced. It missed the mitten and clawed Sara's hand instead.

"Damn you, cat." Sara straightened, her jaw

clenched. "Now you are going to have to be punished." She searched the screened-in back porch. Her eyes lighted on the long-handled spatula which her father had hung from a hook above the grill. Then she noticed the lighter fluid and wooden matches.

Elliot rinsed the last plate and turned off the water. He started to fix himself another drink. The album ended with a click. Leaving the half-completed drink, he went to flip through the albums.

Sara seized the fluid and the matches. She scooped up the kitten, who was now cleaning itself, from the floor. "Bad kitty. *Bad!*"

Elliot came back to his drink. He heard the screen door slam. He looked out the window to the driveway beyond. It was Sara! He went out the back door to the porch. *What the hell is she doing out at this time, and with a fever, too?* He was about to shout at her when she started to talk. He pulled back into the shadows to watch.

"Bad! Bad!" She took a swing at something Elliot couldn't see and knelt down on the hard concrete. She appeared to be holding something in place with one hand; her other hand struggled to uncap something else.

Fascinated, he continued to watch from his hiding place. He snickered. *What is she going to do? Punish Raggedy Andy?*

He heard the soft *glug, glug* of some liquid being poured out of a bottle. He turned his head so that his ear faced the direction of the sound, trying to recognize it. For some reason, it seemed hauntingly familiar, bringing with it a feeling of déjà vu.

Whatever she held thrashed and fought because his

daughter started to curse. *Where did she learn all those words?* He didn't wonder for long, because then he heard the bloodcurdling meow of a cat in pain.

"Oh God." He groaned, glued to the spot. His mind leapt back in time to the day Shelley had torched the family pet, Fluffy, a kitten barely three months old. "Jesus, not again—not Sara."

She struck something against the concrete drive. A match flared. She put it against the cat's tail, and it went up like a Roman candle.

Released by the sudden flash of light, Elliot headed for the screen door. *"Sara!"*

He ran down the porch steps and stopped in confusion. Images and time merged, superimposed over each other. *Sara, Shelley, or both?*

Sara saw her father standing in a daze at the foot of the stairs and abruptly let go of the kitten. The flames lapped eagerly up the tail to its body, and it started to howl. Elliot moved to his daughter's side. He grabbed her roughly by the shoulders and reached for the kitten. Too late, it ran streaking in a trail of brilliant color, flaring into the stand of trees.

He got down on his knees and pulled Sara around to face him. He shook her. "What did you do, Sara? Tell me, what did you do?" She didn't seem to notice. Her head was turned in the direction of the burning cat.

"Meow!" it shrieked, running in frenzied, flickering circles through the trees.

Sara looked at her father and smiled enigmatically. "So pretty. So, so pretty," she said. "Don't you think it's pretty?"

He could still hear the kitten's agonized screech.

The sound seemed to echo, reverberating in the quiet winter night. Elliot looked at his daughter in disgust, pushing her away. He turned to the side of the drive and threw up upon the lawn.

Elliot crawled away from the steaming mass, and what was left of his mind snapped. The fire, the house, the beast who roamed its halls, Shelley and Sara all converged in time and place, and he knew now what he must do.

Elliot helped Sara into bed. His head throbbed, and his sides ached from the violence of his retching. He felt her forehead. It was hot. He could feel the radiant heat despite the slight chill left on her skin from being out-of-doors.

"You stay here, little girl. Don't get out of bed," he ordered emphatically.

"Are you mad at me, Daddy?"

Elliot looked down at her flushed red cheeks. "No, just a little . . . uh, disappointed. I'm going downstairs to fix you some cocoa. Now, stay in bed!"

He put the kettle on a burner and went rummaging through the kitchen cabinets. He pulled a prescription bottle from the shelf. *Good, they're still here.* He was thankful now that Jane—like her deceased mother—never threw anything away. He dumped several child-dose tranquilizers into the palm of his hand.

Out the window, he could see the small fire, which had once been a cat, flicker in the stand of trees. It silhouetted the spindly branches of the dead brush and cast ghostly, leaping shadows. The small blaze looked deceptively cheery, like a distant camp fire.

The kettle whistled, and he poured the boiling water into the cup, stirring in the hot-chocolate mix and a couple of pills. He picked the mug up, thought better of it, and added a dollop of vodka. Elliot took this concoction up to Sara and handed it to her. "Drink this."

She lifted the cup to her lips, wrinkled her nose, and peered questioningly at him over its rim.

"Go head, drink it."

She took a sip. "It tastes funny."

"I don't care. Drink it, all of it." He held out the tranquilizers. "And take these."

"But?"

"You've got a fever. Mama gives you aspirin when you have a fever, doesn't she?"

Sara wasn't fooled. "But these aren't aspirin. These are those pills I had to take after Shelley. . . ." She didn't finish the sentence. "I don't want to take them. They make me feel funny."

"Well, Nana died yesterday so I think you need them. Now, take them like a good little girl. They won't make you feel funny tonight. They'll make you sleep. I don't want you up wandering around anymore tonight. You made a mess, and I have to go outside now and clean it up. I want to know you'll be in bed sleeping."

Elliot sat on the edge of the bed and watched as she took the tranquilizers. "Good girl." He kissed her fevered brow. "I'll sit with you until you fall asleep—and remember, Sara, no matter what you do, Daddy will always love you."

He held her hand. Sara settled against the pillow,

dragging Raggedy Andy onto her chest. Elliot started to hum a soft lullaby. Sara nestled a little closer to her father. She loved it when he sang to her in his deep, rich baritone. She drifted into a gentle slumber, soothed by his voice.

Elliot looked out the window at the skeletal branch. *Tap, tap, tap.* When he was sure she slept, he pulled the covers closer around her and tucked them in. He caressed her cheek. "I love you," he whispered in her ear. Then he got up and went to the master bedroom. He opened the top drawer, looking for his gloves. Jane woke.

"Wha'cha doin'?" she said in a sleepy slur.

"Oh nothing. I didn't know you were awake."

"I wasn't until you came in." She patted the bed next to her. "Why don't you come to bed?"

He moved next to her and touched her hand. "I don't think I'm ready yet."

"Brrr. Your hands are freezing. Don't tell me you're coming down with something, too."

"No, I'm fine, just fine," he said distractedly. He stooped down and gave her a kiss.

She caught the ghostly aroma of Scotch. "Oh, Elliot, you've been drinking. I thought after last night we agreed that we were going to cut down."

Taken aback, he cocked his head. After what had happened tonight, he had forgotten the previous vow. Defensive, he yelled at her. "Look, I'll cut down when I'm damned good and ready. Get off my back. I've had a rough night."

Jane shrank away from him. He noticed the movement, and it angered him more. "Did it ever occur to you that I just might have more important things on my mind?" he snarled. "As a matter of fact, I think I may just go downstairs and fix myself another one."

He slammed out of the room. Jane listened to the sound of his heavy footsteps clumping down the stairs.

"Shit." She rolled over on her side, punched the pillow, and buried her face in it. "Just grand," she said, her voice muffled by the cushion.

CHAPTER 19

Jane tossed uneasily in the tangled sheets. Shelley stood by the side of the bed. She wore the checked pajamas she had worn that night months ago. In places, they were blackened; in others, they had melted into the flesh, becoming almost indistinguishable from her skin.

The hair on the left side of her head was gone. What remained of her skin was bubbled and blistered. The musculature on that side along the jawline had been totally destroyed. The lipless mouth revealed pink gums and grinning teeth.

Her one eye drooped, sealed shut. The other was opened, staring at her. The right side still retained some semblance of normalcy, with its long blond hair and delicate features unravaged by fire. The whole impression was that of a grotesque and misshapen caricature of the human face.

Jane had long ago become used to Shelley's appearing in both waking and sleeping states, but it was only as Jane slept that she saw with grim clarity what Shelley had become. In those nightly manifestations which Jane had come to accept, Shelley usually came to Jane as she had once appeared—fresh, sweet and young, dressed in her favorite dungarees.

This hideous apparition looked solid enough, but gruesome. Jane gagged at the mixed aroma of overly ripe, rotting flesh, and charred meat. She tried to look away, sure that when she looked again, Shelley would be gone. Wasn't that the way it had always happened in the past?

She turned to face the place where her daughter had stood. Shelley grinned back at her. In her right hand, she held—a gas can. With a sharp intake of breath, Jane pulled herself to a sitting position, her left hand reaching for Elliot. She grabbed his shoulder and shook him. Shelley lifted the bright red can.

"Mother." The phantasm spoke, and Jane wanted to cry. She dragged her leaden body toward the head of the bed, one hand still shaking Elliot.

"Mother?"

Jane crab-walked away from the edge of the bed. She stopped. She didn't try to shake Elliot; she hit him with her fists. Her arms whipped around like a windmill; she beat his back. He snored on complacently.

"Elliot!" Jane shouted.

"Mother, what's the matter, Mother? Aren't you happy to see me?"

Jane shook her head and groaned. She made a choked mewling noise in her throat like that of a small animal caught in a trap. Critter walked up behind the charred Shelley, took a small sniff, and backed away, whining.

"Elliot!" Jane leapt on his comatose form. She slammed him against the headboard. He let out another loud snore and rolled over.

"Elliot! Wake up, you bastard."

He sputtered and swept her hand away. "Lemme alone!"

"It won't help, Mama. You know he's too drunk to hear you."

Jane started to cry.

"I'm sorry, Mother, that you don't like me anymore; but I can't help what I have become. You know that."

Jane pushed her entire body flat against the headboard, wishing that she could somehow disappear into the wall.

"I know you don't like me anymore. You're trying to keep me 'n' Sara apart, and that's not right. I don't like it." Shelley paused. She studied her mother and her good eye narrowed to a slit, a crease forming between singed brows. "You must be punished. Remember how Daddy used to punish me? Remember how Daddy tried to show me not to play with matches?" A kitchen match appeared in the fused fingers of her left hand.

"Ever see a match burn twice?" What remained of her lips pulled farther away from her teeth. "Ever see a family burn twice?" Shelley burst into cackling laughter.

"No," she moaned. "You're dead. Can't you leave us alone? You can't have Sara. She never hurt you."

"She's my little sister. Don't you understand?" The

grisly corpse leaned closer. Although Jane could push herself no farther away, she tried anyway.

"She's mine, Mother. All mine now, and I won't let you keep us apart any longer. Do you understand? She's mine."

Jane trembled.

"Do you understand?" The apparition roared, but didn't seem to expect an answer, for she upended the gas can. Pink liquid splashed over the bed. It splashed over Jane and the sleeping Elliot. The smell was overpowering. Jane began to scream.

"Quiet!" Shelley screeched. "Quiet, Mother, I want to enjoy this, and I want to talk. It's lonely where I am now, you know. I have no one to talk to, no one to play with."

Splash. "Remember how Daddy spanked me?" *Splash.*

She poured more gasoline along the foot of the bed. "Remember the night he burned me with cigarettes? Or the night he held my hand over the stove after I lit the fire at school? *Remember?"*

"Yes, yes, I remember," Jane whispered.

"Where were you then?" The specter wept molten tears. "Where was my mama then? My mama who was supposed to protect me."

"Shelley, I'm sssorry."

"Protect me!" Shelley wailed. *Splash!* The remainder of the gasoline came down in a torrent on Jane's head.

"Shelley, I couldn't help it. I couldn't help you!" Her skin, her eyes, and her lips started to sting from the chemical burn. "He would have killed me." Her voice dropped to a whisper.

"So he killed me instead. Is that what you wanted?"

"But . . . but he didn't, Shelley. You killed yourself."

"He did! You did! He and you condemned me to a fiery death!"

Jane turned to Elliot and gave him a few more feeble and futile shakes. Shelley laughed. Critter groveled and cowered in the hall, yapping excitedly.

Jane rubbed her eyes and looked up to plead with Shelley. The image wavered, shimmering in the night and started to fade. Soon an intact and whole child stared back at her, Shelley in her blue coveralls. She leered at her helpless mother. She took the kitchen matches, ready to strike them against the wall. The leer turned to sadness and despair, and again the image began to dissipate as though dispersed to the four winds.

Jane reached out to the vanishing child. "Shelley, please, don't. Please," she implored. Everything blurred; the gasoline which had saturated her hair dripped into her eyes. "Honey, Mommy and Daddy are sorry, and we loved you—love you. Don't do this."

Jane tried to wipe the gasoline out of her eyes and only succeeded in rubbing it in. It stung and her eyes started to water from the pain. She opened her eyes and glanced up, hoping that this time the specter would disappear, but no.

"Shelley . . ." She fell silent. What she was about to say turned into a gasp because Shelley no longer stood by the bed. *It was . . . it was Sara!*

Tears fell from Sara's eyes, rolling down her pink and rounded cheeks.

"I'm sorry, Mama. I don't want to, but I have to. Don't you see? Shelley's making me." Sara brought the match against the rough wooden surface of the headboard. It flared with blue-yellow light.

Jane shivered at the horrifying revelation. *It had been Sara.* She had thought after last night that it was Nana, but it had been Sara all along.

Jane screamed, a long soul-wrenching cry that bounced off the faded gold walls, and the house laughed. Her head swung around. *What's that?* Had she finally lost what was left of her mind? The eerie laughter surrounded her.

"Oh, no." She buried her face in her hand, relinquishing herself to the agony.

Sara held the flame in front of her face. "So pretty. So, so pretty." She gave her mother a beatific smile. "Good-bye, Mama. I love you." She dropped the lighted match upon the bed.

The bed exploded with a brilliant flash. The flame lapped at the blankets and sheets. It leapt in a kinetic frenzy, and Jane found herself engulfed in her own funeral pyre. She shrieked and thrashed upon the bed. She felt her hair go up with a crackle and her skin grew taut. It peeled and split from her face. With her remaining strength, she struck Elliot over and over again. She could hear Critter yipping in the background over the roar of the fire.

A fierce howl echoed off the brocade walls. Jane sat up in bed and realized it was the sound of herself screaming. She examined her hands and ran her fingers through her hair. She got up and rushed to the mirror. She looked normal—her face puffy from sleep and today's tears.

"Whew." *That was one hell of a dream.* She checked the clock. It was early yet, too early to be awake. Elliot's side of the bed had not been slept in. He had probably stayed downstairs. She hesitated, unable to decide if she should check Sara. Exhausted, she climbed into bed, pulled the covers over her head, and slept.

Elliot swayed in front of his daughter's grave. In the half-light of the distant street lamp, the cold marble tombstone read: *Michelle Anne Graves, June 29 . . .* He didn't read the rest. He knew what it said. To him, the slab said a great deal more than what the anonymous dates implied. Etched there upon the stone were his pain, his anguish, his loss, and—in essence—his ultimate failure. Yet it spoke little. It did not tell of the vibrant child who once laughed and played in the sun. Neither did it tell of his passionate and obsessive love for her—a love which destroyed.

To either side of the forlorn bare patch, the grass grew uninterrupted and unmarked by headstones or plaques. Those plots would someday hold the rest of the family. Sooner, perhaps, than either Jane or Elliot had expected when they had bought them a year ago. In two days, Nana would be interred here, and then . . . who knows? He dropped to his knees in the damp grass and rubbed his chin, feeling the slight stubble.

The smell of fresh, wet earth surrounded him. A gentle, but chilling, breeze played with his hair.

Branches whispered overhead, their old, dead leaves rustling in the wind. Stars twinkled in the heavens. He could hear the soft murmur of voices coming from the street. It was a beautiful night, crisp and clear, but still unseasonably warm for February. Despite the hour, a young couple strolled along the street arm in arm, and Elliot wept.

He knelt upon the cold, wet ground. The dew saturated his pants, soaking through to his knees, and the damp seeped into his bones, into his very soul. His fingers tugged at the grass to the side, pulling out small tufts.

"Shelley, no," he moaned. He clawed the earth, digging deeper into the sod, pulling out clumps of dirt. "Shelley, I'm sorry." Elliot swayed again and lurched, falling facefirst upon the grave. He lay, panting. His chest heaved as he tried to catch his breath. Finally, he rolled over. His eyes searched the heaven for strength, for an answer to the madness. The brilliant constellations winked imperturbably, apathetic and mocking.

His daughter did not rest easy. Death for her was no sweet peace of oblivion, but one that cried for justice —for revenge. No apologies were going to give her peace; only one thing would—or might. *Vengeance is mine own, saith the Lord.*

Elliot laughed without humor and righted himself. The chill had spread throughout his body. He could little afford the luxury of grief. It would only prevent him from doing what he knew he must do—avenge her death and make the sacrifice she demanded. He flexed his numbed fingers and reached for the shovel. A large package lay forgotten by the grave. He drove the spade into the reluctant earth, raised his foot, and put it on the blade, using his weight to drive it deeper. He lifted a clod and threw it next to the blanket-wrapped bundle.

Again Elliot pressed against the blade, driving it into the cold dirt. His muscles strained under his shirt. He went through the motions—a sharp jab, a step, a lift, and a throw—and the ground yielded to him unwillingly. Again and again, he repeated the movements until they became automatic. His mind lulled, his senses dimmed. He no longer noticed an occasional car or the distant barking of a solitary dog.

The false spring and recent thaw had done little to melt the frozen earth. Elliot grunted and groaned. Sweat poured over his brow into his eyes, and it stung. He stopped every so often to wipe it away with a handkerchief and to take another sip from his pocket flask. Unused to manual labor, his shoulders began to ache, then his biceps and forearms. His hands felt raw. Soon the hole was deep enough that he had to chip his way through black ice. By then the searing pain brought brief moments of clarity.

When this happened, his mind would shriek at him: *What are you doing? Why are you here in this cemetery in the middle of the night when the sane lie safe and secure in their beds?* But always the answer came: *I'm giving my daughter her due. She stays in an unquiet grave, lonely, bereft of her family. I'm only giving her her due.*

And the calm would descend so that he could jab, step, lift, and throw one more time. The movement became monotonous by repetition and soon he didn't think at all. What lights remained in the surrounding houses blinked off. Fewer and fewer cars drove past the graveyard. Even if they had, he wouldn't have noticed them. His world had become so small that the only thing he understood was the motion—jab, step, lift, throw. He had already gouged a deep hole in the mahogany coffin before he became aware of it.

Elliot stood upright. His back screamed in protest. He looked down at his hands and could see even in this dim light that they bled. The tacky liquid mixed with the dirt to coat his hands with brownish slime. He looked up at the gray rectangle above his head. He stared at the sky and realized that the stars had lost their brilliance and were disappearing one by one.

His hand reached over the lip of the open grave but couldn't find purchase. The grass was wet and slippery, and his hands were slick, covered as they were with mud, blood, and slime. Elliot wondered, perhaps a little belatedly, how he was going to get out of the pit he had made. He took another pull from the flask, and with a sudden inspiration, he tore small steps along the earthen wall with the tip of the shovel. He made these at regular intervals, climbing as he went. Elliot pulled himself onto the dead brown grass.

He knew he had to hurry, that he mustn't get caught, but Elliot ignored this querulous, urgent voice. *It doesn't matter now. It will be over soon.* The bundle stirred. He pulled a corner of the blanket away to reveal a tousled blond head. Sara stared at him groggily.

"Daddy, I'm cold."

"Yes, honey, it's cold out."

"Out?" She struggled to get loose from the restricting blanket which he had wrapped like tight swaddling around her legs, torso, and arms. She twisted and turned, noticing the stars, the trees, and finally the grim gray slabs.

Elliot kissed the top of her head. The medication, the tranquilizers had worn off. He hadn't meant it to be like this. He hadn't meant for her to wake up. He hadn't wanted her to be conscious, but in a way, now that it had happened, he was glad. This way he could say good-bye. "Don't worry, Sara, soon it won't be cold. It won't be cold ever again."

Sara wiggled and squirmed. "Daddy, I'm scared."

"I know you're scared, but you mustn't be."

"Daddyyyyy!" Her voice raised above his gentle, reassuring murmur.

"Don't, pumpkin, you mustn't. Be quiet now. You'll be with Shelley soon. You've missed Shelley, haven't you? You've wanted her to come home."

Sara lay still, bug-eyed. Even in the starlight he could see the yellowing bruise underneath her eye and Nana's ragged red scratches along her cheek. "Now you can be with her. You would like that, wouldn't you?"

"Daddy, Sh-sh-sh-shelley's dead," she stuttered and stammered.

Tears rolled down Elliot's cheeks and sprinkled Sara's hair at this admission. Jane had worried about Sara's absolute refusal to believe or acknowledge Shelley's death. As he had often told his wife, the knowledge would come in time, and it did—but why now? he moaned.

"Yes, Sara, Shelley's dead."

"Daddy, wha'cha gonna do?" Again Sara started to struggle, but was helpless against the tight, binding blanket.

"I'm going to give you to your sister. You see, Sara, she's lonely. She needs a friend. She needs you. She wants you." He looked at the sky which had grown perceptibly lighter. He frowned. "And you see, she already has you."

"Daddy! No!"

Elliot placed his hand over her mouth and nose. "But she does, Sara. Remember the cat?" Sara's eyes pleaded with him silently. "You killed a cat tonight, just like Shelley."

Sara shook her head. Elliot released his hold. Panting for air, Sara said, "No, Daddy, that wasn't me. That was Shelley."

This time her father shook his head. He kissed each cheek. "I'm sorry it has to be this way. I'm sorry I have to do this, but I do."

Sara started to scream. *"Daddy! Daddyyyyy, pleeease noooo!"*

"Good-bye, Sara. You be a good little girl so your mother and I will be proud of you." Elliot dropped her over the lip of the open grave. Her body hit the coffin with a heavy thud. She rolled, still screaming. Free from the imprisoning blanket, she scrambled to her feet. Standing on her tiptoes, her small white hands searched for something to hold onto in the slippery walls of the pit. She reached out to her weeping father.

"Daddy? I'll be good. I promise I'll be good. *Daddy!"* she wailed.

Elliot looked around at the houses that surrounded the graveyard. Suddenly afraid, he fell to his knees, begging her to be quiet. "Sara, pumpkin, hush. You don't understand. I have to do this." She shrieked, not forming words, just one long continuous, tormented howl.

"Sara! Now, you be quiet!" he warned her sternly. He threw a worried glance over his shoulder.

"Sara! No more racket. You could wake the dead." She continued to scream.

"Sara," he whispered, "please don't make me do it. Please?" She kept screaming. He seized the shovel and jumped into the pit. He swung. The delicate skull gave easily. Elliot swung again. "When I tell you to be quiet, goddamn you, you be quiet."

Weeping, he raised the shovel above his head and brought it down upon her limp body over and over again. "Sara, I'm sorry, I'm sorry, I'm sorry," he sobbed. Silence. Elliot slumped against the mud-slimed walls of the grave.

His breath came in ragged puffs; then it, and his heartbeat, slowed. He pulled Sara's broken body onto his lap, cradling her in his arms. He rocked her gently back and forth. Her head flopped and rolled with the motion. Elliot looked down at her face, oblivious to the ravaged features. The left side of her skull had been crushed and her left eye sealed shut forever. Her right eye stared at the heavens. He started to sing the same lullaby he had sung to her earlier that night.

Close your weary eyes and drift away. It's all right.
I'll be here until the break of day brings the light.
. . . I won't let no bad dreams come and bother you,
Just put your trust in me. Put your trust in me.

His voice faltered and broke. His gaze turned to the ashen sky. "Shelley, I love you," he whispered softly and lowered Sara to the casket. Elliot climbed back to ground level, shovel in his hand. He stared down at the torn, bloody blanket, the disheveled, tangled mass of blond hair, and the shredded green Dr. Denton's.

At long last he moved—jab, step, lift, throw. Dirt pattered on the wooden box and lifeless form below. *No hurry now it's done.* Jab, step, lift, throw.

As he covered his daughters with earth, lights began to go on in the houses around the cemetery. People were getting ready to greet a new day of work, of play, of living. Like before, Elliot didn't notice. He continued his odious task, contented now that he knew Shelley had found peace.

Car doors slammed and engines roared, but no one seemed to care about a man covering a solitary grave in the dawn light. More and more people moved about. Horns honked, and cars zoomed by while Elliot went through the motions. Jab, step, lift, and throw.

By the time he finished, the sun was up, and the streets were getting crowded with grumpy Monday morning commuters. The shovel fell from lifeless, numb fingers onto the fresh mound. Again he swayed over the tombstone, reading the drab gray letters—*Michelle Anne Graves*—which by all rights should now also say *Sara Jane Graves.*

The traffic increased in crescendo, reached its peak and died. Still Elliot stood motionless above the torn and ravaged earth. The sound of his hiccuping sobs set a counterpoint to the shrill whistle of commuter trains.

* * *

Officer Jerry Thaxter drove along Second Street. A country-western band sang of unrequited love on the little transistor radio he kept in his patrol car despite department policy. A cup of coffee left a ring of mist on the windshield. He swung into the graveyard, part of his regular route.

In the distance, he saw a young man standing over a newly dug grave. *Sad,* he thought. He skirted that part of the cemetery to allow the mourner some privacy. After he had completed his circuit, he slowed, peering into the distance. The man was leaning on something. *What? A stick? No, a shovel.*

"Holy shit." He felt queasy and ill. He put on the flashers and pulled over onto the turf near the site. Hand on his holster, Thaxter got out of his car. The man, not all that young now that Thaxter had a closer look at him, turned a despairing face toward the officer. His hands were caked with mud and something else—blood.

Wary, Thaxter unsnapped the holster and placed his palm against the comforting metal of the 357 Magnum. He moved to the man's side. His heart sank as he read the date on the grave. Whoever had been buried there should have been left undisturbed. Jerry placed a cautious hand on the man's forearm. Thaxter stood tensed, poised—ready for resistance, ready for a fight, ready for just about anything except what happened. The shovel fell and the man collapsed into Thaxter's arms, weeping.

Jane awoke to the persistent ringing of the telephone. The morning light was insipid and weak. She checked the clock and ran groggily toward the stairs.

Somewhere in the back of her mind she registered Sara's empty bed, but the phone kept ringing. It jarred her nerves. Jane stumbled down to the foyer, wondering where Sara was at this ungodly hour.

CHAPTER 20

Officer Andrew Brady sat at the front desk. Men in blue dragged cuffed, recalcitrant and belligerent teenagers through mesh glass doors, but Brady's mind was elsewhere. His eyes followed an agitated young woman as she paced up and down an aisle of cheap, dirty plastic chairs and overflowing metal ashtrays. She spun and walked toward the bulletin board, ignoring the drug posters and mug shots of the "ten most wanted." Her hands fluttered like two birds trapped in a cage, and it seemed that she carried on a turbulent internal debate.

"Who's the looker?"

Brady jumped at the sound of the voice and turned to see the shift captain, Ralph Madison. "That's Graves's wife."

Madison gave her an appreciative look before returning his attention to the man at the desk. "What's she here for?"

"She's getting him out."

Shock registered by degree. "She's *what?"* Madison's voice rose above the continuous hum of activity. The blonde turned to eye him with an expression which would freeze a man's blood.

Brady felt the same creepy sensation he had when she identified herself and told him her purpose. The skin on his balls turned prickly. "She's getting him out."

"Can she make bail? The judge put a high price on him. How the hell did she get the money?"

"I didn't ask. Figured it was none of my business."

"With what he's done, you'd think . . ." Madison didn't finish his sentence. He watched her as she brushed past a cop, oblivious to his presence. The supervisor chomped down on an unlit cigar and eyed her speculatively. "You don't think . . ." Again the question floundered as another officer brought Elliot Graves into the room.

Brady pulled the proper papers from a drawer to begin the final processing. He muttered irritably to no one in particular, "No, I don't think. That's not what I'm paid to do. I just process 'em, that's all."

Madison rapped the desk with his knuckles. "Yeah, go ahead, process him. You're right, we're not paid to think."

They drove away from the station in hard, stony silence. Elliot sighed as the blue Nova turned up Elm Street and stopped in front of 413. He studied the imposing facade and the skeletal oak to the side. He felt suddenly chilled. Jane opened her car door and waited for Elliot to get out. He huddled against the car seat, refusing to move.

He examined the house as Jane stepped from the vehicle. He didn't like it. It frowned at him. Elliot listened to the murmur of voices inside his head. Despite the brisk weather, sweat dripped in his eyes. The blond lady—his wife, they said—had brought him here. *My wife?* Personally, Elliot doubted it. He would remember a wife like that.

He stared into space, searching for memory. There was none, just an emptiness where logic told him should be a history or even a name. Graves, they called him. So be it. He didn't question them. He figured they knew; they must. And he had done something awful—at least if he could gauge by their rough treatment of him, he had—but he couldn't remember what. "Elliot Graves." He whispered the name to himself as though trying it on for size.

Elliot shifted in the front seat and returned to his examination of the house. Now that he sat there, he wished the lady hadn't come to get him. The thought of being someplace without barred windows had appealed to him, but this place was *Bad*—with a capital *B*. If the woman was his wife and had brought him home, then he lived here, but he didn't believe it. Elliot wouldn't have lived here. The house was menacing, sinister. It exuded a cancerous evil that threatened all it touched. It breathed with inhuman hatred.

He sighed. The cell hadn't been so bad after all. It didn't matter that the guards shoved him around or that the other prisoners shunned him. He had found a measure of contentment as he read the graffiti and pondered the gap where memories should be. Compared to this house, the jail sounded cozy indeed.

The lady—what was her name? Jane—walked around the car and opened the door. She took his arm. He resisted.

"Come on." She tugged at him. Sensing the problem, she said, "Come on, it won't bite you."

Elliot looked at her, skeptically. She pulled him out of the car. He stood by her side and looked down the street longingly. She headed for the stairs. If this was freedom, he didn't want it. He shuddered and tried to back away. She grabbed his arm. Her fingers dug deeply into his flesh. He winced. She didn't let up, only dragged him toward the house. Reluctantly, his feet took him up the walk to the porch.

She attempted a reassuring smile while she fumbled with her keys. He shook his head. She pushed him gently, but firmly up the stairs. Outside the door, she let go of him, inserting the key in the antique lock. Elliot shivered.

"It's okay. We'll be inside where it's warm soon." She propelled him through the door into the foyer. Elliot peered up to the second floor and started to shake. A hand touched his arm; he flinched. He turned to her and then looked into the dusky study. He spied the gleaming sax. For a moment his eyes came alive.

"Oh, you remember that, do you? And they said you had amnesia.

"Go on into the kitchen. I'll bring it to you." Elliot looked confused. She pointed through a door. "It's there, through the living room. I'll be right in."

Uneasily, he walked through the living room. He felt an icy finger run down his spine. He knew he was being watched. He turned to find Jane staring at him. She shot him another smile. It too was cold.

"Go on, I'll be with you in just a minute. I'll fix us a drink."

At the sound of the word *drink,* his fears subsided. Elliot rubbed his lips with the back of his hand. A drink would taste good right now. Maybe it would silence the buzzing inside his head. He went into the kitchen and sat. She followed, holding the sax in her hands.

"Remember anything yet?"

"I don't know what I'm supposed to remember."

She handed him the sax. He reached for it eagerly. It felt comfortable in his grasp. He put it to his lips and blew a few sharp, strident notes.

"See, you remember that. How about that drink?" She bent to the kitchen cupboard.

"It's funny," Jane mused, speaking more to herself than to him. "Memory is such a selective thing. You can still play the sax. You remember that, but not me. How about Shelley, Sara? You don't remember them, do you?"

Elliot cleared his throat. He would have liked to have told her that he remembered her, them, but he didn't—he just didn't. So he nodded as she opened the cupboard, not even thinking that she couldn't see him with her back turned. A row of bottles caught the kitchen light and sparkled. He felt himself start to salivate.

Her eyes narrowed as she straightened to look at him. "Maybe I can help you—remember, that is." She placed a Scotch bottle on the counter and reached into her pocket, extracting another key.

In a single fluid motion, she unlocked a drawer. "But you don't want to remember, do you? You don't want to know what happened here."

"No," he said in a small voice, chastised.

"Too bad, let me refresh your memory." The lady spun back to face him. In her hand, she held a twenty-two caliber revolver. The cold blue-black barrel seemed to absorb the light.

Elliot watched, fascinated at her graceful, confident movements, not noticing the death weapon in her hand. This woman wouldn't be a bad wife to have, but he wished she would forget about trying to make him remember and fix that drink.

She cocked it. The faint click resounded like a gunshot in the silent kitchen. Elliot gasped as its presence and its meaning dawned on him. The images —of Shelley, of Sara, and all that had been before— came flooding back to him in a blinding rush.

"Jane, I'm s . . ." The word died on his lips. A loud report echoed throughout the house. It was followed in rapid succession by another and yet another. Jane stood over Elliot's prostrate form, smoking gun in her hand. Blood pooled where he fell, facefirst, to the floor. His head was twisted at an awkward angle and terrified eyes stared blankly at the ceiling. A door slammed somewhere above her head. She moved like a sleepwalker through the kitchen doorway into the living room.

The sound of children's laughter rang like chimes. Jane smiled and walked into the darkened foyer. The door to Nana's old room opened. Sara and Shelley emerged hand in hand. They stood at the head of the stairs. Golden hair floated like a nimbus around them. Jane beamed at the pair. Her daughters were home.

"It's done. You're safe now. You can come down."

They parted. Only then did Jane see the gaunt little boy dressed in a lacy shirt and shorts. He gazed at her with starved eyes. Dried blood marred his thin ivory legs. Jane turned questioningly to her daughters. They let him through.

"Mother," Shelley spoke hollowly from a face which had begun to melt and weep, "meet William."

EPILOGUE

Tommy ran screaming through the vacant lot from the field beyond, followed by his brother. Freed by spring vacation and turned loose after church, they played. Tommy came to an abrupt halt in front of 413 Elm Street. David careened into him. Tommy fell to the pavement.

"Ow!"

"Sorry, why'd you stop?" David extended a hand to help his brother up.

Ignoring his hand, Tommy pointed to the ancient oak beside the brooding house.

David looked up, bemused. "What?"

"The tree."

"I know it's a tree. It's been there for years."

Getting to his feet, Tommy brushed the dirt from his jeans and wandered to the side of the house. He jumped and grabbed a branch, pulling it down.

"This." He indicated the fresh green buds. David examined the branch and shrugged.

"So?"

"It's budding."

"Of course it is, you dummy; it's spring. All the trees do."

Tommy let go of the branch and wiped his hands on his pants. "Don't you remember?"

"Remember what?"

"Last summer"—he peered expectantly at David—"it was dead."

David's face clouded and he shuddered. He poked Tommy in the ribs. "Come on, let's get out of here. This place gives me the creeps."